EVENTUALLY THEY ALL FALL

WHEN IMAGINATION DEFIES REALITY

JENNA MARCUS

Design and distribution by Bublish, Inc.

ISBN: 978-1-647044-97-8 (paperback)
ISBN: 978-1-6470449-6-1 (eBook)

C O N T E N T S

DEDICATION

To my grandma, Carmela Sconza, who once told me, "I'm so very blessed to know the wonders you will do because you are my granddaughter, and I believe in you." We can be our best selves and positively contribute to the world because of supportive, loving people like my grandma.

Thank you for your unwavering support, Grandma. Rest in peace.

CHAPTER 1

THE ORIGINS OF DRAGONS AND RABBITS

"Eventually, they all fall." This alleged aphorism is not only the first and last memory that I have of my father, but it is my first memory, in general. How messed up is that? The first memory I have is a phrase that is so completely out of context that I can only guess at its meaning. Mind you, these are wild guesses. Maybe he had been looking overhead to see a flock of geese flying in perfect synchronicity, in their victorious V, and he felt like taking them down a peg. Or, maybe, he was nodding in the direction of high school bullies in their element, tinged with an air of superiority, and he was making an apt observation about their impending future. Eh, probably not, that would be giving my father too much credit. On the other hand, I did not know how much credit to give or not to give him because I barely remember him. I only remember that phrase uttered offhandedly as he looked down at me with his dull gray eyes, freckles like constellations etched around the corners of his eyelids, permanent and pulling me in like a black hole. Aside from this, I don't have any other memories. He dropped the phrase and then just disappeared from my life.

Who does that? Who just throws down a random phrase, without explaining what the hell he meant, and then leaves? Not only did he *just leave*, but he left his only five-year-old son. That's messed up, right? I was a kid. How the hell was I supposed to understand what he was trying to tell me without any context? It could mean anything, or nothing. Or, even more likely, it could be an answer to a question I may have asked, such as what is the meaning of my name? Well, what's the meaning of my *first* name? My last name is no mystery, *Garrison*. A "garrison" just means that troops are stationed at some location that they are there to protect. Great. So, am I supposed to live up to that? The valiance and fortitude needed for that do not pair well with me in general or my first name specifically, *Domino*. So, if I am supposed to live up to my *full* name, then by design I am meant to eventually fall but simultaneously stand and protect a civilization? Isn't that a contradictory expectation? It's like saying, "Okay, dive into the depths of the ocean. Since you don't have gills, you will need to come up for air, but your job is to stay down there and protect the merpeople." What exactly are you supposed to say to *that*? Don't be confused about the merpeople part. Just pay attention to the impossible mission.

Okay, maybe I'm overthinking this name thing. A name is not necessarily tied to one's supposed destiny. It's not like my father chose for my last name to be Garrison, but he definitely had a hand in choosing my first name; that's at least what my mom told me. Suffice it to say, it's ridiculous to name your *only* kid—or any kid for that matter—after a game piece. Potentially, he could have had a hankering for pizza when I was born and named me after a fast-food chain. It's probably the former, given the last thing that he said to me. Either way, it's just absurd, but then again, so is my life, so maybe it's fitting.

I know many people, maybe millions if not billions, state that their life is absurd, and maybe they are right, but if we are measuring the absurdity of one's life against each other, then compared to me, they are not contenders. I can almost guarantee this, that is unless their life is similar to mine, or weirder. If this is the case, then I abdicate my throne and wish them a lot of luck. Trust me, I would do this gladly. If I could have one wish in the world, it would be to hand my life over to someone else and to just walk away. I don't know where I would go, or what I would do. As a fifteen-year-old high school sophomore, it's not like I have a lot of options; however, I would still take my chances.

You probably think that I am just being dramatic, or hyperbolic, right? And, yeah, I am pretty verbose for a fifteen-year-old. Blame the PSATs. However, I can assure you that I am not exaggerating one bit. You see, my family is made up of one person, my mom. We live in one of the most run-down apartment buildings on our city block. Imagine if a turn of the twentieth century tenement housing still existed. Great, now add a splash of grimy green moss to the side of that building and some rusting black fire escapes. Got the picture? Now imagine this building at night with dimly lit, narrow alleyways on either side of the building. In one alleyway, you should see a woman with long, black wavy hair leaning up against the grimy moss, her eyes glued to the vibrant display on her iPhone as she waits for her dealer. Got that picture? That's my mom leaning up against our home in Hell's Kitchen.

She intermittently peels herself away from this state, and promises me that she will "quit cold turkey, once and for all." I merely roll my eyes at the empty promise, and respond with, "Right, Mom." Calling her out on an empty promise is futile. At the time, she may mean what she says, but her promises never stick. Everything about her is Teflon.

I think that she knows it as well because eventually I catch her sliding her needle in between her toes. Yeah, she's that good; she knows how to hide the track marks. Initially, when she is caught, her piercing blue eyes are pools of startled liquid, but in a split second they become congealed ice as eyes narrow and her brows furrow in defiance, as if to say, "Who are *you* to judge *me*?" I am neither startled nor aggravated; I am merely resigned to this reality. So, in turn, I ask something innocuous like, "Do you need me to take out the trash?" It's not because I'm avoiding the issue or enabling her in any way, but trying to stop my mom from using drugs is like trying to stop an oncoming train with a flashlight and a wave of the hand. Why even bother?

However, having a drug addict for a mom and living in a run-down apartment building is not why my life is absurd. In fact, I am sure that many kids have drug-addled parents. Okay, maybe not *many*, but a fair number for sure. It is an unfortunate situation, and for some kids it causes a great deal of strife and loss. For me, I am just used to it. Shockingly enough, my mom has never ODed. Maybe that's because she does not take heroin on a daily basis or because her intake is strategic. For whatever reason, she survives in spite of her continued usage. This, however, is not weird. What *is* weird is what happens after I offer to take out the garbage.

In that same alleyway, where I need to dump our garbage bags because our incinerator is broken, again, I'll find a 20-foot dragon with purple teeth wearing a vibrant pink tutu rifling through the dilapidated dumpster brimming with practically a week's worth of pungent trash. Sometimes it's a Pegasus, but it's usually a dragon. Immediately, I find Hermon adorned in paint-smudged overalls, another user and neighbor, sliding to the ground, eyes transfixed to his hallucinogenic creation. He usually names these hallucinations after himself, as if they are his imagined descendants.

"Hello, Hermon the Third," he slurred as his head sagged forward.

"What happened to the Second, Hermon?" I asked human Hermon, knowing that he cannot hear me. He is so enraptured by his hallucination that reality no longer exists for him. Unlike my mom, his drug of choice is PCP. How do I know this? The dragon—sometimes Pegasus—told me.

The very fact that I can have a conversation with a psychedelic manifestation of a drug-riddled mind is why I have earned my crown.

As if distracted by my presence, the dragon turned to look at me and tilted its head to the side, studying me.

"I have nothing for you, Hermon the Third," I stated, throwing our trash bags on top of the garbage heap. "That is, unless you like garbage. I don't know what dragons eat."

Dragon Hermon gave me a slight nod, and then turned back to the dumpster. His scaly claws pawed through the black, robust garbage bags.

Before heading inside, I took a close look at human Hermon to see his fluttering dark eyes still mesmerized by his fantasy.

"Take care, human Hermon. Don't stay in the land of dragons too long." At that, I leave Hermon to his imagination.

Now, I know what you are wondering, *How in the world can you see a dragon in an alleyway?* Then you may also be wondering, *Aren't you afraid that the dragon will burn you to a crisp?* I'll answer this question first. Hermon's dragons usually do not breathe fire, but even if they do, they are imaginary. While I would feel the heat from the fire on my skin, I would not feel the intensity of actually being burned alive for the sheer fact that this dragon is not real.

To answer the first question, *that's* why my life is completely and unequivocally *absurd*. Ever since I can remember, I have had the uncanny, useless ability to perceive other people's imaginings. This is not only reserved for those on narcotics. Oh no, I can perceive anything that *anyone* imagines. I say *perceive* and not *see* because I experience these fantasies with every damn sense I have, and all five are in perfect working order. That's right, I can even taste someone else's fantasy. Yeah, sometimes it's not appetizing, especially when someone imagines a cafeteria food fight in which bologna sandwiches are practically catapulted across the room, and I find the taste of bologna repulsive. This does not happen often, but when I was six years old and saw a bologna sandwich headed right for me like a heat-seeking missile finding its target, I ducked for cover, which looked pretty ridiculous in a room where nothing was happening except for inane conversations about *Power Rangers* or math. Okay, maybe not math. No one talks about math at lunch, but still, I don't know many people who would literally dodge a conversation about math.

I flung myself underneath the cafeteria table as if a grenade just fell in front of me, and a fantastical blob of egg salad managed to fall from the ceiling and land right on top of my head. I spent the rest of the day rubbing imaginary egg yolk chunks out of my hair and trying to hold my breath as often as possible because the imaginary egg salad was imagined far past its expiration date. I never found out who fantasized about the food fight because it never came to pass. It was only a figment of some elementary school kid's imagination. It could have been the lunch staff, but I doubt it. Why would you fantasize about flinging around the food that you prepared?

Well, in any case, this is just one small example of what I am likely to experience on a daily basis. I say *likely* because I have learned how to control it...well, kind of. Most of the time I sense a sizzle in the air around me, as if the fantasy is burning itself into creation. It's at this moment that I close my eyes, take a deep breath, and silently repeat a little mantra to myself: "You're not real, go away." I know, it's a very intricate little chant. Give me a break, I thought of it when I was that six-year-old kid dodging imaginary food fights. Well, whatever you may think about it, it does the job. The fantastical figments disappear and I can once again experience reality. Unfortunately, this is not 100 percent effective. While I can *usually* block out the imaginings, if the emotions of the fantasy's creator are intense, then it's incredibly challenging to suppress what I perceive. In these cases, I just need to wait until it passes. However, when I have to experience these imaginings, it's almost impossible to wait it out. I have to resist the fierce temptation to lock myself inside my bedroom with the lights out and the shades drawn, as if I am trying to create a makeshift sensory deprivation chamber.

I know what you must be thinking—*Domino, how do you know that this is not all in your head? Maybe they are your fantasies, and you just have a vivid imagination.* I follow your reasoning; in fact, if I did not live my life and was an observer of it, like you are now, I may agree with you. However, your reasoning, unlike my life, is logical. Trust me, I wish that everything that I perceive was a figment of my own imagination. In that case, I could just see a psychiatrist and get a lifetime subscription to mind-numbing meds, so my mom and I could challenge each other to every drug abuser's favorite game: who can fall into a drug-induced coma first. However, this is just wishful thinking. Well, if I were granted an *actual* wish, it would be to be normal, whatever that may be. I guess to only perceive reality and nothing more is at least a step in the right "normal" direction. Nevertheless, I cannot even imagine this reality because therein lies the problem. While I can perceive other people's imaginings, I can't *imagine* anything. I've tried...a lot. However, nothing ever comes to mind other than what I have actually experienced, and what I actually experience is the worlds, ideas, and dimensions that other people create in their heads. I perceive wish fulfillment, manifestations of worst- and best-case scenarios, and just bizarre oddities that I couldn't make up if I tried. In essence, I literally have the opposite of a vivid imagination.

Domino, you may assert, *that still does not answer the question. How do you **know** that this is not all in your head?* I get your point—how can I prove that these figments are not just really my imaginings despite the fact that I just told you that I do not have the ability to imagine anything? Yes, it's possible that I am just lying to myself, that I am even delusional; however, I know that that is not the case because I have accidentally confirmed that I perceive other people's imaginings.

At five years old, I saw other people's fantasies, but I had no idea that they were not created by my own mind. Like you, I just thought that I had a vivid imagination. However, something just felt odd about the fantasies. While I perceived them, and therefore should have sustained some sort of intimacy with them, I felt this strange sense of detachment from them, as if these wild creatures and bizarre worlds I saw were so outside of myself that they felt foreign to me. Nonetheless, like any five-year-old, I didn't ponder these feelings, nor did I investigate further. I merely disregarded these feelings, and just played in the park.

The closest park to my apartment building was several blocks away. At five years old, it felt like an eternity before the fragrance of Central Park, the comforting pungent odor of horse manure mixed with horse pellets, hit me. Even before I could see the park's entryway, I could hear the rhythmic clanking of the horses' hooves as they dutifully pulled the carriages strapped to their harness.

I would practically drag my mom into the park as she would gripe about how I could have just played on the sidewalk in front of our building. Usually, I would reason that going to the park was like our version of a vacation. Maybe she felt guilty, or agreed and needed a "staycation" herself. Either way, this argument usually did the trick. However, this would only work on the days when she didn't have any shifts at the diner. On a waitress's paycheck-to-paycheck existence, you can't forgo earning a living in exchange for a day in the park. At least that's what she would tell me. I could have told her that the park was free, whereas her drugs were not, but I was five years old. I was not that snarky, not yet anyway. At least that's what my mom tells me.

It was on one of the days that my mom had off from work when we traversed into the depths of the park and stopped at my favorite spot, the playground. My mom usually plopped down on a nearby bench as I stood on the outskirts of the play area, deciding which contraption I wanted to dive into first. What else would you call interconnected wooden and metal constructs? Play elements? Whatever they may be, I was pretty strategic about which one I was going to try out.

On that fateful day—or maybe it wasn't fateful, maybe it was just random, the jury's still out for me when it comes to fate—I saw a boy about my age entangled in the chain link climbing net. How he managed to loop his scrawny legs through the metal netting and twist them to such a degree that the taut chains looked as if they were cutting into his thighs, I had no idea. Maybe it was out of curiosity or pity that I was compelled to head toward this boy. Either way, I stopped inches in front of this kid, who was hanging upside down with his arms dangling down and his fingertips skimming the springy black mat below. From the way his limp body slightly swayed, it looked like he was making zero attempt to get himself out.

"Hi," he buoyantly exclaimed as I stopped inches in front of him.

"Hi," I returned. "Um, are you okay?"

He eagerly nodded, as his rosy cheeks were quickly becoming an unnerving shade of magenta.

"Yeah, I'm fine," he enthusiastically declared with his toothy smile.

"Do you need any help?" I offered.

"Sure!" he pronounced.

As he continued to limply dangle from the chains, I gingerly untwisted the netting and pulled his legs through. Unfortunately, I forgot to warn him to brace himself for the fall. He hit the ground with a disconcerting thud that made me cringe. However, from the way he sprang up, he seemed to be unfazed.

"Thank you!" he practically sang as he adjusted his overalls. "I'm Griswold Griffin. Nice to meet you."

He excitedly offered me his hand to shake, as if we were businessmen who just brokered a deal. I tentatively shook his hand; never having shaken anyone's hand, I clumsily pumped it up and down before I quickly pulled away.

"Yeah, it's nice to meet you too," I responded, shoving my hands in my pockets. "So, how did you get in that thing?" I asked, nodding toward the netting.

Still smiling, Griswold took a quick look at the chain link netting and just shrugged.

"Don't know," he pronounced. "It just happened. Hey! Do you wanna play hide-and-go-seek?"

Before I could respond, he quickly announced that he would hide. He instructed me to close my eyes and count to twenty-five. Why twenty-five? He never said, and I didn't ask. He just declared that I must count to twenty-five as if it was an unwritten playground rule.

I did as instructed, slowly making my way through the count. And it was a real count, but way of the one-Mississippi, two-Mississippi persuasion. By the time I opened my eyes, Griswold was safely hidden.

It took me less time to find him than it took for him to hide underneath the silver metal slide. The slide was pretty sizable compared to lanky, average-sized Griswold. Normally, it probably would have taken me a few minutes to locate Griswold; however, I had an unfair advantage: I was able to follow his rabbits.

At the time, I did not think it was at all odd that when I opened my eyes, I found a pristine, fluffy white bunny looking up at me, rhythmically wiggling its heart-shaped soft pink noise. Its ears were perked up in perfect unison, as if it were extending this appendage to the utmost degree to hear an anticipated call to action. Before I could even move, the rabbit energetically hopped toward another rabbit. While this one was more robust, it was just as fluffy and alert. In eerie synchronicity, the rabbits hopped over to a group of rabbits. These rabbits were of different sizes, shapes, and colors, as if they were trying to prove the variety of their species through their selective cohort. Once again, as if they had a hive mind, they simultaneously hopped over to yet another group of rabbits, and that group hopped over to an even larger group, until there was literally a bunny swarm around the slide.

I awkwardly waded my way through the pool of rabbits to find a giggling Griswold crouched beneath the underbelly of the cool steel slide.

When I bent down to take a closer look at the collection of rabbits, I found a smiling Griswold with his knees pulled tightly toward him.

"You found me!" he declared. "You're really good at this game. How did you find me so quickly?"

"What's with all of the rabbits?" I asked, ignoring his question.

At the mention of the word "rabbits," his eyes widened.

"You see them too?" he practically whispered, crawling out from under the slide.

"Yeah," I confirmed, looking down at the furry ocean of rabbits, all staring up at me, contentedly wiggling their pink noises. "I have never seen so many rabbits."

"You see my rabbits, really?"

"*Your* rabbits? You have *these many rabbits*?" I asked, gesturing to the pool of fur surrounding us.

"No, I mean, I wish my mommy and daddy would let me have rabbits. I love rabbits. I love every type of rabbit, but they said that they are dirty, so I can't have them, but I like to imagine them. I imagine all of the rabbits in the world," Griswold admitted.

"Umm, all of the rabbits in the world?" I echoed as the waves of rabbits clustered around us, enveloping our feet in pillows of fur.

Griswold excitedly nodded as the rabbits began to multiply. It was as if every time he moved his head, another rabbit popped into creation. Each one was just as vigilant and fluffy as the next. Although each one was a unique shade and size, every single one had the same perfectly pink heart-shaped wiggling nose.

"I want to have all of the rabbits in the world," Griswold enthusiastically announced. And with that, the group of rabbits quadrupled in number. As they replicated at lightning speed, each one stared at me with their glassy, beady dark eyes. The pairs of eyes matched the innocence of their creator. Their stare was neither imposing nor threatening, but just their pure existence felt suffocating.

"Can you stop?" I squeaked, claustrophobia closing in among the rabbit clones. "There are too many."

"You *can* see them," Griswold announced in amazement. "You see the rabbits in my head."

"I—I don't know," I stammered, squeezing my eyes shut, as if by closing them I could shut out the growing sea of rabbits. "Can you make them go away?"

"I just won't picture them," Griswold simply stated. "Okay, I'm not picturing them, is that better?"

I gingerly opened my eyes, expecting to see an ocean of wiggling pink noises; however, I was relieved to see the openness of a typical playground.

Heaving a big sigh, I thanked Griswold.

"So, you see my rabbits," he affirmed.

"I guess so," I admitted, not yet realizing that I could see more than Griswold's imaginary rabbits. I quickly turned away, preparing to run in case the rabbits intended to return for a bunny apocalyptic revolt. But, before I could leave, Griswold asked, "Hey, what's your name?"

Turning, I said, "Domino Garrison."

"Well, Domino Garrison, you're my new friend."

And just like that, I was. In fact, Griswold has been my best friend since that day on the playground. He is also the only one who knows that I can perceive the imaginary. At least, that's what I thought.

CHAPTER 2

TWO LIONS. ONE TIGER. NO BEARS. OH MY

"You have to quit it with your bunny militia."

"I don't know what you're talking about," Griswold said innocently.

I could feel the weight of one of Griswold's rabbits perched on my head, its palpable pulse practically beating into my scalp.

Pinning him with a look, I said, "It's definitely a militia."

"It's not a militia," Griswold countered.

"It is," I insisted.

"Oh yeah, why do you say that?"

"Because this one," I began, looking directly into Griswold's gaze, as I pointed to the top of my head, "is holding a machine gun in his paws." I scanned the room to find a menagerie of ammo-wielding bunnies wiggling their heart-shaped noses, poised to attack who knows what.

Griswold sheepishly looked away as I closed my eyes to block out his fantasy.

"Were you watching *Rambo* again?" I asked, as I felt the weight of the rabbit dissipate from atop my head.

"Yeah, but wouldn't that movie have been so much cooler with some badass rabbits?" he announced, rolling his office chair over to his desk, where he speedily typed on his keyboard. He then turned the screen toward me to reveal a brown and white rabbit adorned in camouflage fatigues, holding enough ammunition to take out a city block. Griswold's rabbits' soft pink heart-shaped wiggling noses were juxtaposed to the fluffy mammal's sneer, making it a comical representation of a war-hardened vigilante.

"Is that what you saw? I tried to imagine them exactly like this."

I smirked as I studied Griswold's CGI creation.

"Mission accomplished, Grizz. A rabbit army invasion would have made that movie a whole lot different."

"*Good* different?" Griswold asked, hopefully.

"Umm, *different* different," I admitted, and then quickly added, "but you *like* different different, right?"

"True," Griswold acquiesced as he closed his laptop and slid it into his backpack. "It's still a good different though, right?"

Standing up, I flung my backpack over my shoulder and said, "As long as you keep them off my head, they are the greatest form of different ever. Ready?"

Griswold nodded as he placed his rotund backpack upright on his bed, turned his back to it, crouched down, and slipped both arms through the straps. He practically fell over as he hoisted himself up. I instinctively grabbed his arms to help him keep his balance. He took a tentative step forward and then nodded again, the signal that I could let go.

"Why don't you just use the wheels?" I asked as we walked down the spiral staircase toward the foyer.

Griswold shrugged before stating, "I just didn't feel like it today."

Rolling my eyes, I said, "Whether you feel like it or not, don't you think it would be *easier* just to wheel the backpack?"

As Griswold descended the last step, he pulled his house keys off of the key rack beside the front door. Slipping into his sneakers on the mat beneath the marble-embossed vanity mirror, hanging on the wall adjacent to the door, he declared, "When do I take the easy route?"

"Exactly. Don't you think it's time that you started?"

"Never!" he decreed with a little too much tenacity for a Monday morning.

"You need to take it down like nine notches."

"Why not ten?"

The only thing that prevented me from responding was the smile melting from Griswold's face as we heard the click-clack of high-heeled shoes growing more pronounced.

The room grew silent as Griswold's mother came to a stop in front of us. Clad in her white dress suit, matching blazer, and leather-bound briefcase, she was clearly a prime example of the phrase "all business." Griswold's mother may be shorter than he is, but with her arms firmly crossed over her chest and her eyebrow raised in that almost permanent air of disapproval, she seemed much taller and more imposing.

"Griswold Griffin, what in the world are you wearing?" Griswold's mother asked, slowly scanning her son from his neatly knotted bow tie attached to his knee-length black cape to his black patent leather dress shoes.

"I'm auditioning for the talent show," Griswold meekly admitted.

"And what *exactly* are you auditioning for?"

Not moving an inch, with his shoulders slumped forward and his mouth agape, he said nothing.

"He's a magician, Mrs. Griffin," I interjected. "You know, magic, rabbits, all that jazz." I quickly slipped on my Converse sneakers and reached for the doorknob. "Well, we don't want to be late."

"Always with the rabbits and the magic. I don't know what we're going to do with you, Griswold."

Even before she finished this sentence, I felt it; the usual sizzle in the atmosphere was unmistakable.

Before I could close my eyes and repeat my little mantra to myself, out of the corner of my eye I saw Griswold, except it wasn't him, not quite anyway. This form of Griswold had brushed and gelled his blond hair to an unnatural state of perfection. His hazel eyes calmly looked into mine as he adjusted his red and white varsity jersey. His cheekbones were a little sharper, and he stood a little taller, as if he were wearing lifts. This Griswold looked eerily similar to our high school quarterback, Tom Hamilton. Seeing as Griswold and Tom's families vacationed together, it wasn't surprising that she would reimagine her son into someone that she knew, but that didn't make it any less off-putting.

"Oh jeez, not this again," I muttered.

Closing my eyes, I hurriedly opened the door, and shoved Griswold out.

"Gotta-go-bye," I blurted out, as if this string of words had melded into one long, multisyllabic word.

With my eyes firmly shut, I walked in perfect darkness for at least a block before I heard Griswold talking to me.

"You saw something," Griswold affirmed.

Gingerly opening my eyes, I breathed a sigh of relief when I saw Griswold's unkempt hair and the lack of any athletic clothing anywhere on him.

"What did you see?"

"You know, the usual craziness. I just couldn't block it out right away, you know?"

"From my mom? What sort of craziness did she imagine?"

"Nothing worth mentioning," I claimed.

You may think that it *is* worth mentioning that Griswold's mother constantly reimagined her son as a nonmagician jock, and not *any* nonmagician jock but her friend's son's twin; however, I couldn't disagree with you more. I tell Griswold practically everything, except for this. I don't know how he would react if he knew; he probably would not be surprised, but why risk hurting him? Some secrets, you just have to keep to yourself.

"So, I didn't hear about a talent show. Does our high school even *have* a talent show? Did they *ever*?"

In my peripheral vision, I saw Griswold grinning as he plunged his hand into his pocket to pull out a folded piece of paper.

"Not exactly," he began to explain as he unfolded the paper to reveal a blank, lined sheet with one crudely written signature on top. "I am creating a petition so that we can have one at our school."

"Uh, Grizz?"

"Yeah?"

"How will anyone know this is a petition?"

"There's a signature," Griswold stated matter-of-factly, and then pointed to it as if I had missed it. "See? Right there. That's mine."

Shutting my eyes once again, I gave my head a good shake.

"Are you seeing something?"

"Nope," I announced. "I'm just wondering how your mind works, Grizz."

"That's funny."

"Yeah, why is that?"

"I wonder the same thing about you."

I could not help but smile at that. Maybe that's why we have been best friends for the past decade—we can never quite figure each other out, but we really don't need to. I have never questioned why he chose to dress like a magician every once in a while, or imagine a guerrilla army of bunnies—yeah, he watches *a lot* of war movies—and he never grills me about my "gift" or "curse," whatever you want to call it. Sure, he asks about what I perceive, especially when the fantasies are intense, but he does not barrage me with questions as if I am under interrogation.

"You may want to put a header or something on that petition to explain what you are petitioning," I offered.

"You think?" Griswold pondered, gripping the paper with both hands and holding it out in front of him.

"Well, unless you expect whoever you are going to hand the petition to, to have ESP, you may want to include something on there that makes it obvious that it is a petition."

"Hmm, well, if you think so," he said. Then, after a brief pause, he added, "Will you sign it?"

"For you, Grizz, sure," I responded, as Griswold handed me a pen he pulled out of his pocket. I was careful to not touch the chewed-up pen cap as I placed the paper flat on my thigh and scribbled my signature right underneath Griswold's.

"How many do you need?" I asked, handing the paper back.

"Two hundred," he gleefully announced as he folded the paper back up and shoved it in his pocket along with his pen.

"And you are dressed up for the talent show today because...?"

"Oh, it's due today," Griswold admitted with a brimming smile.

Once again, I closed my eyes. Anticipating Griswold's question, I stated, "Nope, I'm not seeing anything, I'm wondering the same thing as before, Grizz."

As soon as we got to the school, Griswold unabashedly walked up to every person we saw and asked them to sign the petition. I had never heard anyone explain the purpose of a petition in a single breath, but Griswold managed to do it several times as he tried to cajole everyone into signing the paper.

After fifteen minutes of watching Griswold buzz from person to person only to be turned down with a firm shake of the head, ignored completely, or for some to roll their eyes as they reluctantly signed his paper, Griswold walked over to me, holding up the paper.

"So, how many did you get?"

Griswold furrowed his eyebrows in concentration as he tallied the signatures.

"Twenty-five," he admitted with a frown. He then carefully folded the paper back up and shoved it in his pocket. As soon as he did so, the security guards at the school's entrance blew their whistles and signaled for us to come inside.

"Well, that's more than just ours," I said, trying to cheer him up, which is pretty easy to do. Griswold usually does not get dejected, or if he does, it is only temporary. It is as if being jubilant is his default mode.

"That's true," he chirped as we walked past the guards. "Some were costly though."

"What do you mean, *costly*? Did you actually pay people to sign your petition? Grizz, I know that your parents have money, but don't you think that bribery is a step too far?" I asked as we stopped in front of our lockers.

"Well, I didn't offer money," Griswold began, as he rapidly spun his lock's combination dial to the right, then to the left, and back again to the right before firmly pulling the body of the lock down, but to no avail.

Pulling my world history textbook out of my locker, I turned my attention to Griswold's lock as I worked through the combination.

"Then what did you offer?" I asked, as I pulled the lock down and the shaft pulled away from the lock's body.

"Well, I just made one offer," Griswold admitted, opening his locker and kneeling down to take his backpack off of his shoulders. "And you may not like it."

"Uh, Grizz, what did you do?" I asked warily as I closed my locker and looked down at him.

Without meeting my gaze, he said, "Well, I told Lucy Jenkins that you would go on a date with her."

"Excuse me?"

"She likes you," he stated, matter-of-factly.

"I know. You *know* I know that. You also know why I haven't asked her out," I explained.

"Yeah, I know," Griswold admitted as he put the last of his books in his locker. "Desperate times call for desperate measures. She likes the zoo. That's where she wants you to take her."

I scowled at Griswold as we made our way to our homeroom. Unsurprisingly, Lucy Jenkins was sitting in the front row, hands folded on top of her textbooks neatly stacked on her desktop. As if she was expecting me to walk into the classroom at that moment, her smile widened, revealing her multicolored braces.

"Hi, Domino," she practically sang as I hesitantly walked past her.

"Hi, Lucy," I responded, secretly wishing that she had completely forgotten about the deal she made with Griswold; however, when I felt the familiar sizzle, I knew that this was not the case.

I instinctively cringed as I saw a version of myself in my peripheral vision. This Domino's hair was much longer than mine; his silky, wavy black locks hung just over his sturdy shoulders. Somehow my blue eyes shone a luminous azure on Lucy's version. The imagined Domino was wearing a form-fitting black T-shirt and matching jeans, which were made out of the thinnest magical material possible because you could see every taut muscle. Looking down at my own loose-fitting black T-shirt and baggy jeans that covered my lanky body, it was hard to not feel inferior to my doppelgänger.

My fantastical clone's smile revealed teeth so white and pristine that they put all pearls to shame. He was looking at an imagined version of Lucy, whose perfectly straight brown hair was laced with streaks of gold. She was wearing a blue sequined prom dress, the bottom of which just touched her transparent high heels.

As if this scene was out of every Harlequin romance novel ever created, imaginary Lucy ran into imaginary Domino's perfectly sculpted arms in an impassioned embrace. He lifted her up into the air as if she were as recreating the iconic *Dirty Dancing* leap and threw her down on the desk in front of the classroom. Before this scene went any further, I closed my eyes and whispered to myself, "You're not real, go away." I gingerly opened one of my eyes to see the fantastical characters still making out on top of the desk.

"Dammit," I said to myself, as I squeezed my eyes shut and shook my head.

"Are you okay, Domino?" The real Lucy asked as I tried to block out her fantasy.

"Yup, never better," I said, wincing at the ripping of fabric that was undoubtedly my doppelgänger's T-shirt.

"Oh, okay," Lucy said hesitantly, and then added, "but why are you closing your eyes?"

"Uh, I thought I felt something in them," I said as I rubbed my eyelids.

"Oh, do you want me to take a look?" she asked.

"No!" I said a little too loudly as I heard her go to stand, and then I cleared my throat. "I mean, it's okay. I'm just going to go to the bathroom and wash them out."

As I felt my way to the doorway, I heard Lucy call after me. "I'm looking forward to our date!"

The piercing ring of the school bell echoed throughout the halls as I opened my eyes. I tentatively looked around to see if the overtly romantic versions of Lucy and myself had followed me. Although I saw a few kids heading toward their classes, I didn't see any sequins or luminescent eyes, so I thought that I was in the clear.

With a sigh of relief, I headed toward the bathroom to throw some cold water on my face.

However, as soon as I opened the bathroom door, I regretted this decision as I saw Bryan Trevor pinned up against the tiled bathroom wall, with Colin Jenkins's, Lucy's older brother, index finger aimed at Bryan's acne-covered face.

"I don't want to see you in here again, you got that crater-face?" Colin hissed inches away from Bryan, who cowered as he nodded in compliance.

"Real original," I muttered to myself, or at least I thought I did until Colin slowly turned his head to look in my direction.

"Got something to say?" Colin spat, his tone as guttural as it's always been.

Before I said anything, I heard the bathroom door swing open behind me, followed by a familiar, cheerful voice saying, "Mr. Monty is asking where you went—oh" The timbre of his voice flattening at the sight of Bryan wincing in preparation for whatever physical assault Colin had in mind.

"Yeah," I involuntarily uttered.

"Let him go," Griswold yelped, and then quickly cleared his throat.

Smirking, Colin glowered at Griswold as he removed his hand from Bryan, who quickly picked up his backpack from the floor. Like a skittish deer, he quickly zipped into an open bathroom stall and slammed it shut.

"You've got a problem, *Griffin*?" Colin seethed, cracking his knuckles as if loosening them up for a fight.

Griswold puffed up his chest and cleared his throat again, as if he were preparing to throw out a verbal onslaught, but when he opened his mouth, nothing came out except for carbon dioxide.

"That's what I thought," Colin scoffed as he looked Griswold up and down. "You think you're some type of hero in that getup?"

"I-I'm a magician," Griswold stammered, gripping the edges of his cape.

"A magician?" Colin's caustic laugh reverberated off of the bathroom walls. "More like a caped loser."

"Enough, Colin," I ordered.

"Yeah, or *what*?"

"Or I tell everyone that you have a crush on Tom Hamilton."

For a moment, Colin's eyes widened in disbelief, but then he grimaced as he indignantly moved toward me. His face was practically inches away from mine. I could practically see all the blood vessels in his insipid eyes.

We stood like that for a palpable beat, as I waited for Colin to make his move.

His nostrils flared as he let out a grunt.

"You better watch your back, *Garrison*," Colin growled, as he shoved past me to exit the bathroom.

I let out a breath I didn't even realize that I was holding in.

"How did you—?" Before Griswold could finish his sentence, I gestured toward the feet sticking out from the bathroom stall.

"You can come out, Bryan," I called, at which the bathroom stall slowly opened, and Bryan crept out, suspiciously looking to his left and right before making his way out completely.

"Um, thanks," Bryan timidly said, as he looked down at the tiled floor.

"Don't mention it," Griswold cheerily stated.

"You okay?" I asked, to which Bryan quickly nodded while still looking down.

"I-I have to get to class," Bryan stammered as he jetted past us and ran out.

"So, how did you know about Colin's crush?" Griswold asked.

"We are in a high school where almost everyone we know has hormone-induced fantasies," I explained.

"Got it," Griswold stated.

"Speaking of which," I said, turning to him, "why would you make that deal with Lucy?"

Griswold smirked as he walked over to one of the bathroom mirrors, looking in as he adjusted his cape.

"That's the only way that she would sign the petition. She got her friends to sign it too. She's still fantasizing about you?"

"Uh, yeah."

Turning toward me, Griswold tilted his head to the side as if contemplating something, and then asked, "Well, can't you just, you know, block it out?"

Closing my eyes, I pinched the bridge of my nose as I said, "Yeah, that's what I was trying to do. It's harder to do when someone's emotions are so intense. And to top it off, her fantasy version of me belongs in a GQ magazine."

"Well, that's flattering," Griswold said, smirking.

"It's ridiculous. And, thanks to you, I need to watch this fantasy play out on our date, which is when exactly?"

"Oh, I didn't tell you? After school."

"What!" I exclaimed just as the bell for the first period rang.

"Are you mad at me?" Griswold sincerely asked.

I gave him the side-eye, but then said, "No, but the next time you plan on using me, at least let me in on it."

"Noted," Griswold beamed, as he wrote something in his notebook. I leaned over to see him scribble "Don't use Domino without permission."

At that, I smirked and shook my head.

"You are something else, Grizz."

"Really?" Griswold perked up and turned to face me, innocently asking, "What exactly?"

Before I could respond, I heard the resounding sound of the classroom door slam shut, which was punctuated by Mr. Humphries's exaggerated throat-clearing.

"Page twenty-three, class," Mr. Humphries exclaimed. No introductions, no easing us into the lesson. If Mr. Humphries could be described in three words, they would be "to the point."

"The Roman Empire was rife with acrimonious battles, many of which took place in the famed Colosseum as well as in other Roman arenas," Mr. Humphries began, pensively closing his eyes and smiling.

"Oh boy," I whispered to myself, feeling the sizzle of history shimmer into existence.

"Ah yes, these battles were truly glorious and oftentimes deadly. However, it is a misconception that Roman gladiators squared off against animal predators. Only warriors known as the *venatores* and *bestiarii* tangled with such beasts, such as your legendary king of the jungle, the lion." As if answering his call, Mr. Humphries's fierce twin lions pawed at the ground. Baring their impossibly sharp, bloodstained teeth, they growled at an oblivious audience.

This was one of the many reasons why I sat in the back of Mr. Humphries's class. When he said that he could bring "history to life," little did he know that that was all too true. Others were either taking notes or were looking down at the social media feed on their phones under their desks.

As Mr. Humphries continued to lecture on about how convicted criminals and Christians were offered to ravenous predators as their dinner, the twin lions skulked up and down the classroom rows.

I squeezed my eyes shut and silently repeated the mantra to myself.

"Is there something wrong, Mr. Garrison?" I heard as I gingerly opened my left eye to find Mr. Humphries standing in front of me with his hands on his hips, adorned in a red loincloth, matching brown leather elbow and wrist bands, a plumed helmet perched on top of a metallic visor with crude eyeholes, and pretty much nothing else. Luckily, most of him was covered up by his comically large shield.

I would have laughed if not for the twin lions standing in the row next to mine, licking their chops and eyeing me as if I were one of those convicted criminals or Christians they were promised as their meal.

"Nope, just listening," I said, and gulped as the lions met my gaze.

As much as I realized that these predators were merely a figment of my history teacher's vivid imagination, I could not get over the fact that they looked extraordinarily famished.

"Well, it may be helpful if you take notes. Unless you can take precise notes with your eyes closed, I suggest that you keep them *open*," Mr. Humphries said as he pointed to my closed notebook with his sharp stout sword.

I heard a few snickers and giggles as I nodded and dutifully opened the notebook to a blank page. Once Mr. Humphries pivoted and walked back up my row, I felt Griswold lean toward me.

"What do you see?"

Without looking up, I said, "Lions. Two of them, and they are hungry."

"They can't hurt you though, right? You said that something imagined can't hurt anyone," Griswold whispered. As if trying to defy this fact, both lions let out guttural growls.

"Yeah, I know, but real or imagined, when a lion jumps at your throat, you tend to have a visceral reaction."

"Visceral?"

"Instinctive," I noted, and then added, "but what makes it worse is that Mr. Humphries has reimagined himself into a Roman gladiator."

"A what?!" Griswold hollered, and then clapped his hands over his mouth to suppress a laugh.

As if they had a hive mind, everyone in class turned to look back at Griswold.

"Something you want to share with us, Mr. Griffin?" Mr. Humphries asked, his annoyance accentuated by yet another growl from his twin lions.

Griswold quickly shook his head, uncovered his mouth, and said, "No, sir, just listening."

"I see. Well, maybe you can be a little more placid as you listen, yes?"

"Yes, sir," Griswold replied, and then turned to me to ask, "Placid?"

"Calm and quiet, unlike Mr. Humphries's lions," I noted as the lions continued to eye me.

Once Mr. Humphries turned his back to us, I shut my eyes once again. After a solid beat of darkness, I tentatively opened them to find a pleasant lack of animal predators in the classroom.

Although Mr. Humphries deeply cared about his subject, it's a little odd that he felt that strongly about Roman gladiators. However, you can never really tell what a person is and is not impassioned about, that is until you realize that you cannot block out their fantasy. Well, not *you*, necessarily. As far as I know, I am the only one who has this unique issue, which I would be more than happy to transfer to literally anyone, not that that's possible.

By the time the last bell of the day rang, I had perceived enough exams magically turning into puffs of smoke, a literal dodgeball war in gym class, and enough hormone-induced fantasies for a lifetime. So, overall, it was a typical day. The only thing out of sync was Griswold missing lunch to meet with the extracurricular activities coordinator about his petition. After lunch, in English lit, Griswold told me that he had waited outside of the coordinator's office for about twenty minutes before someone told him that the coordinator was out and would not return until the end of the day. That is why instead of exiting the school, I am leaning up against the wall, waiting for Griswold to exit the coordinator's office.

While waiting, I sent my boss, Miles Godare, a text, letting him know that I would not be in today.

Domino [3:42]: Hey Miles. Sorry. Won't be in. Got roped into something.

Miles [3:43]: This is late notice.

Domino [3:43]: I know. I'm sorry.

Miles [3:46]: It's a slow news day, but Bill can pick up your shift.

Domino [3:46]: You know you sell books, right?

Miles [3:47]: Yes, and for longer than you've been alive.

Domino [3:47]: I'll refrain from the eye roll emoji.

Miles [3:50]: Don't forget about your shift tomorrow.

Domino [3:50]: Do I ever forget?

Miles [3:52]: Well, just don't. We have inventory tomorrow.

Domino [3:52]: Got it.

"So, she said no," I heard Griswold say, realizing that he was now standing right in front of me.

"Is that a surprise?" I asked as I slipped my phone into my pocket.

Griswold shrugged as he adjusted his cape. "Not really, but I thought that *maybe* if she saw at least *one* great act, then she would be convinced."

"Oh no, you didn't cut her money in half, did you?" I sighed.

As if on cue, he pulled a pair of halved twenty dollar bills out of his pocket.

"I can never get that trick to work out," he stated, examining the bills.

"Yeah, I know. That's how I've lost part of my pay," I said as we walked toward the school's front doors. "Speaking of which, you owe me for today. I am missing work, you know."

"You had a shift today?" Griswold innocently asked, as if he didn't already know that I worked in the bookstore every day after school.

"Yeah, so you owe me," I said as we both pushed open the front doors.

The minute we stepped outside, as if waiting for me, Lucy walked toward the entrance, her widening smile revealing her multicolored braces.

"More than you know," I added, seeing the romanticized versions of us following close behind her.

As we walked under the red brick-laden archway, Lucy brushed strands of wavy brown hair out of her face, as her imaginary clone ran her fingers through her far too silky, straight brown hair.

"Your hair is beautiful the way it is," I offered.

Lucy ran her fingers through her wavy brown locks as she timidly smiled and shook her head.

"It's okay, but sometimes I wish it was straighter," she admitted.

"I know."

"You know?"

"Yeah, I mean, a lot of people want what they can't have," I quickly stated.

"And what is it that *you* want, Domino?"

To say that there was not a one straight answer to this question would be an understatement. Then again, this is what you would term a "loaded question," and one that I have not had to answer before.

I guess we all want *something*; scratch that, I *know* that everyone wants something because they all fantasize about it. Fantasies usually manifest themselves as desires. Sometimes they are superficial desires, such as imagining yourself instantly rich and literally swimming in money. I have had to block out way too many visions of nude people diving into a pool filled with money. I never understood the appeal of diving into a container filled with money, but it's a pretty common fantasy. Sometimes, they are fantastical yearnings, like imagining yourself reformed into something mystical or magical, like picturing yourself as an elf traveling across Middle Earth. And then there are those deep-seated longings, such as picturing oneself belonging to a group, or envisioning your unrequited love being re-created into an everlasting and fully reciprocated eternal love. These fantasies were the most powerful and were therefore the most difficult to block out. I was never entirely sure why. Maybe it's because the intense emotion that drives the fantasy makes it feel that much more real to the creator. For whatever reason, if possible, I try to avoid being in the vicinity of those fantasies, which is usually difficult, especially when your friend sets you up on a date with a girl who is always having one of those intense fantasies about you.

While I am hyperaware of the fact that Lucy is infatuated with me, I never understood why.

As we neared the large octagonal sea lion tank, I responded, "I guess I want to know why you like me."

I didn't know if it was the candidness of my statement, or the fact that I could feel the heat of the afternoon sun's rays blazing behind me and therefore shining into Lucy's eyes, but whatever the reason may have been, she squinted as she met my gaze.

"I don't know, Domino. Maybe it's because you are so unabashedly you," Lucy said with a shy smile as she took my hand in hers. Hers was a bit clammy but I didn't mind.

"I'm not sure what you mean, but okay."

"You just seem comfortable in your own skin," she explained, giving my hand a light squeeze. "I just like that. I wish I were more like that."

I looked over her shoulder to see Lucy's imaginary version of herself smiling with perfectly straight, braceless teeth. With her shoulders back, she looked as if she was poised to take on the world.

"I know who I want to be, but I'm just not that person," Lucy admitted.

"You don't have to be anyone else," I said, and then surprised myself when I added, "You are beautiful just the way you are."

She smiled brightly, revealing her braces' vibrant elastics.

"And that's another reason why I like you. You always seem to accept who someone is, rather than who someone can be. You are one of a kind, Domino Garrison."

I felt a splay of heat spread across my cheeks as I looked into Lucy's amber eyes. I had never noticed how effervescent they were until that moment. Maybe it was because I tried to avoid her and her Harlequin romance versions of us as a couple. Maybe it was because I had never stood this close to her or looked this deeply into her eyes. Either way, I could not help but be drawn to her. However, before I could act on this newly discovered feeling, a sharp, shrill scream sliced through the air between us.

At first, it sounded as if this piercing scream was singular and its creator was somewhere off in the distance; however, the screams began to multiply and accumulate into one shrieking mass.

Instinctively, I looked around to see the cause of such terror.

Before I could see its mosaic of orange, black, and white stripes, or its gleaming golden eyes, I heard its minacious roar.

Similar to Mr. Humphries's imagined twin lions, the tiger skulked around, its eyes glistening and hyperalert.

Immediately, I closed my eyes and silently repeated my mantra to myself, believing that when I opened my eyes, the assumed animal activist's freed predator fantasy would disappear from my sight.

Instead, the screams grew louder and people rushed past me, some bumping my shoulder. When I opened my eyes again, I knew that I was not seeing a fantastical manifestation of a tiger, but instead the real artifact that had escaped its habitat.

Without saying a word, I pulled Lucy forward, darting for the exit. We quickly caught up with the human stampede and joined the mass of bodies literally running for their lives.

Lucy's bones practically dug into mine as we hit a bottleneck of screeching humans, all throwing themselves toward an exit that could maybe fit thirty really thin people at most, not the hundreds trying to simultaneously squeeze through.

Random limbs pushed and shoved into us. Bodies were pummeling into my shoulders, as if they were the barrier standing in between gruesome death and sweet freedom. I stood a little straighter and spread my legs apart in an effort to gain a firmer balance, so that I wouldn't fall to the ground.

I heard a crescendo of high-pitched "move, move!" coming from all directions, as we were enveloped in a mass of terrified humans. On top of this crescendo, I heard stern voices emanating from a PA system. The steady voice kept urging the frightened crowd to "remain calm" and to "exit in an orderly fashion." Yes, because when you tell people to be calm and orderly, that usually works like magic. Unsurprisingly, this plea was ineffective.

Gripping Lucy's hand a little tighter, I continued to pull her along as we did our best to keep our footing. My eyes darted around, looking for a sliver of light, or a hole that we could squeeze through among the heaving, terrified bodies. However, all I could see were limbs, smooshed into one another.

I finally turned to look at Lucy. Her wavy hair was disheveled, and her pupils were so dilated that her amber irises were barely visible. Both of her shirt sleeves were torn, revealing splays of yellow and purple skin blossoming on the exposed parts of her arms.

I took a deep breath, wishing that for once what I was seeing was only a figment of someone's imagination.

I managed to pull Lucy toward me, so that we were standing next to each other.

Leaning in, I shouted, "We just need to move with the crowd. We can't lose our footing."

Memories of others' imagined grotesque stampedes with the remains of fallen animals lying on the ground, perforated skin revealing fragmented bones sticking out and brain matter oozing onto the trodden floor, flooded to the surface of my mind.

I shook my head as if I could shake the memory out of mind.

"It can get really bad," I shouted.

The air around us became stiflingly hot and restrictive, as the mass of bodies worked to squeeze through the zoo's all too narrow exit. Maybe it was the mixture of suffocation and sweat messing with my vision, but I could have sworn that the exit was narrowing.

In desperation, I closed my eyes and silently said, "Move." As if it was a collective wish, I felt the crowd loosen as we moved more swiftly toward the exit. I had no idea how that happened, but I was grateful that it had.

In what was a few quick moments, Lucy and I throttled forward through the exit and were practically thrown out onto the sidewalk, our hands still holding onto each other in a vise-like grip. Without letting go, we ran down the sidewalk.

We ran for miles, it seemed, but we finally stopped in front of a brownstone, only to fall, wheezing, onto the sidewalk.

We both stared at each other as we continued to pant from exhaustion.

Although my throat was raw and I could barely breathe, I said the only thing that came to mind. "For our next date, let's not go to the zoo."

CHAPTER 3

THE SEISMIC CATASTROPHE

My thighs were throbbing as I made my way back to my apartment. It felt like my backpack was lined with lead and filled with boulders, but I managed to keep it on my shoulders. In fact, I'm actually shocked that I didn't lose it in the terrified crowd.

Once inside my building, I shuffled to our one elevator only to see strips of bright yellow police tape strewn over the doors. Great. I took a deep breath before heading toward the stairs, regretting the fact that we lived on the damn fifth floor.

After what felt like the Mount Everest of all climbs, I finally stepped out of the stairwell, only to find our apartment door ajar and the distinct mixture of marijuana and BO wafting in the air. I scrunched my nose, knowing that could only mean one thing: Jeff.

Jeff probably had a last name. Not everyone is Ke$ha or Beyoncé. Jeff does not have their fame or gravitas; however, learning Jeff's last name, or anything about Jeff, would be absolutely pointless. I cannot even say with absolute certainty that his name is *actually* Jeff, but it is what my mom called him. He hasn't corrected her yet, but then again, they have only known each for about a week, and based on the grunting that I cannot help but hear through our paper-thin walls, they do not have intimate conversations about their hopes and dreams. I am pretty sure that he doesn't know my mom's name, that is unless he is dumb enough to think that her name is actually "Babe."

Jeff is one in a series of "Jeffs" that my mom sleeps with, until she grows bored and/or her Jeffs turn violent. Once that happens, she immediately detaches. Very few have been abusive, but such men did find their way into our lives, especially when I was a child. The worst was Mike.

Mike was deceptively kind, at least at first. He was a customer at The Silver Spoon diner where my mom works, who came in each evening, despite the fact that he worked and lived downtown. The Silver Spoon is on the other side of town, nowhere within the vicinity of where Mike even existed. His world was a richer one, where he worked as a stockbroker and went to "business events" and cocktail parties. A world of tailor-made suits imported wines, and golf. His lifestyle was so foreign to us that I could not help but question why he pursued my mom. Even at ten years old, I was suspicious, so, naturally, I questioned his motives.

When I first met him at the diner, he kept calling me "kiddo" and ruffling my hair, as if he was my long-lost father. Hell, I don't even think that my dad would have done that. Then again, I don't know anything about my dad, except that he left.

You may think that this behavior is pretty standard for a boyfriend who is trying to get to know his girlfriend's ten-year-old son, and you would be right; however, my life is anything but "standard." Behind his benign behavior was his hidden desire, which was dripping with malice.

As he was ruffling my hair, he imagined himself gripping my scalp and throwing me to the floor; in his fantasy my mom merely looked on with approval. In fact, she smiled with gratification as if this was a shared desire. He then smirked in her direction as the soles of his wing-tipped shoes slammed into the side of my head. He continued to pound the imaginary me until I was unconscious, and the side of my head was horrifically malformed and concave, as if he were trying to reform my skull into a salad bowl.

His fantasy was so vivid that after he left the diner, I kept checking my head for indentations. Since that moment, I could not help but wince every time I saw Mike.

When my mom asked me the inevitable, what I thought about Mike, I had no idea what to say. I couldn't exactly tell her the truth, that he was a sociopath who imagined beating me to a pulp for no apparent reason. Other than perceiving his fantasy, I had no proof that he was a sinister human being. That definitely would not hold up in court.

So, in response to this question, I said the only thing that came to mind, "I don't know."

It was only days later, when I found Mike sitting on our sofa, that I knew that my opinion of Mike made little difference to my mom. My mom and Mike cozied up to one another as I swiftly walked to my room, where I would spend most of my time until I heard Mike leave.

At the beginning of their relationship, Mike never spent the night. He came over most evenings to take my mom out. I never knew where they went, nor did I care to know; I was just relieved that we were not in the same room, that is until he *did* begin to spend the night. My mom had had many relationships with men, but she had never allowed any of them to spend the night. I never knew why Mike was the exception. However, it was evident that he was when I got up in the middle of the night one time to find him in the kitchen, helping himself to the last of our orange juice.

Before I could make my way back to my room, Mike called me over to the kitchen table. Well, it's not technically a kitchen table. It's more like a small, circular patio table that just happened to be in our kitchen.

"Dom, take a seat," Mike said, gesturing to one of the mismatched chairs.

I tentatively sat across from him, unable to hide my cringe at the shortening of my name.

"I get this funny feeling that you don't really like me," Mike said. His brows furrowed over his piercing stare.

In response, I shrugged, not knowing what else to say or do, especially knowing what he would probably do to me if I admitted the truth. However, I didn't have to because he already knew how I felt.

"No, it's not just a funny feeling. You don't like me," Mike affirmed, gripping the empty orange juice jug.

"So? Why do you care? My mom's going to date whatever scumbag she wants," I said. I did not know where that boldness came from, but from Mike's grimace, I could tell that I had hit a nerve.

"What did you call me, you little bastard?" Mike hissed as he flung the orange juice jug against the wall.

The bottom of the kitchen chair's legs screeched against the linoleum floor as I shot up. As if following suit, Mike bolted up, and leaned over the table, with his knuckles pressed down into the tabletop.

In response, I opened my mouth, but nothing came out, not even a sound.

That is when the air started to sizzle.

"No, no, no," I whispered as I saw a series of blades appear, as if released by an invisible force. They all darted in my direction.

Instinctively, I ducked under the table to dodge the weapons; however, that gave Mike the perfect opportunity to crouch down and grab my leg, dragging me out.

"I'll teach you to talk to me like that," Mike growled as he continued to drag me out of the kitchen and toward the bathroom.

Once inside the bathroom, he locked the door, and turned on the shower. Still lying on the floor, I could feel my pulse beat throughout my body as I remained still.

Lifting me up from the floor by my shirt collar, Mike threw me into the tub and ordered me to stand up. Feeling the searing pain in my back from being slammed into the porcelain-enameled tub indicated that this was not a fantasy, even though it felt like a nightmare.

Despite the warm cascade of water showering down, I was shivering as I stood, staring at Mike's menacing grin and dilated black eyes.

"You think you're a tough guy, talking to me like that? Well, do you?" Mike barked, at which I flinched. "You think you're tough? Yeah? I'll show you what it means to be tough," Mike hissed as he balled his hand into a fist and pulled back his arm.

"Mom!" I wailed as I squeezed my eyes shut, bracing for the impact of Mike's punch.

I stood that way, cowering, for what felt like far too long, without feeling any impact.

With my eyes still closed, all I heard was the steady stream of water falling on my skin and clothes, but nothing else.

Hesitantly, I opened my eyes to see my mom standing behind Mike. His hands were raised in surrender. Her right elbow was raised, as if she was holding something and pressing into his back, but I couldn't tell what it was, that is until she told me to get out of the tub and I saw that the tip of a kitchen blade was kissing Mike's spine.

"If you ever go near my son again, you're dead," my mom said, her tone even keeled and firm, almost as if she was making a promise.

Without uttering a word, Mike exited the bathroom and our lives.

After Mike, my mom's relationships seemed to dwindle to one-week increments, and none of them stayed the night. For the most part, the other Jeffs, Toms, Dicks, and Harrys pretty much ignored me. As I mentioned, there were very few who were abusive, but none imagined killing me with levitating knives.

Similar to how she would not let anyone come after me, I protected her. As far as I knew, only one managed to hit her. When I was twelve years old, I had come home from playing ball to find one of the Jeffs throwing a right hook, which landed squarely on my mom's cheekbone, knocking her out instantly.

Instinctively, I gripped the base of my bat and held it parallel to the ground with my arms extended, slightly bending my knees. With my bat poised at the small of Jeff's—of whatever my mom's attacker's name was—back, I yelled, "I've been practicing my swing, and I rarely miss."

This Jeff spun around to see my makeshift weapon, which was now aimed at his ribs.

Compared to this Jeff's 6-foot-tall frame, me being a good 6 inches shorter than he was could not have been that imposing, but then again, I was wielding a Louisville Slugger. Sure, it was not exactly brand new, but with enough force, I am sure that I could have done some damage.

Maybe this Jeff was smarter than I gave him credit for because he quickly jetted out of the apartment. Once again, another creep was out of our lives, that is until my mom found the next one. She had a penchant for locating them.

I don't know if the slew of drugs in my mom's system had anything to do with it, but she recovered pretty quickly, and her cheekbone was only swollen and bruised for a day.

You would think that that instance would have been traumatic enough to ward her off dating, at least for a while, but my mom has always been a "get back up on that horse" type of person—well, metaphorically speaking. If she has ever actually ridden a horse, she never mentioned it to me. Then again, my mom usually does not talk about her past, so it's possible that she could have been a horse polo champion for all I knew.

Suffice it to say, the present Jeff was only one of the countless Jeffs in her life. There were no other Mikes. However, unlike some of her other boyfriends, the present Jeff seemed relatively harmless.

I pushed open the ajar door to find Jeff on our couch, which was grimy enough without his odor stinking it up, taking a hit off of his bong. My mom, who sat adjacent to him, held the sole of her foot while she aimed the syringe's needle in between her big and second toes. The needle eased into the toe webspace as she pushed the plunger down. When I was my younger, my stomach would churn whenever I saw this image, but over the years, that feeling faded away. I guess that I have become desensitized to it by now.

I pushed the door closed and headed to my bedroom, if you could call what should technically be a large walk-in closet a bedroom. Hearing me come in, my mom pulled the needle out and placed it on the coffee table.

"You're home late," my mom said, smoothing out her light blue and white waitress uniform. Her black hair was still sleeked into a neat bun, so she must have just come home from work.

"Yeah, I'm going to my room."

"There's leftover pizza in the kitchen, if you want some," my mom said, to which I shook my head.

I threw my backpack on my bed and rubbed my shoulders as I cracked my neck.

Sinking down onto my bed, I pulled my phone out of my pocket, tapped the screen, and input the passcode. When the phone lit up, it showed ten missed calls and several texts, all from Griswold.

Griswold usually did not call, so without even looking at the texts, I quickly called him back. He picked up on the first ring.

"What, did you throw your phone down a well?" he asked, anxiously.

"Hi to you too. What's up?"

"*What's up?*" Griswold said in disbelief. "Are you seriously asking me *what's up?*"

"Umm, yeah, it's a pretty standard question."

"*What's up* is that you were at the zoo today, right?"

"Yeah, you knew that. You set the whole thing up," I reminded him.

"Dude."

"Yes?"

"Dude."

"What?"

"*Dude!*"

"Okay," I said, annoyedly. "You have hit your 'dude' quota. What are you trying to say?"

"I mean, you were there, with the tiger?" Griswold asked excitedly.

"How did you—?" Before I could finish my sentence, I realized that a tiger freely roaming in a pretty well-known zoo was pretty newsworthy. "Hold on, I'm opening up a news app."

Scrolling through my phone, I tapped on my local news app. I did not have to scroll too far down before I found the news feed. What I read didn't make sense.

Only a few hours ago, a Bengal tiger allegedly managed to escape its habitat in the Central Park Zoo. While the tiger maimed two zookeepers, who were trying to shoot it, neither zookeeper was seriously injured. Although the whereabouts of the tiger are currently unknown, Harold Bernard, the Zoo Director, stated that his staff is well trained to find the tiger. Bernard is referring to the biannual drills carried out by his staff, who Bernard noted are "well prepared for this scenario."

A curfew has been instituted across Manhattan and every animal control agency is currently searching for the tiger.

When asked how the animal could have escaped, Devon Talbott, the zoo's Operations Director, stated that there were no apparent break-ins or any structural damage to the tiger habitat. Furthermore, Talbott indicated that when Emily Diamond, the General Curator, checked her records, it seemed like all of the tigers were accounted for.

Incidents of animals found on zoo grounds, outside of their habitats, are happening more frequently. Recently, the San Diego Zoo's zookeepers tried to sedate a roaming white lion, which is indigenous to the Timbavati region of South Africa, but the white lion evaded capture. At the time, the white lion was not a part of the animal collection, so the staff were baffled by its appearance. Soon after, a Tasmanian devil was found roaming outside of the primate habitat of the Smithsonian Zoo in Washington, D.C. Considering that it is a rare sight to see this creature anywhere other than the island state of Tasmania, the zookeepers stated that they had no idea where it had come from. Similar to the white lion, the Tasmanian devil was also never found.

"Hello? Are you still there?" Griswold asked, as I finished reading about that Tasmanian devil.

"I can't believe that they haven't caught it yet," I said.

"Yeah, they have no idea what happened to it. It's like it just... disappeared."

We both sat in silence for a moment. As if I could read his mind—which I can't, by the way—I said, "It was real, Grizz. I *know* it was real."

"*How* do you know that it was real?"

"Well, for one thing, other people saw it," I definitively noted. "As far as I know, the world did not suddenly develop the ability to see other people's fantasies. That delightful nightmare is only reserved for me."

Griswold paused for a good beat before he finally asserted, "Well, something weird is happening. Tigers just don't vanish."

"Look, just because they haven't found it yet, doesn't mean that it vanished," I stated, but I did not know who I was trying to convince, Griswold or myself.

The next morning, I opened up the news app to see if there were any further developments about the tiger. Although the articles provided a few more interviews with witnesses who were at the zoo at the time, none of the news feeds stated that the tiger had been captured.

I then logged onto our school website to see whether or not school had been canceled. However, to probably all of my classmates' chagrins, school was in session, but there was a special notice in the announcements section, the purpose of which was to assure families that every precaution was being taken to safeguard their children while they were at school. I am not sure how in the world they were going to protect us from an escaped tiger, but I guess we would find out about that at the special assembly that apparently, as the announcement read, all students were required to attend that morning.

I arrived at school to find Griswold capeless. He was wearing ordinary jeans and a black T-shirt with a tuxedo print. With no talent show in sight, there was no point in wearing a cape; however, knowing Griswold, he would try to find another way to perform magic tricks for an audience, even if they did not always go as planned.

He dragged his rolling backpack on the ground as he walked toward me, holding up his phone.

"They still haven't caught it," Griswold announced, shoving his screen in my face.

"I know, I checked my news feed this morning," I said, lowering his phone.

He looked around, as if he were checking to make sure that no one was listening to our conversation, before he whispered, "And, you don't find that *odd*?"

Raising an eyebrow, I warily asked, "Odd *how*?"

"*Paranormal odd.* I mean, they had everyone looking for that tiger. Even the police were looking for it. They canvassed Manhattan. That's at least what one of the latest news feeds said. And, nada, zip, zilch. It's like the tiger just disappeared."

Before I could respond, I saw Lucy in my peripheral vision.

As she came closer to us, I noticed that her amber eyes were pink and puffy, as if she hadn't slept.

"Hi, Lucy, are you okay?" I concernedly asked.

She shrugged as she looked into my eyes.

"I didn't really get that much sleep. I just kept thinking about yesterday."

I felt the familiar sizzle in the air as the events of yesterday played out in front of me. However, instead of the Harlequin romance versions of us running from a predator, Lucy imagined us as we were, two terrified teenagers running for our lives. While we looked relatively like ourselves, the tiger was about triple its size and its fangs were dripping with blood. It was only inches away from the fantastical versions of us, as we ran in place, like we were running on a treadmill.

"Hey," Lucyd said, waving her hand out in front of my face. "Are you listening to me?"

I closed my eyes to block out her fantasy.

"Yeah, sorry, I didn't get that much sleep either," I lied, opening my eyes again to see that her fantasy had disappeared. "What did you say?"

"I said that you saved us, and I never said thank you, so I'm saying it now. Thank you, Domino."

Before I could respond, Griswold interjected, "That may not be the last time he saves you because they still haven't found the tiger."

I gave his shoulder a shove, and gave him a look as if to say, "She's already scared enough as it is, don't make it worse."

"What?" he innocently asked. "It's not like it's a secret."

"You don't need to remind her," I reproached him.

"It's okay," Lucy said, twirling a strand of hair. "It's all over the news anyway. I was following the story last night."

Before I could say anything, the security guards blew their whistles and announced that all students were to go to the auditorium for a special assembly.

"I don't suppose they are going to tell us that they are hiring tiger tamers to protect us, right?" Griswold joked as we headed into the building.

"That's unlikely, unless that's magically in the school budget," I responded.

"Where's Siegfried and Roy when you need them?"

"Didn't you tell me that one of them was attacked by their tiger?" I asked, as we walked down the hallway toward the double auditorium doors.

"Yeah, but that was one time," Griswold responded as we stood behind the crowd pooling into the auditorium.

"It only takes one time."

"It didn't kill him."

"I heard that he died from COVID," Lucy interjected.

"Yeah, that's right," Griswold said, surprised. "How did you know?"

Lucy shrugged as the crowd began to move forward.

"I read and watch a lot of news. I guess that comes with the territory when both of your parents are journalists."

Once again, before I could say anything, our principal, Dr. Wexler, tapped the microphone, sending waves of high-pitched electronic noise throughout the packed auditorium.

"Take a seat, everyone," Dr. Wexler instructed.

In a few moments, aside from a few whispers, everyone seemed to settle in.

"Students and faculty members, most of you heard the news about the escaped tiger. I know that this is a frightening situation; however, I can assure you that we are taking every precaution to ensure that you are safe. While you are in school, we are instituting lockout measures, where you will not be able to leave the building during lunch. Your families and legal guardians have already been notified."

Dr. Wexler's speech was interrupted by snickering and a rise in perturbed whispers.

"Quiet, please," Dr. Wexler ordered as he held up his hands to silence the grumbling crowd. "This measure is being put in place to ensure your safety. This is only temp—"

Before Dr. Wexler could finish his sentence, the ground began to shake and I could hear the resounding sound of the Earth crumbling outside. The former snickering morphed into high-pitched screams.

My field of vision vibrated as I held onto the armrests. Lucy gripped my wrist so tightly that I thought she was going to cut off my circulation. Griswold's eyes darted from left to right as the color drained from his face. Similar to Lucy and me, he remained seated, staring up at Dr. Wexler, who was screaming at the packed auditorium.

"Stay calm, everyone! Stay calm!" Dr. Wexler shouted. Even though he was yelling into a microphone, it was still difficult to hear him over the crescendo of screaming. "Drop, cover, and hold onto something!" Dr. Wexler instructed to deaf ears as students and even some adults ran to the exits, blocking the passageways with their mass. Some of the adults followed Dr. Wexler's instructions and tried to convince the panicking students to do so as well. While some followed the directions, others dropped to the ground, curling up on their side in the fetal position with their eyes squeezed shut. However, some were scrambling to escape the auditorium.

Following Dr. Wexler's instructions, I closed my eyes and repeated my mantra to myself.

Before even opening my eyes, I knew that my little mantra didn't work as I felt barraged with the collective screeches growing to a head-splitting frequency.

"This is real," I whispered to myself as the rumbling and screams were joined by the sounds of squeaking metal followed by a distinct whooshing, as if something massive had fallen.

My eyes snapped open to find a darkened stage, covered in reams of red fabric. The black beam once above the stage that held descending stage lights lay on top of a still, seemingly unconscious Dr. Wexler.

Even though I didn't think that it was possible, Lucy gripped my wrist even tighter. I looked past her to see spider vein-like cracks inching along the auditorium walls.

"We need to get out of here," Griswold resolutely hollered, shooting up out of his seat.

I quickly pulled him down to the floor. Still holding my wrist with her vise-like grip, Lucy slid off of her seat and crouched down.

"Standing isn't going to help," I shouted over the screams. "We need to find an exit."

"The stage!" Lucy announced, grabbing the back of the chair in front of her to pull herself up to look just over the back of the seat. "There's a door at the back of the stage!"

Before I could ask her how she knew that, she tugged me to follow after her, releasing her grip on my wrist. I didn't look down to see if she had left a handprint, but I knew that there would probably be one there in the morning, that is if we didn't die from the auditorium caving in on us.

The ground steadily rumbled as we carefully crawled out of our row and down the aisle. I tried to concentrate only on the feeling of the rough carpet on the heels of my palms as we continued to move forward.

It seemed like eons before we finally made it to the stage stairs, which were covered in shards of glass.

I bit down on my bottom lip as I felt pieces of glass pierce my skin as I continued to crawl forward. I just considered myself lucky that I wasn't wearing shorts, otherwise my palms would not be the only part of my body covered in cuts.

"There!" Lucy shouted, pointing to the beige wall once hidden by the massive red curtain, now crumpled on the stage floor. A small golden knob protruded from the wall of beige.

As the three of us crawled toward the back of the stage, I cringed as I looked to my side to see Dr. Wexler, his glasses cracked and a stream of blood trickling out of his ear. I paused to press my index and middle fingers to his neck. His pulse was very weak but still present.

"He's alive, but barely," I affirmed.

"We're almost there," Lucy yelled, crawling faster toward our only exit.

Quickly bouncing up, she determinedly gripped and turned the doorknob. The door flew open to reveal a stream of light and debris.

"Come on!" Lucy shouted to Griswold and me, as she dropped to the floor and quickly crawled through the exit.

My eyes darted between the opening and the unconscious Dr. Wexler before I slid my fingers underneath the light fixture lying on top of his back.

"Help me!" I screamed to Griswold as I gripped the metal pole pinning our principal to the ground, but it barely budged.

Griswold slid his hands alongside mine, underneath the fixture, and attempted to pull it up, but to no avail.

Realizing that this wasn't working, I climbed over Dr. Wexler and grabbed his legs.

"We need to pull him out," I instructed, and then added "Now!"

Griswold quickly crawled over Dr. Wexler and we both pulled with everything that we had. Although I am sure Dr. Wexler's back would be severely bruised, and from the liquid seeping through the back of his shirt, I am not sure if we were causing further damage to his spine, we did manage to slide him out and pull him through the stage door.

"Now what?" Griswold asked, as we crouched in the hall outside of the doorway.

"Now we get the hell out of here and try to survive," I said, feeling the rumbling begin to subside as we looked toward the once brightly lit exit sign, now flickering and hanging by a single wire.

CHAPTER 4

AFTERSHOCK

D r. Wexler's body was barely out of the school's double doors when the exit sign's wire snapped and fell to the debris-covered ground.

"What the hell?" Lucy cried, running to us.

She quickly ran to us, knelt down by Dr. Wexler's shoulders, and slid her arms underneath his armpits.

"We've gotta lift him," Lucy exclaimed.

"What if he has a spinal injury?" I asked.

"Well, then dragging him out didn't help. On my count."

Before Lucy said three, Griswold and I stood up and repositioned ourselves so that he was lifting Dr. Wexler from underneath his mid-section and I had his legs.

"How did you know about the door?" I grunted, feeling a sharp pain in my shoulders as I gripped Dr. Wexler's ankles.

I carefully sidestepped onto a patch of ground that had not been ruptured.

"I wrote a few articles about the school plays, and had to inter-view members of the drama club. You learn a lot about behind-the-scenes stuff. Here's a good spot," Lucy said as she began to lower his shoulders.

After we eased him onto the ground, I took a look at his pant legs to see bloody palm prints. Before wiping my palms on my pants, I examined them to see exactly what I expected, an array of fresh, superficial cuts on the heels of my palms.

"I can't believe I didn't see him," Lucy said, punching something into her phone. "I'm so stup—Hello, 9-1-1? Yes, our principal is unconscious. He was in the earthquake..."

Lucy's voice trailed off as I stepped away to survey the damage.

The once-level grass and pavement were upturned and scored by vein-like cracks etched into its surface. The windows of the nearby buildings' glass were either fragmented and jagged or completely missing. The buildings looked like severely bruised faces that barely made it out of a boxing match only to come away with broken and missing teeth. Cars were parked at incongruous angles; some had flipped onto their side under the now lifted pavement. A nearby cab had managed to wrap itself around a telephone pole in a crumpled mess, almost as if it was some type of avant-garde sculpture.

A thick gray dust hung in the air like a dirty fog that was just not ready to lift. The stoplights flashed a rhythmic red as if it were communicating a warning in Morse code to whoever bothered to listen.

More and more people spilled out of the school's side emergency exit doors. Some stumbled out, some shoved through and continued to sprint down the unstable street, while others slowly made their way out and looked around dismayed as if they had entered a whole new world and were trying to figure out what to do next.

To my side, Griswold panted as he scrolled through his phone.

"What are you doing?" I asked, massaging one of my shoulders.

"Looking at the news feed to see if they have anything to say about this earthquake," Griswold said, furrowing his brow with a determined look in his eye. This was the same look that came over him when he was making his CGI creations.

"It just happened. I am sure there is—" Before I could finish my sentence, Griswold gripped my shoulder to which I winced.

"Found it!" Griswold announced, and then proceeded to silently read the feed to himself.

"Are you going to share with the rest of the class?" I asked, pulling his hand off of my shoulder.

"Yeah, sorry. I haven't gotten far, but there were several earthquakes today, and not only in New York. This article says that there were earthquakes along the East Coast." Griswold looked up from the screen, his eyes widening in fear. "That's just not normal."

"I mean, we have experienced earthquakes before," I reasoned.

"Sure, but this one felt pretty massive. And the article said that all of the earthquakes occurred at the same time. That's just *weird*."

"So, what are you trying to say, Grizz?"

"This just doesn't seem real."

"Trust me, this is *real*," I affirmed. "Look around you," I instructed, gesturing to the once bustling city street, now left empty and in disarray. "If this was imaginary, then you wouldn't be able to see this."

Before Griswold could respond, Lucy made her way to us, still holding her cell phone to her ear.

"An ambulance is coming, but it may take some time," she said, then thanked whoever was on the line and ended the call. Lucy looked around, surveying the devastation. "The streets are a mess, so I have no idea when they will get here."

As if the Earth was trying to further delay the EMTs, underneath our feet we felt the stirrings of another earthquake. Before what was happening could register, someone yelled "Aftershock!"

Remembering Dr. Wexler's instructions, I screamed, "Drop, cover, and hold on!" I pulled Lucy and Griswold to the rumbling ground, covered my head, and squeezed my eyes shut. Other than the grass, gravel, and dirt beneath my feet, there was nothing to hold onto. At least I had two out of three.

Stop shaking, stop shaking, stop shaking, I mouthed. As if the Earth was listening to me, the rumbling stopped and everything settled.

Gingerly, I removed my hands from the back of my head and turned to Griswold, who was looking back at me, head covered but still gripping his phone.

"What the hell is causing this to happen?" Lucy asked, perhaps to no one in particular, but I answered anyway.

"I have no idea, but it's bad."

A telephone pole suddenly fell on top of a parked car, almost splitting it in half.

"*Really* bad," I added, yelling over the car alarm.

Suffice it to say, school was canceled for the day, and perhaps for a while, considering the structural damage that the earthquake had caused.

While Griswold and I sat on one of the few Central Park benches that was not covered in debris or had fallen victim to the earthquake's devastation, Lucy was near the edge of the lake, speaking to her parents on her phone.

Griswold read through the news feed on his phone.

"The seismologists are estimating that some of the earthquakes had a magnitude of 6.5, including the one that hit the city, but they need to run more tests to confirm," Griswold stated.

"Yeah, it was pretty bad."

Griswold slowly looked up, pointing at his screen.

"They are saying that it's record breaking. According to this, the worst earthquake in New York occurred on September 5, 1944, and the magnitude was *5.9*," he said, stressing the number as if a decimal of .6 was supposed to send me into shock.

"And? Records are broken. It was bound to happen eventually. The earthquakes caused a lot of damage, but I wouldn't say that that is weird. Devastating? Yes. But weird? I don't think so."

"I mean, first the vanishing tiger and now this? I don't understand why you don't think that this is weird. You are like the king of weird," Griswold exclaimed, to which I smacked his shoulder and pointed to Lucy, who was still on her phone.

"Should I give you a damn podcast so you can announce that to the world?" I said.

"What?" Griswold asked, looking back at Lucy. "I didn't say that you are the king of weird *because* you can see other people's fantasies."

"Dude!" I exclaimed, smacking him in the shoulder again.

"Oh, so you can say 'dude' but I can't? Plus," Griswold continued, looking back at Lucy, "I highly doubt that she is paying attention to us." Griswold nodded in Lucy's direction as she walked farther along the edge of the lake, stepping over fallen tree limbs and overturned grass.

Griswold pulled his phone out, tapped the screen, and then quickly shoved it back into his pocket.

"How many times have they called?" I asked while checking my own phone. In response to my earlier text, asking my mom if she was safe, she simply said, "Yeah. You?" Monosyllabic texts, a Rosa Gomez Garrison staple. In the same vein, I sent a quick text back, "Yeah."

Scrolling through my other messages, I noticed several texts and a few missed calls from Miles. In the texts, Miles kept urging me to come in to work, *immediately*. I sent a quick text back, letting him know that I was safe, and that I would be in later.

Now, what *was* weird were these texts from Miles. He *never* begged me to come into the bookstore. If someone has to miss a shift, he will either move around the schedule and ask someone to cover, or if that's not possible, he will make do with the staff he has. If he does ask you to come in, he will send you one text, maybe two; however, he would never *beg* you to come in. Also, I am the only staff member who is still in high school. Miles can ramble on about the importance of education for hours on end, so the likelihood of him asking me to miss school to come into work is incredibly slim. I would expect to see a yeti standing in the middle of his bookstore before I would expect Miles to ask me to skip school for anything.

"About six, maybe seven," Griswold responded.

"The 'I'm not dead' text just didn't cut it, huh?" I asked, sliding my phone back into my pocket.

"Well, I'm not!" Griswold exclaimed, and as if he needed to prove it, he stood up and gestured to himself. "See? Completely alive."

"You don't need to convince me. You are one of the most 'alive' people I know."

"Yeah, but that may not be for long," Griswold stated, pointing at one of the slain trees. "*This*, all of this, is not normal. If it's not some type of fantasy, it has to be the result of magic or something paranormal. Something very strange is happening, and I am not sure why you are not convinced."

Griswold tended to believe that something strange was happening even when there was a logical explanation. I may be the "king of weird," but Griswold is the one who is eager to wear the crown.

For example, Ms. Ackerson, his first-grade teacher, always seemed to know when he was trying to sneak extra snack-time treats, or when he had not completed his homework before she collected the assignment. Instead of deducing that she just knew him well enough to predict what he was going to do next, he immediately declared that she *must* be a witch.

As a result, we went on a wild goose chase trying to find witch hazel in Central Park. It would have helped if, one, we knew what witch hazel looked like, two, if we knew *exactly* where you can find witch hazel, three, if we knew whether or not witch hazel would affect a witch in any way, and finally, whether or not Ms. Ackerson was *actually* a witch. Spoiler alert, she wasn't. I want to say that witches don't even exist, but who am I—the kid who can perceive other people's fantasies—to say that? I think that's what you would call a "pot calling the kettle black" situation.

Whether or not I believed Ms. Ackerson was a witch did not make a difference; I still went along with it because there was no convincing Griswold otherwise. When he was determined to root out the cause of the strange and unbelievable, I have learned to go along with him for the ride, at least for a while, otherwise he will drive you nuts until you do.

"Okay, fine," I conceded. "Explain to me why this is so weird."

"Because this type of stuff *just does not happen*," Griswold emphasized, sitting down again. "A tiger mysteriously escapes from the zoo, but all the tigers are accounted for, and now they cannot even find this tiger. The next day, we have record-breaking earthquakes. If it was *one* record-breaking earthquake? Okay, chalk it up to climate change—which they will probably do, by the way—but *multiple* earthquakes? Happening at the same time? *Most* of them being record breaking? And an unaccounted-for tiger is pulling a disappearing act? I mean this all seems out of the realm of possibility."

Admittedly, Griswold's points were somewhat valid, but that did not mean that there wasn't a reasonable explanation for the tiger and the earthquakes.

That is, until black sludge began bubbling up from the ground right beside me.

I heard the gurgling before I saw the thick, syrupy black liquid. Yellow foam began to form on the edges of the liquid, which began to bleed onto the Earth's surface. It resembled a sea of boiled slugs that were folded into hot tar. As the black tar-like substance dyed the ground, I heard a distinct sizzle as if acid were pouring onto the dirt and grass. The ground began to sink, forming into a widening hole.

Immediately, believing that this had to be someone's warped fantasy, I squeezed my eyes shut and said my mantra to myself.

Down by the lake, Lucy squealed, "What the hell?"

Before opening my eyes, I groaned. "Shit, it's real." I opened my eyes to see Lucy running toward us. The black liquid covered the toes and soles of her sneakers. Blades of grass and dirt stuck to the sludge, which she kept trying to shake off.

Griswold pulled out his phone and tapped the screen.

The bubbling increased in intensity and volume as Griswold scrolled through his phone.

"Ouch!" Lucy screamed. Like the ground, the black liquid began to eat away at Lucy's sneakers. I didn't know if this substance was also flesh-eating, but I didn't want to find out.

"Quick, take them off," I instructed, going to her side and offered my shoulder for balance. She leaned on my shoulder as she quickly undid her laces and slipped off her sneakers.

With only thin white socks covering her feet, we quickly moved to a concrete-laden path. Brows furrowed, Griswold continued to scroll through his phone.

"Guys, this is really, *really* bad," Griswold stated, still staring at the screen. "There have been other sightings of this black stuff."

"It's like acid," Lucy said, looking down at her sneaker-less feet.

"Come on, we can't stay here," I affirmed.

"Where *exactly* are we supposed to go then?" Lucy asked.

I took a deep breath before saying, "Follow me."

"So why are we stopping at a bookstore?" Lucy asked, looking up at the ripped, bright red awning with faded plastic letters that read *Booklet*. Why Miles chose to name his store after a thinner version of what he actually sold, I will never know.

"The guy who owns this store is my boss and he kept asking me to come in. There has to be a reason why. Maybe he knows something," I explained, reaching for the door.

Lucy placed her hand on top of mine before I could make contact with the door.

"How is it possible that your boss knows what's going on? We need to go to the police, the hospital, a lab, somewhere where we can find people who can stop this," Lucy insisted.

"They don't know what's causing this," Griswold asserted, looking down at his phone. "I've been looking and everyone is baffled. This black stuff is coming out of the ground, eating away at everything it touches. They can't even figure out how to take any samples."

"It would be *way* too early to figure out what it is, but they *will* figure it out. My parents said that every journalist in the tristate area is reporting on the earthquakes, and probably now on that sludge too. Someone is bound to get to the bottom of this. I mean, there *has* to be a logical explanation," Lucy said, looking into my eyes as if she was trying to urge me to agree with her.

Maybe Lucy was right. Maybe a scientist, a doctor, or the police could provide us with a reasonable explanation. Maybe even Lucy's parents would break the story. Maybe I should listen to Lucy, but my gut told me to brush those maybes aside.

"Your parents are probably worried about you," I began, and then sighed. "You should go home, but I need to be here. I just can't shake the feeling that Miles may know something."

With that, Lucy took a step back, her brow furrowed. She slid her phone out of her pocket, but she didn't turn it on. Her thumb hovered over the screen for a beat before she determinedly shoved it back into her pocket.

"Okay, let's see what Miles has to say."

It was as if Miles had sonar hearing because before I could even touch the door, it swung open, smacking into the wall with a distinctive thud that should have pulled the door off of its hinges.

"Get in," Miles commanded, his head barely peeking through the crack in the door.

The three of us were barely inside before Miles slammed the door shut and slid the dead bolt into place. The once-smooth blue walls were etched with jagged, vein-like cracks. Books were strewn across the wood floor; some were piled in a disjointed heap as if someone were preparing to burn them. Most of the books were covered in bits of fallen plaster. The once perfectly aligned wooden bookcases were toppled over onto one another like a deck of cards that was poorly shuffled.

One of the lights above the counter flickered, creating a strobe light effect that was bound to give us all migraines, that is if this insane day didn't beat the lights to it.

Miles turned toward us, adjusting his cracked horn-rimmed glasses. Similar to his inventory, Miles was covered in a coat of white plaster that powered his black sweater vest and matching pants.

"Miles, what's going on?" I asked, and then added, "I mean, it's not like there is an emergency inventory situation here. I could have helped you clean up later, I just don't get it."

"That's not why I wanted you here," Miles stated. He crossed his arms as he looked at Griswold and then at Lucy before he added, "I should have asked you to come alone."

Griswold raised both of his eyebrows, looking taken aback. He turned to me as if I understood why Miles wanted me to come to the bookstore alone. In response, I just shook my head. Griswold's guess was as good as mine. Lucy looked at Miles expectantly, waiting for him to explain.

"Why? I mean, a disheveled bookstore that survived a series of earthquakes isn't a secret. Why should I have come alone?"

Miles pulled off his glasses and looked down at the crack in the lens. He ran his fingers halfway through his hair before he determinedly lowered his arms to his sides.

"Because what I have to tell you is for you, and you alone, to hear."

I quickly glanced from Griswold to Lucy, and then back to Miles.

"Well, I can't magically make them disappear, so whatever you need to say to me, you can say in front of Grizz and Lucy."

Miles sighed before he said, "Fine, but what I have to tell you isn't going to be easy to hear. I'd tell you to sit down, but as you can clearly see, there is nowhere to sit." Miles took a deep breath before he continued. "You have obviously been outside, so you know about the earthquakes and that sludge."

In unison, we nodded.

"And the tiger," Griswold added.

"No one knows what's going on," I explained.

"Not *yet* anyway," Lucy added.

"Well, I highly doubt that they will," Miles said, sliding his cracked glasses into his pocket. "It's not real, none of it."

While Lucy tilted her head to the side and slightly furrowed her brow in confusion, Griswold's eyes widened in amazement. He quickly turned to me, as if to ask the same question that was on my mind: *If the sludge and earthquakes weren't real, how could everyone else see them?*

"What do you mean that it's not real?" Lucy asked. "It's unbelievable what is happening outside, sure, but it's *real*. Are you saying that it's all just a giant conspiracy?"

Miles chuckled and then shook his head.

"No, I am not proposing any conspiracy theories. What I am saying is that I know who is responsible for everything that is happening. There is only one person who could do all of this."

Even though I could hear Miles perfectly fine, I still leaned in just to ensure that I did not miss a syllable. Miles took a few steps closer to me, looked into my eyes, and placed his hands on my shoulders.

"It's your father."

CHAPTER 5

THE MAKINGS OF THE NOT-SO-REAL REALITY

Have you ever just woken up to find yourself sprawled out on the floor, feeling so out of place that it took you a moment to realize where you were? Well, it's even more disorienting to experience this sensation when you aren't even asleep. I shook my head as if my brain were an Etch-A-Sketch that needed to be reset.

"My *father*?" I echoed.

Bits and pieces of Miles's words, specifically "not real," "responsible," and "father," kept replaying in my head. I don't know about you, but a million questions were just on the tip of my tongue. I know that I am being hyperbolic, but if any day was the perfect day for hyperbole, it was this one. The questions that made the top five list were: How could the tiger, earthquakes, and that black sludge not be real if everyone else can perceive them? How could my dad be responsible for them? If my dad was responsible for them, how could he be responsible for something that is *not real*? If he was responsible for every weird event that happened yesterday and today, why was he doing this, and why *now*? How much does Miles know about my dad?

Miles gave a determined nod as he gave my shoulders a firm squeeze. He must have noticed me wincing because he quickly pulled away.

"Wait, you're saying that Domino's *father* is the cause of the tiger who tried to attack us, the earthquakes, and the sludge that burned through my sneakers?" Lucy asked, with a healthy dose of skepticism in her tone.

"Yes," Miles responded to Lucy, but he was still looking at me.

"How is that even possible?" Lucy asked, crossing her arms over her chest.

A reiteration of question two. How in the world could my dad be responsible for a vanishing tiger, a series of the worst earthquakes that New York has ever experienced, and for creating a substance that has the potential to dissolve anything in its path? Well, at least I *think* that it has this potential. I have not put my theory to the test, but who would want to? I mean, it ate through sneakers. I'm not letting my hand be its next victim.

"'Once you eliminate the impossible, whatever remains, no matter how improbable, must be the truth.' Sir Arthur Conan Doyle may have written that approximately a century ago, but it perfectly applies here," Miles asserted.

"We haven't even had a chance to eliminate *anything*," Lucy insisted, roughly running her fingers through her wavy hair. Throwing up her hands, she added, "I knew that we should have gone to the police. This is ridiculous."

A soft, rhythmic hum rose from Lucy's pocket. She pulled her phone out and slid the bar on the screen to the right before she pressed the phone to her ear.

"Colin? Are you okay? Mom couldn't reach you," Lucy stated and then turned away, carefully making her way through the book graveyard.

My eyes followed Lucy to the back of the bookstore before I turned my attention back to Miles.

"How could all of this," I said, gesturing at the cracked walls and fallen bookcases, as if Miles's store was a representation of today's chaos, "be my dad's doing?"

Miles looked down and slightly shook his head before he stated, "He should have told you, but you were too young, far, far too young, when he left."

"What should he have told him?" Griswold asked. Griswold had been so uncharacteristically quiet that I almost forgot that he was standing right next to me.

"He should have told Domino about himself," Miles responded, and then, looking into my eyes, he added, "You may not know this, but you are more like your father than you realize. As you know, I knew your father from when he was younger than you. Max Garrison was special, but not in the same way that others may say that a person is 'special' because of their character attributes. Your father was—*is*—special because he has the ability to project his own fantasies into reality."

"What?" Griswold and I asked in unison. His "what?" sounded way more enthusiastic than mine. Mine was laced with disbelief and a sense of dread. So not only did my dad leave, stamping this departure with a cryptic message, but he also had supernatural abilities that were somewhat like my own. If I did not perceive countless fantasies on a daily basis, I would have argued that Miles's notions about my dad were fallacious; no, scratch that, I would have told him that they were downright *wrong*. However, in my world, where reality and fantasy were consistently fused together as if they were the result of some horrible science experiment gone awry, I had no choice but to keep an open mind.

Miles nodded, continuing, "Yes, if Max imagined something—*anything*—he would bring it into reality."

"*Would* bring it into reality?" I asked.

"Well, I shouldn't say 'would.' Sometimes he was able to control what he brought into reality, but sometimes he couldn't."

I put up my hand and said, "Wait, wait, how in the world do you know this?"

Without skipping a beat, Miles responded, "Your father imagined enough scenes from *Fantasia* when he was working here as a stock boy that it was hard *not* to notice."

"Great, he fancied himself a wizard," I said, running my hands down my face.

"That's so cool!" Griswold excitedly cried.

"Wait, then other people must have known, right? If he didn't mean to project his fantasies into reality in front of *you*, then he must have accidentally done it in front of others, right?" I asked.

Miles simply shrugged.

"It's possible that others knew, but maybe not. People tend to believe something that seems realistic. Most would not believe that someone has the ability to make their own fantasies a reality," Miles reasoned.

I nodded, reflecting on why I have told no one else, except for Griswold, what I am able to perceive. Not that I would, but even if I *could* prove that I am able to experience what other people imagine, I highly doubt that many would believe me. Plus, I am pretty sure that I would be institutionalized if I told others that I hear imaginary voices and see imaginary constructs. It's not even like it's useful. I mean, how is seeing twin lions in history class or a dragon-sometimes-Pegasus outside of my apartment building at all helpful?

"Max had a hard time controlling what he brought into the world," Miles continued. "Some of his fantasies were harmless, like imagining that he had a new bike; however, as he got older, some of his fantasies were much deadlier. For example, once, after reading about Jack the Ripper, he magically appeared in the middle of the bookstore."

"*The* Jack the Ripper?" Griswold asked in disbelief, and then began looking around the store, as if the homicidal madman was hiding behind a fallen bookcase.

"So, you're telling me that my dad brought a nineteenth-century English serial killer into existence? And where is this serial killer *now*?"

"Your father managed to remove him from existence, but it was hard for him."

"Are you kidding?" Lucy asked, standing behind Miles. I don't know if I jumped because I didn't expect Lucy to be standing there, or because Miles had just informed me that my dad had magical abilities that he couldn't control. Either way, it didn't matter because the resounding gurgling drowned out every thought that I had.

The black sludge began to seep in through the cracks in the floor, overtaking the wood with a thick, ominous coating of acidic black varnish. In severe defiance of gravity, the sludge crept up the walls, heading for the ceiling.

I squeezed my eyes shut, and repeated my mantra to myself, but to no avail.

"We've gotta get outta here!" Lucy screeched, turning toward the exit.

"Wait!" I shouted, reaching out and grabbing her wrist as she tried to bolt. "Look," I said, nodding toward the door that we came in, which was now covered in black sludge. A deafening, sickening hiss reverberated throughout the store as the sludge began to eat its way through the infrastructure.

My eyes darted from left to right, trying to find another way out.

Suddenly, a large, metal door appeared behind the counter.

"There!" I announced, pointing at the metal door. "We can escape through there."

Lucy and Griswold looked at the door in confusion, and then looked back at me.

"They can't see it. It's in my imagination," Miles exclaimed, gesturing to the walls, where identical doors manifested, replacing the sludge infused walls.

"Make them real," Miles instructed.

"Make them *real*?" I echoed. I watched more doors pop into existence as if they were cloning themselves. Doors next to doors covered the floors and ceilings to the point where I could no longer see the black sludge.

"Concentrate," Miles commanded. "I can't keep imagining doors with this sludge eating through my store."

"I can only see what you're imagining, I can't do anything with it," I admitted, and then added, "It's useless, there's no point."

"There's nowhere to run!" Lucy cried. "It's everywhere."

"Concentrate!" Miles desperately yelled, as more doors appeared on top of one another. "This is what you can do. I know, I saw it, just concentrate."

Between just being told that my absentee dad was able to imagine his fantasies into reality and that somehow I was able to make Miles's fantastical doors suddenly become real, my head was spinning. I was tempted to block out Miles's imaginings, but the fear and anxiety that were driving his fantasies were so intense. Plus, if Miles were right and I could make his doors become real, it was our only chance to escape.

I focused on the multiplying doors, not knowing what else I could do other than stare at them.

"Do you see them?" I yelled to Griswold and Lucy.

Blood draining from their faces, they cowered as they shook their heads.

"Shit," I spat and then shouted to Miles, "It's not working. I can't do it."

"You can," Miles insisted, climbing on top of the counter under the makeshift strobe light.

"*How?*"

Griswold, Lucy, and I quickly joined Miles, sitting on top of the counter, bringing our knees to our chests so that we could make ourselves as small as possible.

"Just believe that they are real," Griswold suggested, pulling in his knees closer to his chest.

Nodding, I brought my focus back to Miles's imagined doors. Since I had encountered doors every day, you would think that believing that these doors were real would be pretty easy, but when you *know* that something is imaginary, it's hard to trick yourself into believing that it isn't. Nevertheless, I had to try.

I concentrated on the large metal door that had replaced the wooden one that we had come through. Its patchwork of metal sheets were bolted to one another as if Dr. Frankenstein had suddenly become a carpenter and his first creation was this door. Its silver handle was sturdy and seemed to repel the sludge, which danced along the edges of the metal, but refused to touch it, as if it *knew* that this particular door was different.

"There!" Lucy exclaimed, pointing toward Miles's imagined door. "The door!"

"Great, how do we get to it?" Miles asked, looking down.

Lowering my gaze, I concentrated on the floor where Miles had imagined the other overlapping doors. They had melded into one metallic mass with random handles sticking out in all directions.

I attempted to bring these doors into existence, but a wave of exhaustion suddenly hit me. I tried to push through it as I focused on bringing the door floors into reality.

An intense ringing resounded in my ears, as I willed the door floors into existence. They formed into a single pathway that led toward the massive door in the wall.

"You did it!" Griswold exclaimed as he and Lucy jumped off of the counter and ran for the door.

Miles carefully, but quickly, climbed down and sped toward the door, ensuring that he did not touch the sludge that covered everything but the imagined-now-real metallic doors.

The high-pitched ringing intensified as I eased myself to the makeshift path. I practically toppled onto the door floor as I struggled to stand up.

"Domino!" I heard Griswold and Lucy yell as they ran back into the store. With Griswold standing to my left and Lucy on my right, they hoisted me up and helped me toward Miles's melting bookstore's exit.

Miles flung the door open and ordered us to run.

"Run?" Lucy yelled, "Domino can barely walk."

Miles looked me up and down. He mouthed something, but I couldn't hear him over the persistent ringing. I slumped down as the whole world went dark, as if it were fading from existence.

When I came to, I was lying on something hard. It was too lumpy and bulbous to be the sidewalk. Reluctantly, I opened my eyes to see the orange and golden hues of dusk peeking through the heavy, graying clouds that ominously hung overhead, as if they were threatening to bring forth another natural disaster.

For the briefest moment, I thought I was still outside our high school, waiting for the effects of the earthquake to wear off. However, that moment's oblivion quickly vanished when it all came flooding back—the sludge, Miles's razed bookstore, and the not-so-imaginary doors.

The second I shot up, I quickly regretted it. My brain rattled around in my skull, like a ping-pong noisily slapping against a brick wall. I winced as I rubbed my temples.

"Are you okay?" Lucy asked, kneeling next to me.

The answer to this question should be simple. Usually, it only required a monosyllabic response, but neither a "yes" nor a "no" sufficed. I stopped rubbing my temples long enough to hold my palms out in front of me. The tiny cuts had become a series of small, thin, red lines that were sprinkled on the heels of my palms. I did a quick body scan to determine that nothing seemed to be broken. Sure, my shoulders were still a little sore, and lying on this rock definitely didn't help, but physically I wasn't too bad off. Was I fine *mentally*? Your guess is as good as mine. The simple and complicated answer to that question is an uncertain one: I have no idea. I mean, would you be okay if you just pulled something imagined into reality? Would you be okay if you were being surrounded by an unknown substance that acted like a flesh-eating virus with a vendetta? Maybe *you* would be, but I was still uncertain. All I knew was that I had just done the impossible and I had no idea what any of it meant.

"Where are we?" I asked, skirting the question, looking around to see fallen trees, overturned ground, and a severe lack of people.

"Central Park," Miles answered, standing a few feet away.

"What, does this park have a gravitational pull on us or something? How did we wind back up here?"

"You saved us!" Griswold excitedly shouted. I winced and began rubbing my temples again.

"Just a few decibels lower, huh, Grizz?"

"Sorry," Griswold whispered, and then added, "But you did. You saved us from that stuff. We wouldn't have made it out alive without you."

"This is all just so crazy," Lucy exclaimed. "There has to be a logical explanation for what's happening, right, Domino?"

She looked at me pleadingly, as if she could find that logical explanation somewhere in my eyes.

I ran my hand over my face, trying to figure out how to respond.

Simply put, there was no logical explanation for what had happened. I could tell her the truth, that I have the ability to perceive other people's fantasies, but not only is that illogical, it's not even completely true, because what I did in Miles's bookstore was more than that. I didn't just perceive Miles's fantasy, I pulled it into reality—well, part of it at least—but how exactly do you make something so nonsensical understandable? You literally have to suspend your belief in what you knew to be true, that reality and fantasy are two entirely and unequivocally separate notions. How in the world am I going to begin to explain that the not-so-finite lines between fantasy and reality just blurred? Hell, I am the one who was responsible for blurring those lines, and I was having a hard time understanding it, let alone explaining it in a way that made any sense.

"It may seem crazy but it's not. Domino *did* save us. It's because of what he is able to do. He's always been able to do that, he just didn't know it," Miles began to explain.

"What was he *able to do*?" Lucy interrupted, quickly standing up to be directly in Miles's eyeline.

Miles lowered himself and sat cross-legged on the rock. Lucy and Griswold followed suit, leaning in expectantly, waiting for Miles to continue. Looking to me, he took a deep breath before he began.

"As I said, your dad has the ability to bring his *own* imagination into reality, but while you can also make a fantasy real, I've only seen you bring someone else's imaginings into the real world, specifically mine.

"Your dad used to bring you by the bookstore." Miles cringed at the word "bookstore" as if its disintegration were just hitting him. He waved his hand in front of his face as if he were trying to push the memory aside before he continued. "You were only about three years old when it first happened. I was reading one of my favorite tales, "Little Red Riding Hood," to you. You were sitting on my lap in my office as I held the book out in front of you. Normally, children look at the images in an illustrated book, but you didn't look at them, not even once. As I read, you were looking off to the side, as if something in that part of my office caught your attention.

"It wasn't until I heard a guttural growl that I understood why you were not looking at the images. When I turned, I saw a wolf baring its teeth in the corner of my office. It was wearing a cloth cap and a matching flower print nightgown, the *exact* nightgown I imagined the wolf wearing in the story. Before I could even reach for the phone on my desk to call animal control, you said 'What big teeth you have' and—this I will never forget as long as I live—the wolf grinned and said, 'All the better to eat you with.' At that moment, the wolf lunged at us. Holding you by the midsection, I sprang up from the chair and backed up against the wall. With the door behind the snarling wolf, we were trapped. So I did the only thing that I could think of doing, I told you to close your eyes and to repeat what I heard your father say when he wanted the fantasies to disappear: 'You're not real, go away.' And just like that, the wolf vanished."

I leaned back as I digested Miles's story. So, that's how I came up with my mantra. If I did not know my life well enough, I would think that, similar to "Little Red Riding Hood," this story was merely a fairy tale. That, or Miles had lost his mind.

"That. Is. Awesome!" Griswold enthusiastically cried, giving each word its own weight.

Lucy glared at Griswold and then turned her gaze to Miles.

"Let me get this straight, you are claiming that Domino has this ability to bring what people *imagine* into reality, and you are basing this off of seeing a *talking wolf* in your office about to attack you and Domino?"

In response, Miles simply nodded; however, from Lucy's raised eyebrow and steady glare, it was obvious that a nod would not suffice.

Miles held her gaze, as if they were having a staring contest, before he finally said, "While this was the first time that Domino did this, it was not the *only* time. As difficult as it may be, it's the truth. As Sir Arthur Conan Doyle said—"

"We know, we know, it's just incredibly hard to believe," Lucy interrupted, shifting her gaze to me.

"Why is all of this happening now?" I asked, looking past Miles's shoulders at the thickening gray clouds.

"I don't know," Miles sighed, groaning as he stood up. He extended his hand to me, which I took. It took me a moment to find my balance, but the throbbing had subsided enough that I could stand on my own without having to lean on something or someone else.

"However, what I *do* know is that I have never seen anyone who can do what you or your father can do, so if this," Miles said, fanning out his arms as if he was presenting the world to us, "is not your doing, then it *has* to be your father."

"Perfect," I moaned, running my hands down my face.

A large part of me, like 95 percent, wished that the conversation had ended there, but when you discover that you have the ability to pull figments of people's imaginations into existence, and that your father is probably responsible for producing a predator, massive earthquakes, and a black sludge that can eat through anything except for magical doors that *you created*, well, obviously the conversation needs to continue.

"So, what do we do now?" Griswold asked the question that I was dreading because I knew the answer.

"We have to find my dad," I sighed, and then added, "wherever the hell he may be. I haven't seen the man in ten years, so I have no idea where we would even start."

Without missing a beat, Miles asserted, "I do."

I do not know why I expected Miles to pull a map, a book, or a phone out of his pocket. Perhaps some tangible item would indicate that my dad had left him some sort of clue so that Miles could find him. You know in case my dad went on a supernatural rampage and needed to be stopped. That's always a good reason to track someone down.

However, Miles did not reach into his pockets. He didn't pull out his phone, nor did a map or a book magically appear.

Without a bit of sarcasm or any faltering in his tone, he said "Oblivion."

CHAPTER 6

A DRAGON WE WILL GO

"**S**o not only are you claiming that Domino's father is some type of wizard, but you are saying that this wizard is destroying the world from a barstool?" Lucy exclaimed.

"He's not a wizard. Wizards use spells," Griswold corrected.

Throwing up her hands, Lucy responded, "Whatever he is, he's doing some sort of magic from the inside of a *bar*?"

If someone caught this conversation out of context, they would definitely glare at us. Hell, even knowing the context does not make the situation any less confusing. As the offspring of the confusion's creator, even I find it hard to believe.

Miles examined his cracked glasses before sliding them back into his pocket. He squinted into the darkening horizon and gave an affirmative nod, and then said, "That's at least the last thing he said to me, that he was headed for Oblivion. Aside from its dictionary definition, the only other 'oblivion' that I know of is the bar where he met Rosa."

At the mention of my mom's name, I quickly pulled my phone out of my pocket to see if she had called or texted. Aside from news feed updates about the intensifying black sludge, there was nothing new.

Sliding my phone back into my pocket, I surveyed the desolate city, as if the bar were in my sights. For all I knew, Oblivion was in another city or state. Who knew how far my dad traveled to get away from me? At least now I knew a little more about the man, other than that he liked to mic-drop confusing messages before making his exit. It still didn't explain why he left, but it was at least more than what I knew a few hours ago.

I was still deciding whether I even *wanted* to know this information. It didn't really matter though. Unless I could magically time travel—which at this point, it wouldn't have surprised me if I could—I knew that my dad has these crazy abilities that he can't control, which could be apocalyptic. Well, at least he had a good chance of destroying the East Coast. Maybe his fantasies couldn't extend beyond a certain point, as if he had a magical leash on them. Then again, you would need to have some semblance of control over them to leash them, so all bets were off.

Even if my dad had lost control of his fantasies, which were now running amok, I still could not help but question why this was happening *now*. According to Miles, it seemed like my dad always had difficulty controlling his abilities. While I do not remember anything before I was five years old, I *do* remember the last ten years going by without incident, that is unless what he imagined was too subtle to be on anyone's radar. If that's the case, then why have his fantasies escalated?

That is, assuming that these fantastical events were accidental. Maybe the tiger, earthquakes, sludge, and who knows what else were created intentionally, but *why*? What reason could my dad possibly have for trying to end the world? Or at least to destroy the East Coast. I mean, the crime rate is not de-escalating any time soon, but was that really a reason to create havoc? It wasn't even constructive havoc. If you have the capability to take out a coast, why not just do it? Why create earthquakes, sludge, and random predators to do so?

That's when it hit me.

"The tiger," I whispered to myself, recalling the article I had read after the tiger escaped from the zoo.

I quickly pulled my phone out of my pocket and searched for the article I had read after the tiger attack. I had to scroll through a couple of news apps before I found the article. Once a lead story, it had been pushed into the bowels of the news feed as it had been usurped by articles about the unknown black sludge eating through the East Coast.

I skimmed the article until I found the line I was looking for: *Recently, the San Diego Zoo's zookeepers tried to sedate a roaming white lion, which is indigenous to the Timbavati region of South Africa, but the white lion evaded capture.*

What if the white lion, the Tasmanian devil, and who knows what other random roaming predators were also figments of my dad's vivid imagination? Either that leash got a lot longer or my dad had his sights set on more than just the East Coast. But why would he want to destroy the United States? Or maybe he was just focused on the United States for now, but his fantasies were slowly spreading, like a contagious virus. I did not know which was worse—if my dad was intentionally trying to destroy the world or if it was accidental.

Well, I could keep hypothesizing all I wanted, but the only way I was going to find any answers was if I found him, and this bar was the only lead that we had.

Closing the news app and tapping on a map app, I asked Miles, "You wouldn't happen to have an address, would you?"

I looked up to see Miles shaking his head.

"I don't even know if it's in New York State," Miles admitted.

"Okay, so let me get this straight, you know that Domino and his father have these crazy, magical abilities, but you don't know the address of the bar that he *may* have gone to?" Lucy asked, raising her eyebrow and placing her hands on her hips, obviously irked.

Before Miles could respond, Griswold cut in, holding up his phone.

"Well, wherever it is, I highly doubt that it is open right now. They're declaring a state of emergency across the tristate area."

"Do we have to evacuate?" Lucy asked, pulling out her own phone and scrolling through. "Damn, I missed a bunch of calls from my parents."

Lucy furrowed her brows as she looked down at the screen.

"No, not yet," Griswold answered. "But they may bring in the National Guard, and some organization called the Agency for Toxic Substances and Disease Registry is looking into the black sludge. They still can't get a sample because, you know, it burns through everything."

"Except for the doors you created," Miles said, turning to me.

My thumb hovered over the map app as I met Miles's gaze. His steady gray eyes looked straight into mine, as if he were trying to communicate with me through his glare alone. Again, I cannot read minds, but I knew exactly what Miles was getting at.

"So, you're saying that I could stop it, right?" I sighed.

"That's exactly what I am saying," Miles asserted. "When I imagined those doors, I imagined that they were impenetrable. If you could create an impenetrable substance, then we can combat your dad's creation."

Remembering the deafening high-pitched ring I heard the last time I pulled Miles's fantasy into reality, I roughly ran my one hand through my hair while still holding out my phone with the other.

"I don't know," I said, looking away from Miles and back at the map app. "I don't think that I can."

"But you did it before, so you can do it again," Griswold interjected. I looked up to see Griswold's bright hazel eyes brimming with encouragement and optimism.

If we all had at least a fraction of the hope that Griswold had, this world would be a better place. Nevertheless, his hope did not dampen my doubt, but I was willing to listen to Miles.

"Okay," I breathed, looking back at Miles as I clicked my phone off and slid it back into my pocket. "What do you have in mind?"

Miles began to rub his chin and narrow his eyes as if he were trying to solve a complex mystery. He paced for a bit as he mumbled something to himself before he stopped in his tracks and stuck his index finger in the air like he was trying to predict whether or not it was going to rain.

"I've got it," Miles announced, "but the only caveat is that it is a short-term solution. We will have to get to the source to get rid of the sludge permanently. However, for the time being, I can imagine a preventive shield to cover the Earth, which Domino can make real."

"You want Domino to do *what*?" Lucy asked, taking the words right out of my mouth. She clicked her cell phone off and slid it into her pocket. With her hands on her hips and her eyebrow firmly raised, she was like the poster child for skepticism.

Miles turned toward her, his steely gray eyes softening with patience.

"I know that this may seem impossible, but we have to suspend our belief in what is and what is not possible at this point. I *know* that Domino has the capability of doing this," he said, and then he turned toward me to add, "You can do this."

I let out a breath that I did not even realize that I was holding in.

"I'll try," I conceded, and then added, "I mean, we have nothing to lose."

As if Miles took this concession as his cue, he closed his eyes. The familiar sizzle in the atmosphere tickled my eardrums as the creases in Miles's eyelids deepened.

I heard a slow drizzle gradually escalate into running water, as if every faucet in the world had been turned on. I looked down to see a rush of glittering liquid glide over my sneakers to form into a thin, gelatinous, transparent slip that covered the ground; although I couldn't see it, I felt it cover the Earth's surface, as if the globe was being engulfed in an invisible blanket. Even though it looked like my feet were stuck in the gelatinous covering, they waded through the substance with little resistance.

"Do you see it?" I heard Miles ask. Looking up to see him open his eyes, I gave him a quick nod before I looked back down to concentrate on the Earth's new transparent slip.

Unlike the doors, I had never seen a substance like this one. It was akin to a liquidy yet solid river enveloping the Earth's surface. It felt more like a protective blanket against unknown toxic substances. For this reason, it made believing that this covering was real that much more difficult.

I took a deep breath as I heard the stirrings of the high-pitched ringing begin to emerge. Although its growing volume was hard to ignore, I continued to concentrate on the covering, staring at the glimmering sheen. Instinctively, I extended my arms, hands splayed over the Earth's surface, as if this gesture would help me better perform this strange alchemy. I mean, all alchemy is pretty much strange, but at least with regular alchemy you are transforming something *real* into something else that is *real*. What I was doing was alchemy on steroids laced with unicorn magic, that is if unicorns existed. Well, if I could pull Miles's transparent coating into reality, I am sure that I could fix our lack of a unicorn problem.

The tendons throughout my body felt taut, and I could feel my neck muscles straining as the high-pitched ringing increased with a vengeance, to the point where that was all I heard. Desperately, I wanted to cover my ears to protect myself from the deafening ringing, but I didn't dare move just in case any slight movement would disrupt the process, leading me to have to start all over again.

The edges of my vision were saturated with exploding sprays of vibrant flashes as the high-pitched ringing grew to an impossibly destructive screech. I felt something liquidy slide from my nostril and settle onto my bottom lip.

The taste of metal tinged my tongue as the entire world shrouded in darkness, and I felt myself fall.

"Domino? Are you okay?" I heard a soft, concerned voice ask.

"I think I see his eyelids fluttering open," another voice, this one more of a baritone, stated.

I felt a cool breeze lick my cheeks before I saw the darkening sky, masked by the looming thick gray clouds hanging overhead. In my peripheral vision, I made out the fuzzy outlines of three figures looking down at me, as if I were some type of science experiment laid out on a slab, on full display for anyone to examine. At this point, I wouldn't have been surprised if that was my reality.

"I think he's waking up!" the figure with blond hair sticking out in an array of obscure directions exclaimed.

Before he came into focus, I immediately knew that the excited and quick-paced timbre could only belong to one person.

"I've gotta stop passing out," I said as Griswold extended his hand to help me up.

Standing upright, I felt off kilter, not only because I had blacked out but also because my feet were nestled in the gelatinous goo covering the ground.

I rubbed my eyes with the heels of my hands, attempting to bring the world back into focus. When I opened my eyes again, I was confronted with Lucy's furrowed brow umbrellaing her vibrant amber eyes, which were focused on my lips. Touching my tongue to my lips, the taste of metal brought me back to the moment before I passed out.

"Are you okay?" Lucy asked again, digging something out of her pocket. "Here," she said, offering me a tissue.

I tilted my head back as I pressed the tissue to my nostrils, but the bleeding had already stopped. I rubbed my lips and nostrils with the tissue before stuffing it into my pocket.

"I'm fine," I said, purposely picking up my feet one at a time to feel them settle into the gelatinous substance covering the ground.

"I guess it worked," I added, looking down at Miles's creation.

"It *definitely* worked," Griswold began, holding up his phone. "And people are *definitely* talking about it."

The four of us opened up our phones to find any news feed on the transparent substance that Miles imagined, which wasn't hard because it was at the top of almost every news feed I found.

I had no idea how long I had been out, but it was long enough for people to hypothesize about what Miles's creation was made out of, where it came from, and how it seemed to cover every crevice of the Earth's surface. Some attributed the covering to aliens beaming down and creating a protective coating to shield us from the adverse effects of climate change, while others said that the gelatinous surface was a government experiment used to thwart terrorist attacks. Some theorized that the Earth had created the substance on its own, and this was just a part of the natural evolution of the planet. Many stated that more tests needed to be conducted because no one could determine whether or not the substance was harmful; however, it did seem to keep the black sludge at bay.

"Any chance anyone will figure out that this stuff isn't real?" Griswold asked, still scrolling through the news feed.

"Doubtful," Miles affirmed, clicking off his phone. "As far as anyone knows, it is real, that is unless someone knows what Max and Domino can do."

"How long will it *stay* real?" Lucy asked, vigorously typing something into her phone.

Looking at me, Miles stated, "As long as Domino keeps it that way."

I took a deep breath and then exhaled audibly as I stared at the substance's glittering surface. While bringing the imaginary gelatinous substance into reality was draining, sustaining its existence took no exertion at all. I just believed that it existed because, well, now it did.

"Well, if it's protecting everyone from the black sludge, then obviously your creation needs to stay," I affirmed.

"Can we really live this way though?" Lucy asked, looking down at her phone. "My parents are reporting on this stuff and people are panicking. It does not *seem* harmful, but no one knows that for sure."

"Well, this is just a temporary solution, like a Band-Aid," Miles admitted. "The only *permanent* solution I see is finding Max to prevent him from imagining any more destructive forces."

"And all we have to go off of is that my dad probably went to Oblivion, a bar that is who knows where, ten years ago," I recapped, and then added a "Great" just for good measure.

I looked over to Griswold, who was being uncharacteristically quiet again. He furrowed his brow in concentration as he typed something into his phone. The tip of his tongue peeked out between his lips as he scrolled down, and tapped something on his screen.

"I didn't find any bars called Oblivion in New York, but there are a couple in New Jersey. One is in Jersey City and one is in Newark," Griswold stated, clicking off his phone.

"I can drive us there," Miles offered.

Before I could respond, Lucy interjected, still looking down at her phone.

"That won't work. The roads are a mess," Lucy began to explain as she held her screen out to us. Displayed on the screen was a light green road map covered in blaring, angry red lines. It looked as if Christmas was coming with a vengeance.

"We'll never get there if we go by car," Lucy continued. "I'll look at MyMTA to see if the trains are running."

After a few quick swipes, she shook her head.

"Nothing, they've all stopped, even the subways."

"Dammit," I hissed, roughly running my fingers through my hair.

This was what you would call a "lose-lose" situation. By pulling Miles's gelatinous protective coating into existence, we were able to prevent the black sludge from melting the Earth down into a muddy pulp, but at the same time, by creating another unknown substance to combat the malicious unknown substance, I caused worldwide panic. Well, I wasn't sure if the panic spread across the globe, but I am pretty sure it did. I mean, maybe the arctic penguins were cool with it, but everyone else seemed to be freaking out.

"So, all modes of transportation are a no-go," Lucy affirmed.

Griswold's phone noticeably hummed in his grip, as if it were confirming Lucy's statement. Griswold swiped left, and then shoved the phone in his pocket.

"And our parents won't leave us alone," Griswold noted.

Well, at least *their* parents were contacting them. I didn't even need to look down at my phone to be confronted with my mom's lack of messages and calls. Ironically enough, while their parents were reaching out to them, we were hunting down one of mine to prevent him from potentially destroying the world. I am not sure if there is a dysfunctional family award, but I think that the Garrisons are definitely contenders.

"Mine are on assignment, so they are stuck. My mom is in Chicago and my dad is in Florida. They told me that all flights are grounded right now," Lucy explained.

"Planes, trains, and automobiles are completely useless to us," Miles said, vocalizing what we were all thinking. "So how can we get to New Jersey?"

"By foot?" Lucy asked, sighing as she looked down at her sneaker-less feet, wiggling her toes in the transparent goo.

We were all silent for a beat as we mentally calculated how long it would take us to walk from Manhattan to New Jersey. I literally couldn't even imagine how much our legs would ache after that trek. If you recall, I can't really imagine anything. However, I felt it in my legs when I walked the length of Central Park, so walking from Manhattan to New Jersey would probably feel a lot worse.

Think outside of the box, I told myself as I began contemplating other modes of transportation.

Hot air balloon? No, that wouldn't work. If planes are grounded, then why would it be okay for hot air balloons to fly freely in the sky.

The bus? Nope, traffic. Damn traffic.

A ferry? They were halted, along with the trains.

Motorcycles? We may be able to weave in and out of traffic, but none of us own a motorcycle, and as far as I know, none of us know how to drive one. Well, maybe Miles does. Apparently, I don't know every-thing about him, like that he knew about my dad's paranormal abilities.

Bicycles? Possibly. I don't own a bicycle but we can definitely bor-row a few Citi Bikes. However, since the Earth's new gelatinous coating is pretty foreign, I did not know how much resistance we would have to wade through on a bike.

Electric scooters? Another possibility. They are electric, so that may fare better through the covering, but we couldn't be sure.

The other modes of transportation, such as a space shuttle, sled, and snowmobile, *definitely* would not work. I am not even sure if a sled would be at all useful on a fairly flat surface.

Before I could ask if anyone knew where we could rent an electric scooter, Griswold clapped his hand on my shoulder, and said, "I think I've got it."

Oddly enough, the glitter embedded in the transparent goo was far more luminous underneath the flickering, dimly lit streetlights. It was like it was sparkling in stark defiance of the darkness. The night's hanging, pregnant gray clouds managed to almost block out the moon's illumination entirely, so that we were only left with artificial light to guide us.

If it wasn't for the practically protruding thick layer of moss that clung to my building, and the fact that I have walked these streets countless times, I might have missed the alleyway.

"This is a crazy idea," Lucy said, holding up her phone's flashlight so that we had a better view of the alleyway.

"Acknowledged," Griswold responded, slowing down his pace as we entered the alleyway. "My other idea was probably crazier, so I went with the more reasonable one."

Lucy's eyebrow shot up as she aimed her phone at the familiar dilapidated dumpster.

"Do I even *want* to ask?" Lucy questioned, motioning the light up and down, revealing the dumpster's peeling dark blue paint and a series of indentations, as if it had been in an all-out brawl that did not end well.

"You don't have to," I said, narrowing my eyes as I searchingly looked around the dumpster. "It probably involved rabbits."

"I don't know how *reasonable* this—" Lucy began, but before she could finish, I reached over and placed my hand on top of her hand that was holding the phone.

I moved it slightly to the left and down toward the ground to reveal a man sprawled out on the ground. Adorned in the same paint-smudged overalls he always wore, as if no one would be able to identify him without this attire, Hermon's shoulders slumped forward and his head sagged to the right.

I carefully walked closer so that I could kneel in front of Hermon. I cringed as I felt my knee slide into the gelatinous goo.

Hermon's glassy eyes lacked focus. Like heavy shades, his eyelids kept sliding over his eyes.

"Hermon, can you hear me?" I asked, motioning for Lucy to come a little closer so that I could get a better look at Hermon.

Hermon began to squirm under the illumination, and tried to back into the wall as if he was a caged animal. I quickly motioned for Lucy to back up to calm him down. Lucy lowered her phone's flashlight to the ground to reveal the glittery sheen of the Earth's new protective covering.

"Hermon," I began again, trying to make my tone comforting. "I need you to do something for me."

Hermon opened his mouth as if he were going to respond, but then his jaw went slack and his body began to lean to the right.

I quickly grabbed his right shoulder and tilted his body to an upright position.

"Hermon, it's very important that you listen, can you do that for me? I need to speak to Hermon, the other Hermon," I stated, looking into his glazed stare.

"I don't think that this is going to work," Miles said from behind me. "He's too high to focus. Any one of us can imagine—" Before Miles could finish, Hermon shot up, his eyes suddenly wide open and trans-fixed on the dumpster.

The air's sizzle coincided with the resounding roar beaming from just above the dumpster.

"Hermon the Third," human Hermon corrected, his meek timbre severely contrasting with his hallucination's pronouncement.

Standing up, I spun around to face the shimmering golden eyes staring directly into mine. Hermon the Third's nostrils flared, releasing threads of white smoke that disappeared into the atmosphere. A series of dark brown horns framed its emerald green face. Its taut, dark green wings were pinned to its sides in the narrow alley, severely flattening the frill of the prominent pink tutu.

"It's good to see you again, Hermon the Third," I greeted the dragon. "I'm glad that you're not a Pegasus this time, otherwise this might not work."

"We can't see it," Griswold interjected. In my peripheral vision, I could see Griswold waving his hands, trying to get my attention.

"We need a favor, a very important favor," I began, walking a little closer to Hermon the Third, who lowered his head, supposedly so that he could listen in. "We need you to take us to New Jersey to find my dad," I yelled to the 20-foot dragon, who tilted his head to the side as if he were carefully considering my request.

"Will there be food?" Hermon the Third asked in a raspy voice that sounded as if he had gargled gravel before speaking.

Smirking, I said, "We'll get you whatever you need."

"Then yes," Hermon the Third affirmed, smiling to reveal purple-coated fangs.

Smiling, I held my hands out in front of me, concentrating on pulling Hermon's dragon into reality. The high-pitched ringing came in intense pulsating waves as the edges of my peripheral vision began to darken, but I remained steadfast, continuing to rip open the fabric of reality to pull Hermon's hallucination into existence.

I resisted the urge to close my eyes as I felt my labored breathing become more prominent. I could also feel myself swaying before someone grabbed my shoulders from behind, holding me upright. I spread my legs farther apart to anchor myself.

With my muscles tightening and the air growing thin, I felt my tether to Hermon the Third loosening as my strength gave out. It was only when I thought that the world was going to fade away and that I would live with permanent tinnitus that the ringing subsided. After a beat of silence, I jumped at the sound of a distinct gasp.

"You did it," I heard Miles whisper from behind me, as he loosened his grip.

I sharply inhaled as I lowered my arms, feeling my muscles return to their normal, unflexed state.

"Shit, it's a dragon!" Lucy yelped, backing up into a wall. The small bit of brightness from Lucy's phone faded as I heard the clack of the plastic meeting concrete.

"A dragon, sometimes Pegasus," I panted, drinking in gulps of oxygen after each word. "And he just agreed to give us a ride."

"It's a damn dragon!" Lucy cried again, pressed flatly against the brick wall behind her.

Still panting, I reached out for her, motioning for her to take my hand. Lucy remained still, her eyes widening as she stared into Hermon the Third's golden eyes.

"It's okay," I said, trying to reassure her. "He won't hurt you." Feeling my breathing begin to steady, I inched closer to Lucy as she continued to stare into Hermon the Third's eyes, not daring to look away.

"It's a damn *dragon*!" she repeated as I gently pulled her away from the wall and laced my fingers through hers.

"I know," I confirmed. "We're old friends."

"How in the world are you friends with an *imaginary dragon*?" Lucy yelped, gripping my hand a little tighter.

I nodded toward human Hermon, who was staring up at his hallucinogenic creation like a proud father whose child just scored the winning goal.

I shrugged before I explained. "It's one of human Hermon's drug-induced visions. I've been seeing him for years."

"We *did* tell you about the plan," Griswold interjected, walking over to us. "This really shouldn't be surprising."

Now it was Griswold's turn to back away in fear as Lucy scowled at him.

"I didn't think that you were talking about an *actual* dragon," she sneered.

Tilting his head in confusion, Griswold asked, "What did you think that I was talking about?"

Lucy threw her hands up in the air, including the one I was holding, as she exclaimed, "I don't know! I thought it was a code name for someone or something. Who expects that an *actual dragon* will get us to where we need to go?"

"Who ever heard of anyone named 'The Dragon'? That's just crazy," Griswold chortled.

"But a dragon isn't?" Lucy bellowed.

"Enough," Miles asserted, fanning out his arms as if he were an umpire signaling that the batter was safe after sliding into home plate. "You two can argue about the dragon all night if you want, but at least we have a ride. Now we need to figure out how we're going to get and stay on Hermon the Third."

"And how we're going to hide him," I added, staring 20 feet into the air at Hermon the Third's vibrant purple fangs.

"I got it! I can imagine a saddle that we can all fit on and invisibility cloaks for all of us, so that we won't be seen," Griswold said, giving off a beaming smile. "I can imagine it now—" Before Griswold could finish his thought, I held up my hand to him.

Just thinking about the high-pitched ringing practically ripping through my eardrums was dizzying. My lungs constricted at the thought of extracting a fantasy from an imagination and yanking it into existence.

Instinctively, I gripped my chest with the hand that was not holding Lucy's.

"Are you okay?" Lucy asked, giving my hand a firm, reassuring squeeze.

"Aren't you getting tired of asking that?" I asked, turning toward her. I gave her a small appreciative smile and then added, "It just takes a lot out of me, that's all, but I don't know why."

"It's strange," Miles noted. "When you were younger, you didn't have any reaction when you brought a fantasy into our reality. You just did it, as if it were as natural as breathing."

"Maybe it's like learning a magic trick," Griswold offered. "You have to keep practicing in order to get better. Then, one day, you will master it."

I gave a little laugh as I lowered my hand from my chest.

"Maybe," I began, and took a much-needed deep breath. "But this isn't pretend. This is *real* and it hurts like hell."

Turning toward Griswold, I gave him an affirmative nod before I said, "I'll just grin and bear it. Imagine what we need and I'll make them real."

Griswold's smile widened as he said, "You've got it."

The air sizzled as I looked up to see an enormous, elaborate black saddle appear on Hermon the Third's back. The saddle's harness cut into Hermon the Third's frilly pink tutu, snuggly wrapping around his body. Next, a hooded, black velvet cloak gently parachuted down and fell onto Hermon the Third's back, the hood of which nestled onto Hermon the Third's head, covering his prominent spikes. The black velvet shimmered into a transparent material.

"Do you see it?" Griswold asked. Turning back toward him, I saw four matching invisibility cloaks in the crook of his arm.

Giving another affirmative nod, I let go of Lucy's hand to hold out my arms in front of me. As if preparing for a train to arrive at its destination, I braced myself for the deafening high-pitch ring to decimate my eardrums.

CHAPTER 7

FINDING OBLIVION

After the customary high-pitched ringing subsided, I backed out of the alleyway as I directed Hermon the Third onto the sidewalk.

"Are you *sure* that no one can see him?" Lucy asked, her head snapping from right to left as if she expected paparazzi to appear out of nowhere and dive bomb us with camera flashes.

"Can you see him?" Griswold asked, to which Lucy shook her head.

"Then it worked," I finished, tugging the hood of my cloak to ensure I was well hidden underneath.

Hermon the Third lowered himself onto the sidewalk as, one by one, we lifted up a part of his cloak and climbed onto the saddle. Once we were all on Hermon the Third's back, I grabbed the reins and told Hermon the Third that we were ready to go.

I sat up a little straighter and gripped the reins that much tighter when I felt Hermon the Third crouch to the ground before he shot up into the sky, wings still pinned to his sides. Lucy's arms dug into my sides, wrapping around me as if her life depended on it. I felt myself slide back, our acceleration increasing as we continued to ascend.

Even hidden underneath the thick velvet cloak, the crisp night wind pummeled into my chest as we picked up momentum.

In the midst of the piercing wind, the atmosphere began to sizzle so loudly that I cupped my hands to my ears while still holding onto the reins. I heard Lucy's muffled cries as I felt us suddenly drop straight down.

"No!" I screamed as I felt the reins cutting into my palms.

My pulse was drumming throughout my body, its pace quickening at the fierce acceleration of our drop.

"Domino!" I heard someone scream from behind Lucy. "What's wrong?"

I opened my mouth to say something, but all that came out was silence, not understanding why it was taking us so long to hit the ground. That's when I realized that the sizzle in the air could only mean one thing.

I squeezed my eyes shut and repeated my mantra to myself in between gulps of air.

"Domino?" I heard again, coupled with the flapping of wings slicing into the night sky.

I took a much-needed deep breath as I leaned forward and opened my eyes to see us gliding through gray puffs of cool fog.

As soon as I was able to catch my breath, I leaned back so that Lucy could hear me.

"Try not to imagine us falling," I said, the memory of plummeting still raw in my mind.

"You saw that?" Lucy questioned, as she loosened her grip on me a little.

I nodded, and then said, "I have to give you credit for having a really vivid imagination. I usually know the difference between reality and fantasy, but yours felt pretty real."

"I can't help it," Lucy stated, her voice quavering. "I'm afraid of heights."

"Shit," I hissed, placing my hand on top of hers, while still gripping the reins. "Just close your eyes and lay your head on my back. We should be there soon."

I felt strands of Lucy's wavy brown hair tickling the nape of my neck as I felt the subtle pressure of her head against the top of my spine.

"Grizz," I yelled over the whipping of the wind, "can you pull up GPS? I literally have no idea where we are. I'll direct Hermon the Third."

"Damn!" Lucy hissed, as she shot up. "I left my phone in the alleyway. My parents are going to kill me."

"Should I say we are going by foot, public transportation, by car, or by bike?" Griswold called, and then added, "There's no 'dragon' mode of transportation listed."

Smirking, I called back, "If they have a dragon option, I think we are in trouble because that would mean riding a dragon is more common than I thought."

"How common did you think it was?" Griswold quipped.

"I hope we are pioneers here, Grizz," I responded, and then added, "I guess, say that we are going by car."

"Got it. Head toward the Lincoln Tunnel," Griswold directed.

I squinted into the night air, as if narrowing my eyes would cause the clouds to dissipate. They stubbornly floated around us, obstructing my vision of the roads below.

"We can barely see the ground," Miles confirmed.

"If I imagine a clear night sky, Domino can make the clouds go away," Griswold suggested, but I immediately shot that down.

"Passing out on the ground, fine, but in the sky? That would end badly," I explained, gazing down through the thickening clouds at the tiny brightly lit dots.

Turning my attention to Hermon the Third, I asked, "Can you go a little lower so that we can see?" In response, Hermon the Third slowly descended, at which Lucy hugged me from behind tighter, to the point where I thought that she could potentially crack my ribs.

At the lower altitude, the giant stone archways began to come into focus. I smiled as I told Hermon the Third to continue to fly in the direction of the tunnel.

I will spare you the details of Griswold directing us from the Lincoln Tunnel toward the Holland Tunnel, and flying over side streets until Griswold said that we had made it to Jersey City. There are really no details to relay except for trying to dodge obstructive clouds and wondering when Lucy would release her vise-like grip.

Hermon the Third slowly descended, landing next to one of the many brightly lit high-rises. Once I heard Hermon the Third's claws settle onto the concrete and he lowered his wings to his side, I tapped Lucy's hand, letting her know that we had landed safely.

Letting go of the reins, I slid down from Hermon the Third's back, which was almost impossible with Lucy still hugging me from behind.

"We're here," I grunted, settling my feet into the glittery, gelatinous goo coating the ground. I gingerly peeled Lucy's arms away from my body and took off my cloak.

After taking off her cloak as well, Lucy cleared her throat and muttered "Sorry" as she ran her fingers through her now knotted brown hair.

"How far is the bar from here, Grizz?" I asked, wincing as I touched my ribs, which definitely felt tender.

"It's only a couple of blocks—" Griswold began, but before he could finish, Lucy held up her hand and said, "Hold it. Before we go anywhere, don't you think that we should call to make sure that they're open?"

"Aren't bars *usually* open at night?" Griswold innocently asked, lowering the hood of his cloak, tapping something on his phone.

"Usually," Lucy acknowledged. "But during a state of emergency? I don't think so."

Griswold shrugged as he dialed a number and put it on speaker. My stomach dropped when I heard the mechanical voice state that "this number is no longer in service."

"Shit," I hissed, pulling out my own phone to pull up the bar's website. It took a bit of scrolling, but I found the links to the two bars, one in Jersey City and one in Newark. One was still open, and one was closed, *permanently*. Guess which was which.

"Shit," I hissed again, running my hand down my face.

Without missing a beat, Miles pulled his cloak back on and climbed back on top of Hermon the Third's back, gesturing for us to do the same. Lucy marched up to Hermon the Third, blocking our path, and held up her hand again, which I was beginning to suspect was her favorite gesture.

"We can't go from bar to bar until we are *absolutely sure* that they are open," Lucy insisted. Then, pointing down at her now blackened socks, she added, "And I am not going anywhere until I at least get some shoes."

"Imagine them and Domino will make them real," Griswold nonchalantly stated as he tapped on his screen, supposedly calling the number of Oblivion in Newark.

"Look, it's not a parlor trick, okay?" I snapped, and then closed my eyes and took a breath. "I don't need to bring everything into existence. I'm sure that we can find Lucy a pair of shoes."

"This will be the perfect way to practice," Griswold noted.

Pulling out my phone, I clicked it on and found a shoe stores in the area but none that were open. I let out a deep sigh as I prepared myself for the high-pitched ringing.

"Just imagine something quick, so we can get this over with," I huffed.

Griswold was probably right; this ability was like a muscle that had atrophied. The side effects would lessen the more I used it; however, I could not help but cringe at the thought of hearing that high-pitched ringing and feeling as if the world was fading into darkness, as if by pulling something into existence I was extricating myself from reality. Yeah, maybe practice makes perfect, but is this really something that I want to perfect?

Sure, I may have to use this ability to stop my dad, but did I really need to master it to do so?

Well, at least I had Lucy's vise-like grip to distract me from my thoughts, because right after I pulled her imagined converse sneakers into existence and the high-pitched ringing subsided, we were off again, and Lucy was gripping my midsection like she was a terrified octopus wrapping its tentacles around the first solid object that it found, in this case me.

It took less than half an hour to find a building to land on. Unlike the high-rise in Jersey City, this building was not nearly as tall. When I looked over the edge, a flood of lights illuminated an expansive black awning below.

"Grizz," I said, turning toward him as he clicked off his phone, "Where did we land?"

"On top of Penn Station," Griswold nonchalantly stated, as he slid his phone back into his pocket.

"Well, at least we have a home base. How far away is the bar?" I asked, taking off my cloak once again.

"It's only a block away," Griswold stated.

"Okay, now all we have to do is find a way down from here," I noted, looking around for an exit.

"It's here," Miles called from the other side of the roof. I didn't even realize that he had moved.

Lucy, Griswold, and I placed our invisibility cloaks near Hermon the Third before we walked over to the exit, our first step toward Oblivion. Yup, I never thought that I would say that sentence, but I need to get used to expecting the unexpected. In fact, I should know better by now—the impossible is always possible, especially when the lines between reality and fantasy are an illusion.

Whether the cracked Oblivion sign was an aesthetic choice or a result of the earthquakes, we did not know; either way it seemed to fit the bar's vibe. Aside from the sign, the rest of the building seemed to hold up.

Once inside the bar, it took my eyes a minute to adjust to the smoky haze. The place was pretty sizable, with random barrel tables and matching chairs strewn throughout the bar. The flat-screen TV in the far corner of the bar added to the background noise, which was very low. Again, maybe it was because of the earthquakes and the sludge, but aside from a couple sitting at one of the barrel tables, and two other guys nursing beers at the bar table, there was no one else in the bar.

I was not sure if the barstools were placed so far apart for social distancing purposes, but Miles, Lucy, Griswold, and I each sat at any available spot, trying to get the bartender's attention.

While waiting for a bartender to come out from what I assumed was a door to an office or some sort of wine cellar, I looked at myself in the mirror that was blocked by hundreds of bottles on thin wooden shelves jutting out from the wall.

Maybe it was the refraction of the fluorescent lights on the bottles I was looking through that distorted my image, or just the aftereffects of riding on the back of a dragon, but my reflection revealed bloodshot eyes and a ghostly pale face, which was several shades lighter than my normally tan skin. I rubbed my eyes with the heels of my hands, as if I could expel my exhaustion with this simple gesture. However, I didn't really *feel* exhausted. No, exhausted was not the right word. *Drained.* I felt like a battery that was in desperate need of a recharge but no one was tending to it. Not that I needed anyone to "tend to" me. However, a break would have been great. Sure, a break was a luxury at this point. I mean, when you are on a mission to find your father, who is either purposely or accidentally unleashing random disasters onto the world, breaks are not included.

I looked over to Griswold, who was maybe one of the few people I knew who can look refreshed after surviving the worst earthquake to hit New York, dodging destructive black sludge, and riding over the Lincoln Tunnel on the back of a dragon hidden underneath an invisible cloak. His beaming smile did not waver as he leaned over the bar, looking for the bartender, as if he or she was hiding underneath.

As if the bartender sensed that his sacred space behind the bar was being invaded, a man in a black T-shirt with a logo that perfectly matched the Oblivion sign out front burst through the door adjacent to the collection of liquor bottles adorning the mirrored wall. He narrowed his beady black eyes at us in suspicion.

"We don't serve minors," the bartender curtly stated, looking at Griswold as if he was sizing him up.

Before Griswold could respond, Miles leaned over the bar and said, "They're with me, but they're not here to drink."

The bartender raised his thick brow at Miles, waiting for him to continue.

"We're looking for my dad," I picked up. "He used to come to this bar—or a bar called Oblivion, but we think it was this one."

The bartender nonchalantly started wiping down the table with a rag I didn't even realize that he was holding. Without looking up, he said, "A lot of people pass through here. He could possibly be one of them." I looked around at the practically desolate bar that completely contradicted this statement.

"It's very important that we find him. It could be a matter of life or death," Miles insisted.

Maybe Miles had more of an air of authority than I did as he stared at the bartender with his steely gray eyes, or maybe the timbre of his voice suggested that he had no time for games. Whatever it was, the bartender took notice. He stopped wiping down the table and looked up; however, Miles's authority was short-lived as the bartender smirked in response.

"Life or death, huh? Is the fate of the world at stake too?" the bartender said mockingly, holding up air quotes around "the fate of the world."

Without the slightest hesitation, Miles said—in the most even-keeled tone— "Yes, the fate of the world could possibly be at stake if we don't find him."

That mic-drop statement sent the bartender into a fit of laughter.

After about a minute of us waiting for the bartender to calm down, I said, "Look, we just need to find him. His name is Max Garrison and he has these beauty marks around the corners of his eyes that look like a constellation, just a whole mess of them."

At the mention of "constellation," the bartender's laughter tapered, and he sobered up, no pun intended. Well, maybe it was intended. Either way, I was glad that he stopped.

"We did have a guy who had marks like that on either side of his face. In fact, he came in a lot. He was a pretty strange dude."

"How long ago was he here?" "Do you know where he is now?" "Does he still come in often?" "Strange *how*?" We peppered the bartender with questions, the last one being mine, until he held up his hand.

"He was here a few years ago. That idiot kept going on and on about how he couldn't control anything, and that he was the most dangerous person in the world. That he couldn't even be around his kid, blah, blah, blah." Looking toward me, the bartender paused. "He probably meant you. Sorry, kid."

"It's fine," I said, even though it wasn't. "Keep going."

"Well, he was completely plastered. I had cut him off after a few pints, so he shouldn't have been that drunk, but every time I looked over at him, he had a mug filled with beer. I am not even sure how it was possible.

"Anyway, he kept yammering on until this other guy yelled at him to shut up. That's when things went down. The guy with the constellation marks on the side of his face—your dad—shouted at the other guy, telling him that he could destroy him with a single thought, whatever that meant. One thing led to another, and then they started pummeling each other, right in the middle of the bar. It got so bad that they threw each other through the windows. Believe it or not, they were still beating the crap out of each other, lying on the sidewalk.

"By that time, I had already called the cops. My shift was over so I left before the cops arrived. Billy, the other bartender at the time, said that one of the guys, Max Garrison, was arrested, but I don't know about the other guy. It was strange. Billy didn't really talk about what happened; in fact, he quit shortly after that."

Although the bartender could only guess at what my dad meant when he said that he was the most "dangerous person in the world," I knew exactly what he meant; however, that didn't clarify whether or not he is now purposely trying to destroy the world, possibly from a jail cell, but possibly not. If this happened a few years ago, how likely was it that my dad was still sitting in a jail cell? That is, unless he had committed another crime, which at this point wouldn't surprise me. I mean, world destruction counts as a felony, right? I mean, his methods are highly creative, I will give him that, but I still think that it could be ruled a felony.

"Do you know what police station he was taken to?" Lucy asked, as Griswold tapped his phone.

"Probably the 3rd Precinct," Griswold affirmed without looking up from his screen. "It's the closest one, about five minutes away."

I nodded as I turned on my heels to leave. However, before I could exit, the bartender called me back.

"Hey, kid," he began as I pivoted to look at the bartender, whose beady eyes seemed to soften. "I've seen guys like your dad come in here. For what it's worth, he didn't seem like a bad guy, just a depressed one who had a lot of demons."

I nodded in acknowledgment and said "Thanks" before I turned back and pushed through the exit.

Maybe the bartender was right, maybe my dad was so haunted that he thought that my mom and I would be better off if he weren't around. However, the reasons why he left really didn't matter right now. What mattered was trying to find him before he caused any more damage.

By the way, I totally should not have thought that last thought...I definitely jinxed us.

CHAPTER 8

SINS OF THE FATHER

"So, our next stop is the police station?" Griswold asked, tapping on his phone.

"No," Lucy asserted, taking a step closer to Griswold to look at his phone. "It's very unlikely that he is still there. Let's try to find an article about him and then search for his arrest records."

I must have been giving Lucy a quizzical look because she quickly responded, "What? This is how my parents dig when they have a lead."

"But why would there be an article about him?" I asked, to which Miles quickly responded.

"He caused damage to that bar. Maybe a local paper reported on it, maybe not, but it is worth looking into," Miles said, pulling out his phone.

Following suit, I pulled out my own phone and typed "Max Garrison" in a search engine.

Unless my dad suddenly became a college football star with a Twitter account, the first page had nothing to do with him. I was also pretty sure that he was not an author. I'm not sure if he ever fished, but this website dedicated to Max Garrison, the *Fishing Guide* writer, was probably not him either. Well, if anything, this search definitely helped hone my process of elimination skills. After passing a NASCAR notice, a 1940s census page, an obituary for the dearly departed ninety-year-old Max Garrison, and an MMA fighter website, I jumped to the fourth page of the search engine to find an article about a Max Garrison from over three years ago.

The headline, "Rumble at the Oblivion," indicated that I was probably on the right track.

I tapped on the link and zoomed in to read the practically microscopic writing.

Oblivion, a local dive bar, has seen its fair share of fighting, so no one thought twice when two men, one identified as Max Garrison, thirty-five, and an unidentified man, threw each other through the bar's window, that is until a black hole appeared in the middle of the sidewalk.

One of the witnesses, Billy Talbet, one of Oblivion's bartenders, confirmed that the unidentified man fell through the black hole. Sources say that the black hole disappeared before the police arrived to arrest Max Garrison. Other sources say that the unidentified man ran off when he heard the police sirens. So far, there is no investigation underway into the unidentified man's disappearance.

Before I finished reading the article, Griswold and Lucy announced that they found an arrest record for Max Garrison.

The New Jersey Courts Public Access page included the SBI number, county case number, the sentence data, and a guilty plea. While this information was important to the New Jersey police station, it did not help us find my dad.

I clicked on the "event detail" button, but that didn't reveal any enlightening information.

Returning to the main page, Lucy clicked on the "sentence" button, which included additional information about the statute and place sentencing. According to this page, Max Garrison was charged with disorderly conduct and something called "POSS CDS/ANALOG - SCHD I II III IV," but he wasn't placed in jail. Under place sentencing it read "Alcohol & Drug Rehab."

"Where?" I asked no one in particular, tapping on the arrow that took us back to the main page. "And what the hell is Poss CDS/Analog?"

"Well, since he was sentenced to an alcohol and drug rehab, maybe it has to do with drugs? Or maybe alcohol? Maybe even both?" Lucy guessed.

I didn't even have to research the term to know that she was right. Of course, my dad was in possession of drugs when he was arrested. Why wouldn't *both* of my parents be drug addicts?

"Drug abuse? That doesn't sound like Max," Miles interjected.

I turned from the screen to look into his steady eyes. He looked so certain, so confident in his assertion. Maybe it was just easier for me to believe that my dad was in possession of drugs because I didn't really know the man.

In fact, it was only in the last few hours that I had learned *anything* about him. It's not like my mom provided a wealth of information about the man that she supposedly loved enough to marry. Hell, I had never even seen a picture of him. Then again, I didn't exactly ask for one. Considering that Miles did not pull out a picture of my dad so that the bartender could identify him, it was unlikely that he had a photo of him either.

Maybe Miles knew him for a while, but that didn't mean that he knew him *well*. Sometimes we keep those closet skeletons so deeply hidden that we never expect anyone to find them. Maybe this was one of my dad's many, many skeletons.

"Maybe, but it's like that bartender said, my dad had a lot of demons. Plus, knowing my mom, it adds up."

"What does that mean?" Lucy asked.

Quickly regretting what I said, I took a deep breath before turning back to her.

"She's an addict," I admitted and then looked away to avoid "the look." You know that look, one ripe with pity followed by a sorrowful "Oh, I am so sorry." I cringe just at the thought of hearing it. What's worse is when people pry with follow-up questions such as, "Has she gone to rehab? Is she seeing anyone?" Well, she hasn't ODed, which is the only way that anyone would ever be able to get her into treatment, and aside from her parade of Jeffs, she is not seeing anyone.

However, before either Lucy or I had a chance to say anything, I felt a splash of wintry frost smack the left side of my face.

"What the—?" Lucy began, placing her hand on her now wet cheek. The rest of her sentence was drowned out by a storm of snowballs that began to rain down on us. The perfectly round, pristinely white snowballs dove into the Earth's gelatinous covering, as if they were a wintry army trying to break through a barricade.

The temperature was nowhere near freezing, so it seemed unlikely that it could be snowing. However, snow in early autumn did not seem impossible, that is until the snowballs and snow boulders began defying gravity. That's when I knew that this storm was a fantasy. In mid-air, many of the snowballs moved horizontally and melded into one another, gaining mass. Some even released icy spikes that cut into the Earth's coating.

I am no meteorologist, but as far as I know, snow should not be able to do that.

"We need to get out of here," Miles commanded, which quickly prompted us to run back toward Penn Station.

We skidded to a stop in front of a crosswalk where we were confronted by a line of cars, some slamming into one another, presumably trying to avoid the snowballs being hurled at them by some unknown invisible force.

"Shit," I yelled, jumping back from a gray Honda headed straight for us. Through the windshield, the driver emphatically spun the wheel to the far left and then to the far right, as if she were trying to go any which way to avoid slamming into us.

"No!" I screamed, instinctively holding out my hand, as if I could stop the car with this single gesture. Well, maybe I couldn't, but the giant snow boulder that slammed into the hood of the car definitely did the trick. The car slammed to a stop, pinned underneath the weight of the snow boulder. Ribbons of gray smoke rose from the hood as the dying engine hissed underneath.

"Shit!" Lucy cried, as she took a wobbly step backward. "We need to get out of here."

Before I could respond, I heard the sickening, metallic crunch of a car slamming into the back of the gray Honda. As a result, the driver of the gray Honda flew backward as a white airbag exploded in front of her, taking up all of the space on her side of the car.

"No!" Griswold shouted, running to the driver's side of the car.

Before I could react, Griswold gripped the handle of the driver's side door and pulled, but to no avail. However, this did not seem to deter him as he expelled all of his energy trying to muster up superhuman strength so that he could rip the door off of its hinges.

"Shit!" Lucy cried again, pointing up to a cascade of snow boulders gaining speed, headed straight for Griswold.

"No!" I shouted, one of the most guttural screams that sounded so foreign to me that if I had not felt it come from my vocal cords, I would have sworn that it came from some unknown entity.

I didn't know why, but on impulse I threw up my arms and held out my hands, palms facing up to the sky. I could not tell you what compelled me to do that, but I am glad that I did because the boulders that were aimed for Griswold, rocketing toward him, were suddenly suspended in midair. In fact, all of the snow boulders and snowballs were levitating at different points in the air, as if they were each held by an invisible thread.

It was as if this image created a ripple effect of silence because everything stilled as drivers looked on in amazement at the perfectly round, now innocuous globes of floating snow. As I remained frozen in place, Lucy leaned over and whispered, "Is this you?"

"I think so," I whispered back, not daring to lower my arms.

"Well, I don't think that you can stop," Lucy asserted.

"She's right," Miles noted, tapping on his phone. "This is on live news feed. The snow that, moments ago, was slamming into the ground just stopped in midair."

"Shit," I hissed, looking up at my extended arms. "I can't just *stay* like this. Hell, I'm not even sure how I'm doing this."

"This must be from Max's imagination, and you are controlling it," Miles explained, clicking off his phone and sliding it into his pocket.

"How is that possible? I mean, I *know* that I can pull fantasies into reality, but how am I *controlling* his fantasy-made-real?"

Miles began rubbing his chin in contemplation, head tilted upward, looking at the snowballs and boulders as if he were studying a museum exhibit on display.

Still examining the suspended snow, Miles stated, "I can't really answer how you can control something that was already made real. I've never seen you or Max do that. Yours and Max's abilities don't come with an instruction manual."

Yeah, a magical instruction manual would have been incredibly helpful to have on hand.

"If you are able to control your dad's fantasies, then do we still need to find him?" Lucy asked, looking up at the suspended snow.

She had a point; however, the only issue was that I had no idea *how* I was controlling my dad's fantasy. I mean, I just barely learned how to pull the fantasies I saw into reality. Why the hell did this damn ability have so many different permutations? A few days ago, it was so simple, I saw random fantasies and just blocked them out when I could. Now, all of a sudden, I was making fantasies real and controlling others that have already been made real? What's next, time travel? I mean, that might as well be next. I've already dipped my toe into the crazy water, I might as well just dive in.

"Are you doing this?" Griswold asked, as he sat the gray Honda's driver on the sidewalk. Her face looked sunburnt after being smacked with the giant airbag. Sweaty strands of blonde hair framed her wide, terrified blue eyes, which seemed to be staring off into the distance at nothing in particular.

"Not so loud, but yeah," I said, involuntarily lowering my arms a bit, "But I'm not sure how much longer I can keep it up. I don't know if keeping my arms like this is doing anything, but I can't stay like this forever."

"I've got an idea," Griswold said, smirking. "It's epic."

"To what extent does your idea involve rabbits?"

"To a pretty great extent," Griswold admitted, and then quickly added, "But I think it could work, but I'm not sure how many ninja rabbits we would have to create."

"Pass," I asserted, not even being able to fathom how ninja rabbits could prevent hyper speed snowballs and boulders from plummeting to the Earth.

"Usually, snow forms when the temperature is at or below freezing, right?" Lucy asked no one in particular, but Miles, Griswold, and I all nodded in response.

"However, this is not your normal brand of snow. I am not sure how *imaginary* snow may function."

"Imaginary or not, what if it got *really hot* all over? If the atmospheric conditions didn't allow the frozen crystals to form, maybe the snowballs would melt before they even reached the ground," Lucy hypothesized.

I looked over at Miles to gauge his response. He was back to rubbing his chin in contemplation.

"It may work," Miles noted. "But it will also cause a lot of press."

"What's new?" I grunted, involuntarily lowering my arms a bit more. "I can't keep holding up my arms. Let's just try it."

Lucy nodded and then tilted her head up. The habitual sizzle resembled that of an egg frying on a griddle, the sound of which amplified as Lucy's imagined invisible heat waves obliterated any semblance of cold in the air. The heat was so intense that it felt like a hand brushing up against my cheek. My breathing felt labored as I lowered my arms a bit more.

Closing my eyes, I balled my hands into fists as I pulled this heat into existence. The high-pitched ringing quickly escalated, threatening to shred my eardrums. Instinctively, I grabbed my ears and sank to the ground, which caused the snow boulders and snowballs to continue on their original trajectory.

"Dammit!" I screamed over the high-pitched ringing. Pushing the heels of my hands into my cheeks, I kept going.

The ringing intensified to a single, sharp whistle that was a threaded needle, stitching my brain with a strident frequency that should have sent me into convulsions, but didn't. In fact, as quickly as it came, it left. After it hit a crescendo of sorts, it petered out, only leaving the sound of sloshing snow smacking to the ground in its wake.

I felt the beads of sweat form on my upper lip and brow before I opened my eyes to see that Lucy's imagined heat wave had become a scorching reality.

I gingerly opened my eyes to see the streets crawling with cars, their headlights blaring, slowly wading through streams of water soaking the roads as they dodged the pouring rain, which was dissipating into white puffs of muggy smoke.

"It worked," Lucy said, her smile beaming to reveal her multicolored elastics.

"We better get out of here," Miles said, looking around at the cars. While some drivers were focusing on making it through traffic without skidding, some had come to a full stop and began to get out of their cars. These drivers stood by their car doors, staring in our direction.

"Dammit," I hissed, looking down the street, ready to run.

"Wait, what about the woman?" Griswold asked, nodding toward the driver, who was still staring off into space.

I slid my phone out of my pocket and put in an anonymous call to 9-1-1.

"Okay, they're coming," I confirmed, sliding the phone back into my pocket. "Now let's go."

I'm not in the habit of abandoning drivers who had gone into shock after almost skidding into me, but then again this was the first time I was in that situation. Maybe it would be the last, but who knows. We can't say "never" about anything.

Between running through thick puffs of smoke and trying not to slip on the now drenched gelatinous cover coating the Earth, it took us quite a bit of time to make it back to Penn Station. Luckily, when we made it back, the conductors, ticket takers, and passengers were distracted enough by the news of giant snowballs falling from the sky and then dissipating into clouds of smoke that we easily snuck up to the roof without being noticed.

Fortunately, Hermon the Third kept his invisibility cloak on because he was nowhere to be seen.

"Hermon the Third, where are you?"

"Here," I heard a raspy voice state to my left. I reached out to feel the soft velvet covering Hermon the Third's tail.

"So where now?" Lucy asked, as Griswold searched for our invisibility cloaks.

"I have no idea," I admitted, wiping beads of sweat from my forehead.

"There's a rehabilitation center in Newark," Miles noted, looking down at his phone. "It's only a little over ten minutes away." Miles tapped on his phone and then slid both it and his hands into his pockets. "I texted you the directions," he said just as I felt my phone vibrate.

"Great, let's go," I said, walking toward what I assumed was Hermon the Third's midsection as I lifted up the edges of the cloak to climb underneath; however, before I could, Lucy touched my arm.

I turned to face her pensive amber eyes, underscored with dark circles forming just underneath her bottom lids.

"Wait, you never answered my question," Lucy stated. "If you are able to control your dad's fantasies, then do we still need to find him?"

"Yes," I affirmed. "I have no idea how I did that, and even if I did, I just can't keep trying to control whatever he does. Plus, there's no way to predict what he is going to bring into this world next. I'd have to constantly be on high alert. No, the only way to stop him is to find him."

This explanation seemed to satisfy Lucy since she nodded, but then groaned when it seemed to hit her that we would be traveling by dragon.

"I hate flying," Lucy griped, hoisting herself up.

"Just imagine if he was a Pegasus this time," I said, after pulling myself up and taking hold of the reins.

It only took us about ten minutes to make it to the Newark Rehabilitation Center. As I told Lucy, we needed to stop my dad, but how were we going to do so? Your guess is as good as mine. How do you stop a man who can imagine anything and pull it into reality? And let's not forget that his ability is unstable, so I am not even sure about whether or not what he is doing is intentional. This situation definitely called for a fly-by-the-seat-of-your-pants plan. However, Lucy wasn't having it.

"What now?" she asked, taking in a deep gulp of humid air as she lowered her hood.

"Now we figure out where he is and how to stop him," I stated.

"*If* he's still here," Miles asserted, turning toward me. "He was arrested over three years ago. We need to prepare ourselves for the distinct possibility that he's no longer here."

I ran my hands down my face at the realization that we may have hit a dead end. I hated to admit it, but Miles was right; however, that raised the question, if he deduced that my dad probably was no longer here, why had he waited until *now* to say anything? So, naturally, I posed this very question to him.

In response, he grinned and then stated, "Because I know how we can figure out where he may be now, and the clues we need are right in there." Miles pointed to the beige brick building just off in the distance, illuminated by the surrounding streetlights.

"Care to elaborate?"

"Even if your father isn't there, they must keep records of their former patients. In these records, there could be a clue to his current whereabouts."

"And how are we supposed to gain access to these records?" Lucy asked Miles, raising her eyebrow and placing her hand on her hip. "Just go up and ask? They're not going to just hand over Max's file."

"That's why we're not going to ask," Miles said.

"This is a bad idea," Lucy said, pulling her hood even further down as the four of us walked through the sliding entrance doors. The cool air blasting from the A/C was a welcome relief. Then Lucy turned toward what I assumed was Griswold—it was a little hard to tell, considering that we were all shrouded in cloaks of invisibility—and asked, "I suppose you agree with this plan?"

"It makes sense to me," Griswold simply stated.

"What if we get caught?" Lucy asked.

"How can we get caught if we're invisible?" Griswold responded. He had a point, but if we *did* get caught wearing invisibility cloaks, I had no idea how we were going to explain where in the world we got our hands on invisible clothing. I'm pretty sure The Gap or Target doesn't sell them; then again I don't really go clothing shopping, so I wouldn't be the one to ask, but I could almost guarantee that if any retail store sold magical clothing, everyone would have heard about it.

I couldn't exactly tell them the truth, that I pulled my best friend's fantastical cloaks into existence. That is, unless I would like to spend the rest of my life locked up in a mental institution or being experimented on. Either option was a nonstarter.

"We're not going to get caught," I asserted, nearing the front desk.

"I hope you're right," Lucy whispered.

Behind the desk, the receptionist was focused on a large monitor. Through the reflection in her glasses, it looked like she was on a patient database, but it was a little hard to tell if this was the case without taking a closer look.

I felt someone pull on my cloak. Moving toward the pull, I figured that it was Miles.

"I am going to imagine something that will create a distraction. You're going to have to bring it into reality so that I can search for your dad's files," Miles explained.

I cringed at the thought of the high-pitched ringing decimating my eardrums.

"Can't we just create a *normal* distraction?" I offered.

"What do you have in mind?" Miles asked.

I quickly scanned the room to see what could cause a good enough distraction that everyone would move away from the front desk. I walked past the elevators and stairwells, hoping that something in the hallway would trigger an idea. However, nothing came to mind.

Just as I was about to give up and concede to Miles's plan, I saw it. Grinning, I determinedly walked over to the strip of wall near the stairwell and pulled down the red handle on the fire alarm. The blaring fire alarm was unnerving, but nothing compared to the high-pitched ringing that was reserved for the purpose of trying to destroy my hearing.

The receptionist's head shot up as she quickly jumped up and proceeded to the front door. Other nurses, doctors, and patients followed suit as everyone made their way through the exit as quickly as possible.

Once I assumed that everyone had filed out, I snuck behind the desk and motioned for Miles to follow me. Realizing that he probably didn't see me because we were still wearing our cloaks, I shout-whispered, "Miles, over here!"

With the building emptied out, I heard the rustling of capes as Miles, Griswold, and Lucy made their way behind the desk.

Luckily, the receptionist had not logged out of the computer before she left the building. The patient database was fully accessible but contained so much information that I didn't even know where to begin.

"When I said files, I meant *physical files*," Miles asserted, and then added, "there must be a file room somewhere on this floor."

As I glanced at the list of names in the patient database, I turned toward the direction in which I heard Miles's voice and said, "You look for a physical file, and I will search for a digital one. Hopefully, one of us will come up with something."

I heard Miles's footsteps walk in another direction as the faint sounds of a fire engine neared the building.

"Shit," I hissed, realizing that we had a lot less time than I thought as I scrolled through the names.

"Can't one of us just imagine that you find your dad's file?" Griswold offered.

"You *can*, but that would be an imaginary file, not the *real* one. We need to know exactly where he is," I insisted, continuing to scroll. Looking at the laundry list of names, I realized that this was going to take forever, so I held down both the CTRL and F keys to do a quick search.

After typing my dad's name into the search bar, the screen showed a cell highlighted in yellow. To the far right of the medical record number, under the column "Status" it read "Transfer: Newark Psychiatric Hospital."

"Damn," I sighed as I lifted my hands from the keyboard and ran them through my hair. "Let's find Miles. He's not here."

"So, he's been institutionalized?" Griswold asked as we stood in front of Hermon the Third, looking out toward another brightly lit beige building.

"That's what his file said," I confirmed, pushing off my hood and wiping my brow with my arm.

"Did it say whether or not he was still *here*?" Lucy asked, fanning herself with her hands. "And can you get rid of this heat? It's stifling."

"Best to keep it here," Miles said, lowering his hood and wiping down his brow with a handkerchief. "It may be the only force keeping the snow at bay."

I nodded in agreement. In truth, even if I had wanted to unimagine what I had brought into existence, I had no idea how to do so. Just this morning, I could only see into people's imaginations. Only a few short hours later I was pulling these fantastical images into reality, and now I was controlling my dad's fantasy-made-real notions.

It's possible that unimagining something would be easier than making it real. In Miles's story, he said that I just said my mantra and then the wolf disappeared, so maybe it was as simple as that. Then again, when I was little, pulling fantasies into reality was second nature to me, so maybe the same rules don't apply now.

"Griswold, can you look to see if there is any news feed about the heat wave?" Lucy asked, now fanning herself with the bottom of her cloak.

Griswold dutifully pulled his phone out of his pocket, tapped on the screen and began to scroll. His eyes widened as he slowly scrolled through whatever news feed he was reading.

"How bad is it?" I groaned, walking over to his side and glancing down at the screen to find a distant photo of a teenager holding his arms out to levitating snowballs and snow boulders.

"Damn," I hissed, running my fingers through my hair, now laced with sweat. "I didn't even see anyone holding up a phone."

"What is it?" Lucy asked, walking over to Griswold's other side, and looking down at the photo. "Oh shit," she gasped.

"What is it?" Miles parroted Lucy, pulling out his own phone.

"Someone took a picture of Domino doing," Griswold said, pausing to wiggle his fingers in the air. "You know, his magic thing."

"When have I ever wiggled my fingers when bringing things into existence?"

Griswold shrugged and then said, "I guess you didn't, but I think it needs a little something, you know? To show that you are doing some sort of magic."

"I'm skimming the news feed, and it doesn't mention Domino by name. It just says that an unidentified teenager may have some involvement in the heat wave and the suspension of the snow," Lucy said, and then looked up from the screen to look at me. "No one knows that it's you."

"That doesn't mean that someone won't figure it out," I noted, walking away from the screen. "They can always magnify that photo and sharpen it."

"If they could have, they probably would have done so before publishing it," Miles noted, scrolling through his phone. "Lucy's right, I don't see any mention of your name."

"That means you are safe." Griswold beamed, clicking off his phone and sliding it into his pocket.

Maybe Griswold was right, maybe I was "safe," but only for now. With all of the "magic" that I was doing, it was only a matter of time before someone else discovered what I was capable of doing. Then what? Would I become a lab rat? Would I be institutionalized? Maybe here? Great, a father-son reunion, institution style.

I had managed to spend fifteen years of my life going unnoticed, and now my dad was in the process of shining a light on both him and me because he was either hell-bent on destroying the Earth—or maybe just the United States, that was still undetermined—or he couldn't get a handle on the abilities that he had decades to master. Either way, if I didn't stop him, he was going to expose us both, that is if he didn't destroy the world first. So why do the sons have to pay for the sins of their fathers? This definitely counted as one of those moments, and suffice it to say it sucked.

"For now. This is just another reason why we need to stop my dad," I contended.

"You still didn't answer my question. How do we know that he is *still* here? Or even here at all? Did the file say that he was *specifically* at this institution?"

I shook my head and then added, "It didn't, but this is the closest institution to the rehab center. We at least have to try."

Lucy sighed and reluctantly nodded as the four of us walked toward the entrance, pulling our hoods back up.

Once again, the blasting A/C was a breath of fresh air as we neared the receptionist's large oblong desk, protected by an expansive plexiglass shield. My gaze immediately fell on the fire alarm behind the desk, but before I pulled it, I had to make sure that she was on a patients' database or directory page.

I felt for Lucy's hand. When I finally found it, I gently pulled her toward the exit.

Once back outside I whispered, "Can you cause a distraction while I check the computer screen? I need to make sure that he's actually here and the only way to do that is to check the patient database."

"This may sound crazy, but why don't we just *ask* if he's a patient here?" Lucy whispered back. "I mean, we should have just done that at the rehab center, but you and Miles over-complicated things."

"Do you honestly think that they would have given us *any* information on my dad if I just politely went up and asked them?" I countered.

"You could have at least *tried*," Lucy returned. "Who knows? Maybe you would have been pleasantly surprised," she stated.

"Hey, what's the holdup?" I heard Miles ask from the entrance.

I glanced around just to make sure that no one was looking in our direction before I took off my cloak. Following suit, Lucy, Miles, and Griswold also removed their cloaks and placed them in the crook of their arms.

"Lucy thinks we can get information about my dad without sneaking in," I explained, at which Griswold scoffed.

Scowling at Griswold, Lucy asked, "And you'd prefer to sneak in? Why make something complicated when it doesn't have to be."

Griswold shrugged and then said one of the most profound things that I have ever heard him say. "Because life is complicated." He shrugged again, and looked toward me. "It's your call. What do you want to do, Domino?"

"I don't really care how we get in, just as long as we stop him," I asserted, and then added, "We will try Lucy's way, and if that doesn't work, then we will sneak in."

We hid our cloaks in a bush near the front entrance before we reentered the mental institution. Once again, the blast of the A/C was a welcome relief.

We walked straight up to the desk to find the receptionist reviewing something on one of the computer screens in front of her. Unlike the receptionist at the rehab center, this receptionist was not wearing glasses, so it was difficult to determine what she was reading on the screen.

To get her attention, I tapped on the plexiglass, which caused her to grimace at me.

"Don't tap on the glass," she reproached.

"Sorry, I just need information about a possible patient that you have here. See, he's my father, and I need to see him." As long as we were taking the simple route, we might as well try the truthful one as well. Well, generally speaking. I wasn't about to tell this receptionist, who I had met a few seconds ago, why I needed to see my dad. That was on a "need-to-know" basis, and she *definitely* did not need to know.

"Visiting hours ended one hour ago," the receptionist nonchalantly stated, turning back to her computer screens.

"Well, can you at least let me know if he *is* a patient here? His name is Max Garrison, and I think that he was transferred to this institution a little over three years ago."

The receptionist let out a long sigh as if I were purposely inconveniencing her.

"Give me a sec," she said, typing something on her keyboard.

After what was definitely longer than a second, she said—without turning from the computer screen— "Yeah, he's a patient here, but he is not accepting visitors."

"*Ever?*" I asked in disbelief.

"Afraid so," the receptionist stated.

"Does it say why?"

The receptionist sighed again in exasperation before stating, "There is just a written order from the doctor, but nothing else that I can release."

"So, I can't see my own father?"

At this question, the receptionist looked away from the computer screens and into my gaze.

"If you really want to see him, I would get a lawyer, otherwise there is nothing that I can do to help you."

Without saying another word, I pivoted away from the receptionist's desk and marched toward the exit. Once outside, I pulled one of the cloaks from the bush and threw it over my shoulders, making sure to cinch it at the neck. I then grabbed the other cloaks.

Turning toward Miles, Griswold, and Lucy, who had followed me out, I threw them their cloaks as I said, "Complicated it is."

It was pretty easy to find my dad's room number considering that the receptionist still had my dad's file open on one of her computer screens. However, actually finding said room was a whole other issue. The mental institution was like a maze with brightly lit, long winding hallways that were practically replicas of one another. The only distinction that differentiated one hall from the next was the painted horizontal strip that lined the walls, which must have separated one wing from another.

What made it worse was that every room had a designated four-digit numerical code etched into the beige doors; however, my dad's room was a five-digit alphanumeric code, RA307.

"Great," I whispered as we passed what felt like the hundredth door we saw.

"We're never going to find it," Lucy whispered from behind me. "We must have been on almost every floor and looked at almost *every* door."

"Are you sure that his room number is RA307?" Griswold asked.

"I may see a lot of crazy things, but this was real and pretty sane. The screen clearly showed that his room number was RA307."

"Maybe there's another floor that we haven't been on," Miles noted, pressing the elevator button.

Once the elevator arrived and we piled inside, I glanced at the elevator buttons, recalling that we hit all of them.

"Hey, what's that one?" Griswold asked, pulling up the sleeve of his cloak to point at a pristine button that, dissimilar to the other buttons, had no painted numbers on its surface.

Shrugging, I said, "It's worth a shot."

I expected the button to light up under my touch, but when I pressed it, nothing happened.

"There seems to be a keyhole next to the button," Lucy pointed out. "Maybe it's like a restricted floor or something."

Of course, it is. I mean, why would my dad just be on an ordinary floor with the rest of the patients?

"If I imagine a key that matches the hole, you can bring it into existence," Miles noted, at which I sighed.

I reluctantly nodded as I heard the air sizzle. Once I saw the key that seemed to match the ridges of the keyhole, I began to pull it into reality. The high-pitched ringing came and went so suddenly that its presence and exit sent me reeling back in surprise. I managed to catch myself just in time so that I didn't smack my head into one of the elevator's walls.

With the imagined-now-real key in the keyhole, Miles firmly turned the key to the right, which prompted the mysterious elevator button to light up. The elevator gently ascended a few floors before we reached our destination.

The doors opened to reveal a small, dimly lit hallway. Unlike the other hallways, the walls were a grayish white. However, similar to the other halls, each door was etched with a code, except these were alphanumeric codes.

It didn't take long before we found RA307, which was only a few paces away from the elevator.

Standing in front of the door, I took a deep breath, trying to mentally prepare myself to confront my dad. I gripped the doorknob for a moment before I twisted it to the right and pulled.

CHAPTER 9

DON'T BOTHER SAVING ME

I don't know why seeing the restraints surprised me. Maybe it was because he was obviously asleep, so he didn't technically need to be restrained. Or maybe it was because this little ten-year reunion was punctuated by my dad being tied to a bed with thick beige straps that seemed to be melded to the sides of the bed. It was probably both. Oh, that and having to stop him from doing whatever he was doing to the world...while he was unconscious.

I leaned over the side of his bed, studying the beauty mark constellations on either side of his eyes just to confirm that this man was indeed my dad, and then began to shake his shoulders in order to wake him up. I must have been shaking him for a good minute before I gave up.

I could not help but question *how* my dad was able to cause such imaginative destruction without being awake. I mean, no one sleeps *that* heavily. He was obviously in a comatose state. Maybe he was unknowingly projecting his dreams and nightmares into reality. If this was the case, then it would make it that much harder to prevent him from doing it, as it would be completely involuntary. As far as I knew, everyone except for me can dream, so how could we stop my dad from doing what is neurologically natural for every other human being?

"How can we wake him up?" Griswold asked, lowering his hood.

"If we had some smelling salts, maybe we could wake him up," Lucy suggested, lowering her hood to reveal that she was standing adjacent to Griswold. "However, I'm sure that we wouldn't find them here. There's really nothing around."

Except for the bed and the fluorescent light hanging overhead, the small, box-sized room was completely barren.

"Okay, so we don't really have anything that we can use to wake him up, so what are we supposed to do now?" Lucy asked no one in particular.

"We just have to keep trying to wake him with whatever we *do* have," Miles stated, lowering his hood as he touched the half-empty plastic bag hanging from the IV pole beside my dad's bed. My eyes followed the transparent tubing attached to the bottom of the bag, to the crook of my dad's arm, where the tubing was secured with white tape. A small, thin needle was inserted into one of my dad's veins.

Turning toward me, he added, "We could have an endless supply of resources that you could bring into reality so that we can wake him."

I rubbed the heels of my palms into my eyes as I mentally prepared myself for the excruciating high-pitched ringing.

"Fine," I sighed, resigned to our go-to solution. Honestly, I don't blame Miles for proposing this. If I were in his shoes, I would probably do the same thing, but unlike him, I had to deal with that head-splitting high-pitched ringing. It wasn't as prolonged as it had been a few hours ago, so maybe that meant that the effects were fading? Or maybe it was because what I was pulling into existence wasn't as imaginative and grand.

"It looks like your father was heavily sedated, so we just need something that will counter the effects."

I would have pressed Miles to explain further, but the noise outside stopped me. Although the heavy footsteps in the hallway were a bit muffled behind the door, they were undeniably marching toward us.

"Someone's coming," Miles affirmed.

We quickly pulled up our hoods and flattened ourselves against the grayish white walls. I mean, we were already invisible underneath these cloaks, so I am not sure how trying to meld into the wall was going to help, but I did it anyway. If whoever were coming came into this impossibly small room, I am sure that s/he/they would bump into us.

As if that thought served as an invitation to enter, I saw the doorknob slowly turn. The door barely made a sound as it swung open to reveal three men, one of whom was wearing a long white doctor's coat. They practically marched into the room as they looked from right to left, as if they expected to find someone hiding behind the grayish white walls. Well, technically we *were* hiding, but in plain sight...sort of.

"I don't think anyone is here," one of the men, who was wearing a short-sleeved white shirt and matching pants, said to the man in the white coat.

"Yeah, there's no one in here," the other man, wearing the same exact same outfit as the one who just spoke, affirmed.

The doctor gave the room a quick scan before stating, "Well, someone has to be here. Dr. Sutai and I are the only ones who have authorized access to this floor, and neither one of us used our keys." Then, turning toward the men, he added, "It's very important that we find out who is here. This is a restricted area, especially this room. If anything happens to that man," the doctor stated, turning toward my dad's bed, pointing at his comatose body, "it will be detrimental."

Without another word, both men simultaneously nodded and followed the doctor out into the hallway, presumably to check the other rooms.

As soon as they left, I released a breath that I didn't even realize I was holding in.

I knew that this must have been some sort of restricted area given that we needed a key to get to the floor, but *why* was this floor restricted? I hadn't been in any of the other rooms, but maybe the other patients were dangerous. There's usually *that wing* in a mental institution, where they house patients who are a danger to themselves and others, but something told me that that was not exactly it. Yes, maybe the other patients *were* dangerous, but the doctor seemed to single out my dad in particular, especially when he said that if anything happens to him, it would be "detrimental." Detrimental to whom? How? And what did the doctor mean by "anything" and "detrimental"? Was it possible that he was referring to my dad's abilities? Maybe that's why he was sedated.

Come to think of it, that would make sense, because maybe the doctor assumed that if my dad was unconscious, he wouldn't be able to project any of his fantasies into the world, that is unless my dad *was* able to project his dreams into reality. Is it possible that the doctor did not realize this? I mean, how could he not with everything that has happened in the last twenty-four hours?

Well, the only way that I was going to find any answers to these questions was if we managed to wake up my dad.

I didn't move until I no longer heard the fall of footsteps in the hall as they trailed off.

"We can't wake him up here," I decidedly said, walking over the bed to look at my dad, who was blissfully unfazed by the goings-on in the room. I gingerly pulled the white tape away from his arm and carefully worked the needle out of his vein. If he was being fed a sedative intravenously, then obviously the first step to waking him up was putting a stop to the supply.

As I looked past the familiar beauty mark constellations around his eyes, I saw semblances of myself in him, such as my thick eyebrows and dark hair. His cheekbones were a little rounder than mine, but still just as pronounced. His thin nose and clean-shaven jawline tugged on the strings of my memory, but a specific image didn't come to mind; it was just a lingering feeling of a familial tether.

I brushed my hand in the air, like I was physically brushing away this feeling.

"Domino's right," Miles asserted, lowering his hood to reveal his furrowed brow. "I am pretty sure those gentlemen will be back soon. Domino, if I imagine us outside, can you get us there?"

"Like, teleport us?" Griswold squealed, taking the words out of my mouth, except my tone would have been a lot less excited and a lot more skeptical.

"I don't know, Miles. I mean, what if I just pull carbon copies of us into reality, who just happen to be outside, with a carbon copy of my dad?"

"You won't do that," Griswold asserted. I felt his hand around my shoulder as he added, "You've got this. If one of us imagines that we aren't here but that we are outside, with your dad, then there shouldn't be a problem."

He made it sound so simple, and maybe it was. Maybe I was just overthinking it.

"Okay, let's just do it. We obviously can't stay here, so someone imagine that all of us are somewhere else, and I'll make it happen."

"I've got this," Griswold said, again, sounding way too excited.

The sizzling contrasted with the gentle brush of the cool night air that began to form around us. It was difficult to discern exactly where we were without distinguishable landmarks, but when I felt some unknown thick but firm scaly thing flick the back of my legs, and heard a raspy grunt, I knew where Griswold had imagined us.

I nodded toward him, signaling that I had it, but I had a mountain full of doubts about whether or not I was able to get us there. Well, I guess there was a first time for everything, and today was definitely a day of "firsts" for me.

"Wait!" Lucy exclaimed, but I couldn't hear the rest of what she said as the high-pitched ringing drowned out every other sound. Without actually moving, I felt myself shifting from one existence to another, as if my aura were moving without my body, but was expecting it to follow close behind. With my hands pressed to my ears, I sank to the ground and lowered my head as the night air felt more pronounced, and that much more real.

On my knees, I leaned back and let myself fall onto the damp, gelatinous ground. Panting, I wiped my nose with the heel of my hand, knowing that when I pulled it back, I would find a trail of blood. Instead of looking, I just wiped my blood on my pants and slowly sat up.

"You should have waited!" Lucy exclaimed, pulling off her cloak. Then she took a step back and her eyes widened, probably at the sight of my bloody nose. "Are you okay?" she asked, her tone softening.

I nodded and said that I was fine. Probably seeing that I was, she nodded, and then turned toward my dad's grayish white bed.

"We should have waited because we needed to create a doppelgänger, otherwise they're going to know that he is missing," Lucy frustratedly explained.

"Shit," I hissed, running my fingers through my hair.

"They won't know that it was us," Griswold explained, pulling off his cloak. "I mean, we were literally invisible."

"Yes, but Lucy has a point," Miles noted. "They will still notice that Max is missing. Who knows what consequences that may have?"

I groaned as I ran my hands down my face. Maybe I was wrong before, maybe I wasn't overthinking anything. In fact, maybe we weren't putting enough thought into these improvised plans. Improvised plans usually aren't calculated ones by design, so it adds up. I just needed to think things through a little more before I acted.

In the meantime, we couldn't reverse time—or maybe I could if someone imagined it, who knew—so we needed to deal with this reality where my dad was laid out on a bed, completely unconscious, and probably responsible for all of the devastating events that were taking place. Well, maybe he wasn't responsible for *everything*. I mean, if there was a tornado in Kansas, was that my dad or just nature at work? At this point, who could really tell? And therein lies the issue.

"Well, at this point, we just need to wake him up," I said, standing up on wobbly legs.

"We could try smelling salts," Lucy suggested again, and then bit her lip before adding, "But one of us would need to imagine them because I don't see any around."

"Let's just do it," I sighed, feeling the sizzle in the air before I saw the small, white rectangular packets.

If you ever try to wake someone up by waving smelling salts under their nose for an extended period of time, make sure that you are at least an arm's length away, that is unless you like the noxious smell of ammonia. Then by all means, sniff away.

With my shirt pulled over my nose and my head beginning to throb from the fumes, I continued to wave those damn smelling salts back and forth under my dad's nose for what felt like forever before I just threw my hands up in the air, accidentally flinging the smelling salts to the ground.

"What, is he in a coma?" I asked no one in particular.

"I don't think so. When we found him, he wasn't hooked up to an EKG, so it seems unlikely that he is in a coma. He is, however, definitely out cold," Miles said, rubbing his chin as he examined my dad's annoyingly unconscious body.

"I mean, if he's this much of a pain when he is unconscious, I wonder what he's like when he's awake."

"Do you think that we should try to unstrap him?" Griswold asked, picking up the smelling salts from where they landed on the ground.

"I'm not sure how that's going to help, but why not," I said.

Soon after, I felt the familiar sizzle in the air as Griswold imagined industrial-sized scissors that could cut through anything, including the straps that were impossibly tightly cinched to the bed. Taking a deep breath, I powered through the high-pitched ringing to pull the scissors into reality.

Once we cut through the straps, my dad's limp arm hung over the side of the bed.

"Let's try sitting him up."

Standing on either side of the bed, Griswold and I managed to lift my dad to a sitting position. However, he fell back on the bed once we let go.

After about another hour of sitting around waiting for my dad to wake up, Lucy suddenly exclaimed, "This is ridiculous." Gesturing at my dad, she continued, "He's obviously not waking up anytime soon. I say that we find a motel for the night and try to wake him in the morning."

"It is pretty late, and there's not much that we can do with Max asleep," Miles contended.

"Fine," I sighed, resigning myself to the wave of exhaustion that was hitting us all head-on. "Anyone know of any motels nearby?"

"You *could* just imagine one," Griswold joked; at least I think that he was joking. Either way, the only response that he got from me was the side-eye, as I opened up a map app on my phone.

It didn't take Hermon the Third too long to land in the parking lot of the closest motel we could find. Once we got off, I directed him toward the forest behind the motel, where he could sleep, and bought him a couple of things in the vending machine to eat. Who knew that dragons—who are sometimes a Pegasus—liked Lay's potato chips, Doritos, and chocolate bars? As long as he kept his cloak on and stayed completely invisible, he could eat whatever he wanted. That's all we needed, people discovering a nonexistent-kind-of-real dragon, as if people didn't have enough to read about on their news feed.

With a 6-foot-tall frame and a sizable build, it was a lot harder than I thought it would be to carry my dad to the motel room. Well, "carry" does not exactly explain what Griswold and I did. With my dad's arms swung over our shoulders, his legs were dragging behind him as we pulled him toward the room.

After Miles paid for our rooms—Lucy having her own—Griswold and I flung our dad onto an orange and green checkered armchair near the TV stand.

My dad's head slumped to the side as he slid down in the chair. He didn't snore, grunt, or really make any sound that would indicate that he was asleep. In fact, the only sound that we heard was the hum of Griswold's phone vibrating. He slid it out of his pocket, looked down at the screen, and then headed to the bathroom.

Looking down at my dad's unconscious, limp body, it was pretty difficult to believe that he was responsible for any of the destruction that had happened. In fact, it was hard to believe that he could be responsible for anything, even for himself. Considering that he went from a rehab center to a psychiatric hospital, it was obvious that he was going downhill fast.

"How are we going to stop him?" I asked Miles, feeling him standing behind me, looking down at my dad.

"I'm not sure," Miles admitted, taking a step closer. "I am not even sure how your father has imagined anything into existence in this state."

Turning toward him, I asked, "Couldn't he have projected his fantasies into reality while sleeping?"

Miles tilted his head to the side and narrowed his eyes as if through sheer observation he could determine whether or not my dad was capable of this feat.

"Not sure," Miles admitted. "Your dad never mentioned that that was possible, but who knows? I don't see any other explanation for what is happening. I haven't seen him in a decade, so it *is* possible. Anything's possible."

Again, therein lies the problem. When *anything* is possible, including a single man being able to cause massive destruction with a single thought, most of which he may or may not be having while conscious, then how do you even begin to stop him?

"The only way that we can find out is by talking to him," Miles noted, and then, looking down at my dad's limp arms, added, "It is possible that he may run off when he wakes up, so we may want to strap him down."

"Any chance there's something in this room that we can use to tie him down?" I asked, looking around only to see the TV stand, two twin beds with matching orange and green checkered bedspreads, random pictures of forests bolted to wood-paneled walls, a bathroom door, and pretty much nothing else.

Sighing, I told Miles that if he imagined something, I would bring it into existence.

The sizzle in the air brought forth an impervious, orange satin ribbon that wrapped around my dad's midsection, pinning his arms to his sides. Two other matching ribbons appeared, one that hugged my dad's chest and wrapped around the back of the chair. The other spun tightly around his ankles, bringing his legs together.

"Wow, I never thought that I would see impenetrable satin ties," I stated before concentrating on the imagined fabric, feeling it holding my dad firmly in place as the high-pitched ringing began to resound.

Involuntarily, I took a wobbly step back and checked my nose for fresh blood, but I could only feel the thin layer of blood that had already dried over my upper lip. Although I had not looked at my reflection since we left Oblivion, I imagined that I looked like a bloody mess.

"Perfect," Miles affirmed, leaning down to give the now real satin ties a tug for good measure. Miles looked back to see me inspecting my blood-stained hands.

"It'll get easier with practice," he stated.

"What if I don't want to practice," I countered, wiping my palms on my pants. "What if I just want it to go away?"

"Sometimes people have destinies that are well beyond their own desires. I know it's hard to do, but there are moments, like these, when we need to put aside what we want, and instead do what's needed," he explained. Looking at my dad, he added, "And, in this case, it's trying to prevent someone from causing more devastation."

"*If* he's actually doing it," I added, running my fingers through my stiffening hair, probably coated with blood.

"Well, if he's not responsible for what has happened within the last twenty-four hours, then I am not sure what we will do next."

Unlike me, Miles was usually prepared for anything. Sure, he was going along with our improvised plans, but I am almost certain he had a plan B tucked away in his mind at every turn, so to hear him admit that he did not have an alternative plan just in case my dad was not the cause of this mess was a little unnerving.

I felt my fingers catch in matted strands of hair; the overwhelming feeling of griminess and exhaustion hit me, with griminess winning out. I looked toward the shut bathroom door to hear muffled sounds of Griswold speaking on the phone. My guess was that he was trying to convince his parents to not call the cops. After all, he had been gone for a while, but I highly doubt that the police would come looking for him because he definitely wasn't missing for forty-eight hours. Nevertheless, I could definitely see his parents threatening to take certain privileges away, like laptop access, if he didn't check in.

Sighing, I said to Miles, "I am going to see if Lucy will let me use the shower in her room."

Miles merely nodded as he continued to look at my dad.

A tinge of sympathy softened Miles's steely gray eyes. Miles may have never spoken about my dad, but it was obvious that he cared about him. I mean, my dad worked for Miles for years, and as far as Miles and I knew, Miles was the only other person that my dad trusted with his secret. It makes sense that he would feel some sort of connection to my dad. I, on the other hand, cannot say that I feel the same. Sure, there may be a memory or two tickling the back of my mind, but I don't feel emotionally linked to him in any way. In fact, his existence being a part of my reality has just caused me more strife.

I was completely fine in his absence. I was able to get from A to B, and just exist without causing any disturbance. Sure, I saw other people's fantasies, but I was able to block out most of them. I didn't try to do anything about what I saw. I didn't try to use these so-called visions for any type of personal gain. I'm not even sure how I could have gone about doing that. My world was weird but fine, that is until my damn dad had to disrupt it by causing havoc. Now, not only do I have to stop him by doing who knows what, but I am expected to fulfill some sort of "destiny" by practicing pulling fantasies into reality, which damn well hurts. Frankly, it *should* hurt. Who the hell should have the ability to *do* that? I mean, when you come to think about it, it's just beyond bizarre. Oh, and on top of it, I can also control other people's fantasies but only on instinct in a hyper-defensive state? Again, it's just nuts. It's what comic books are made of, not real life.

And what has all of this gotten me? A reunion with a comatose father in a cheap motel room with blood-stained hands and hair.

Lucy's room was only a few paces away. I gently knocked, not knowing whether or not she was still awake; however, I knew that she was when she opened the door after the second knock.

"Did I wake you?"

"No," she softly said.

We awkwardly stood in front of one another before I asked if I could use her shower.

She nodded as she stepped away from the opening to let me in.

I thanked her as I made my way to the closed bathroom door.

With my hand on the doorknob, Lucy said, "I know I've asked you if you are okay, but are you really?"

Turning back toward her, I saw her tuck her wavy hair behind her ears and bite her bottom lip, revealing her multicolored elastics.

"Yeah, but I know that I look pretty bad," I admitted, smiling and running my fingers through my matted hair.

"All things considered, I think that you look more than fine."

"Thanks," I said, giving her a small smile.

As I turned back toward the bathroom door, I heard Lucy clear her throat.

"Domino, umm, so this thing you have? This ability? Umm, are you able to see everyone's fantasies all the time?"

Turning back toward her, I nodded and then asked, "Why?"

That's when she began to blush and looked down at the orange shag carpet that lined the room, as if she were suddenly too embarrassed to make eye contact.

"This is silly, but did you ever see anything about, you know, us?"

"Oh," I inadvertently said, realizing that she was referring to the Harlequin romance versions of us. Luckily, I had not seen these fantastical visions since our date. Maybe it was because she had learned the truth about me, or maybe it was because almost being mauled by a fantastical-turned-real tiger overpowered any romantic imaginings that she could have of us.

"Not really, I mean—" I paused in midsentence because I had no idea where I was going with that statement.

Lucy's blush deepened as she realized that I did see her fantastical versions of us.

"God, this is so embarrassing," she admitted, lowering herself onto the corner of the twin bed. "I mean, imagine finding out that your crush is able to see your desires and fantasies? It's humiliating."

Seeing her still staring at the carpet, I knew that I should say something reassuring, but my mind was drawing a blank.

"I can't really see desires. I mean, I *can* if they are imagined, and I don't block them out, so I kind of guess that I can, but I usually try to block out fantasies," I stammered.

Yup, super helpful, Domino; try to explain your abilities, as if that is going to make Lucy feel any better.

"It's still humiliating," Lucy grumbled.

"Don't be humiliated. I've seen fantasies that were a lot worse and far more graphic," I explained, sitting next to Lucy.

"Like what?" she asked, still looking down at the carpet.

"Well, like your brother's for one," I said, and then cringed, mentally smacking my head because I had no idea if he had come out to his family yet, or was ever going to.

However, what Lucy said next surprised me, "Yeah, Colin has it really bad for Tom Hamilton."

"Yeah. He hasn't told him," I affirmed, blinking to block out the memory of Colin's graphic sexual fantasies.

"Yeah, part of the time I think that's why he's such a jerk. I mean, not to me, but to everyone else. I wish he could just be himself," Lucy admitted, looking up to glance into my eyes. "Not that it's just that easy," she quickly added.

"Are you referring to this," I said, pointing at my right temple, as if my abilities originated from this part of my head. Who really knew what part of my autonomy was responsible for my strange powers? It could have very well been my kidneys for all I knew, or my appendix. It had to be there for some reason, right?

"I can't even begin to imagine what it's like to see what isn't real, and then have the ability to pull it into existence. It's, well, godlike," Lucy explained, at which I could not help but laugh.

"Sorry, I just never thought of myself as a god."

Lucy raised her eyebrow at me and gave my shoulder a playful push.

"Don't get an inflated ego. All I meant was that you only hear about gods and goddesses being able to do what you are capable of doing."

"So, you are of the polytheistic persuasion?" I teased.

Rolling her eyes, Lucy gave my shoulder another playful shove.

"You know what I mean, Domino. What you can do is just so, I don't know, *grand*. If someone just imagines something, *anything*, you can just go ahead and pull it into reality, just like that," she said, snapping her fingers.

Looking down at my blood-stained palms, I said, "Yeah, just like that, and as I'm doing it, I feel like I am being lobotomized without an anesthetic each time. Loads of fun."

"Well, maybe it's like Griswold said, you need to practice," Lucy suggested.

Running my hands down my face, I said, "Yeah, that's what everyone keeps telling me, but what if I don't want to?"

Lucy paused for a moment as if she needed a second to fully understand what I was saying.

"Well, why wouldn't you want to?"

Taking a deep breath, I explained. "I accept that I will need to stop my dad because who else can stop someone who can make something fantastical real other than someone who can do the same thing? But that doesn't mean that I want to get *good* at it. In fact, after I stop my dad, I just want to forget that I can do whatever the hell it is that I can do, pull others' fantasies into reality or unintentionally control other fantasies made real."

"But why? Why wouldn't you want to use your abilities for the betterment of humankind?" Lucy pressed.

"Me? Be responsible for the betterment of humankind? You've gotta be kidding me," I scoffed.

"Yeah, you. Why is that so unbelievable? Why *not* you? You are the one with the abilities. You can use them to stop war, create world peace, end hunger, and bring climate change to an end. The possibilities are endless," Lucy explained.

Digging the heels of my palms into my eyes, I shot up.

"Well, right now, I'm going to be responsible for taking a shower," I said, marching straight for the door.

My stomach churned at the thought of being responsible for saving humanity. That proverbial question, *why me?* rolled around in my head like a marble being shot across an uneven wooden floor. Yes, there was no denying what I could do, but just because I *could* do it didn't mean that I was the right person for the job. Trust me, if I could hand off the torch, baton, whatever physical manifestation you want to create to symbolize my abilities, I gladly would. However, for now, I was stuck with them.

Maybe by stopping my dad I would inevitably be saving the world, but after that, I think that my career as a superhero would pretty much end.

I did not realize how long I had been in the shower until I noticed my pruny fingertips, and that Lucy had fallen asleep on one of the twin beds.

As quietly as possible, I snuck out of her room and went back to my own.

I slipped the key into the lock, and practically slid into the dark room, trying to make the least amount of noise possible.

"You're back," Griswold exclaimed, turning on the lamp closest to the twin bed that he was lying on. I looked toward the other bed to see a body-sized lump completely covered in the orange and green checkered bedspread.

Pressing my index finger to my lips, I nodded. Looking to my right, I saw that my dad was in the same position, practically dead to the world.

"He hasn't moved," Griswold whispered, nodding to the armchair.

I nodded and then slid off my sneakers. Not even asking Griswold to move over, I walked over to the bed and lay down next to him.

Before I could close my eyes, Griswold said, "What do you think you'll do when your dad wakes up?"

Turning to face him, I said, "I don't know. I'll ask him why he did what he did, that is if he even realizes that he brought the tiger, earthquakes, sludge, snow boulders, and who knows what else into the world."

"You think that it was unintentional?"

"Maybe," I said, yawning. "He's definitely in an extremely deep sleep, so I'm pretty sure that he has not been awake in a while."

"Maybe," Griswold said, almost in the form of a question. "I don't know. Well, either way, I can imagine whatever you need me to, to stop him."

"Thanks, Grizz," I said, yawning again. "Let's turn off the light. I need to get some sleep."

"Sure," Griswold said, but then added, "Is it weird to see your dad again?"

I sighed, coming to terms with the fact that I wasn't going to be able to go to sleep anytime soon.

"Yeah, I guess, I don't really remember him from ten years ago, so yeah, it's pretty strange."

Griswold was quiet for a beat, as if he were processing what I said.

"Are you going to tell your mom?"

"Are you kidding?" I scoffed. "What good would that do?"

Griswold shrugged and then said, "I don't know. Just asking."

"I'm pretty sure that she's done with him. She never mentions him," I said, and then let out a curt laugh as I added, "I can't even imagine them together. Hell, sometimes I don't even know how I'm their son."

Griswold nodded, and then said, "Yeah, I get that. I feel that way too, with my parents I mean."

I was a little taken aback, not because I doubted the truth of the statement but because Griswold had admitted that that was how he felt. In the ten years that I have known him, I don't remember him ever speaking about himself as an outsider in his own family. If he felt that way, he pretty much kept it to himself.

Maybe neither of us spoke about our families because we had a shared experience; our parents didn't really understand us, or cared to do so. His parents wanted him to be a super-jock like Tom Hamilton—scratch that, to *literally* be Tom Hamilton—and mine, well, mine just didn't care one way or another. Apathy was fine, but when their actions start causing mass chaos, well, then we have a problem. Not that this was the case with my mom. She was too busy dividing her time between her parade of Jeffs and heroin to care about my where-abouts. Honestly, the only time she ever really seemed to pay attention to me was when I was in danger, like with Mike. Well, at least she has the protective parental instinct down. One point for Mom.

"At least your parents are concerned enough to blow up your phone," I said, with as reassuring of a tone as I could muster. Then, nodding toward my dad, I added, "And they are not trying to destroy the world with their minds."

"True," Griswold said simply, looking over at my dad, "But when they call, I wish they would stop saying, '*Why can't you be like this person or that person,*' blah, blah, blah. I mean, I'm just not like them, I'm like me."

"Yeah, and that's all you can be. Look, Grizz, you know who you are. You've *always* known exactly who you are, and you shouldn't be any-one different. Parents be damned. They don't know everything. They are just as imperfect as we are, they've just been roaming around the Earth for a while longer, so you'd think that they'd be wiser, but that's not always the case," I said, trying to suppress another yawn.

"Yeah, you're right," he said decidedly. "A leopard can't change its spots, even when its parents are pestering him to do so."

"Exactly," I said, but I was so tired I had no idea what I was agreeing with. "Grizz, can you get the light?" With a tick, the room was enveloped in darkness.

If I ever slept anywhere else other than my bed, I had gotten into the habit of listening to my surroundings before opening my eyes. I'm not exactly sure why. Maybe it was because I was masked in the illusion of sleep, so I would have the upper hand, just in case anyone in the vicinity was awake. I was not entirely certain why I needed this upper hand, but my instincts screamed to keep my eyes shut as I heard grunting emanating from the corner of the motel room.

I kept my eyes closed as I listened to the grunting increase in volume and frequency, which was quickly followed by the rustling of sheets.

"Miles," a gruff voice growled.

My muscles tensed as if they were preparing themselves for battle. They were in defiance of my brain, which was screaming to stay alert but remain still.

"Max, it's been a long time," I heard Miles softly confirm.

"What am I doing here, Miles?" my dad snapped.

"This has to stop," Miles stated, ambiguously.

There was an eerie silence that followed this statement, as if my dad and Miles were in an epic staring contest. However, I had no idea because my eyes were still closed.

Fighting my instincts, I opened my eyes to my dad staring straight into Miles's, as if at any moment my dad was going to eject lasers right into Miles's pupils. Since I knew that this may be a real possibility, I sprang out of bed and ran up beside Miles.

When he saw me, my dad's eyes widened. Apparently, the recognition was immediate.

"Domino," my dad whispered, looking me up and down as if he couldn't wrap his mind around my existence.

Quickly, my dad's bloodshot gray eyes shifted back to Miles. His expression twisted into a grimace as he hissed, "You let him find me?"

Miles swallowed before he said, "We didn't have a choice. We had to stop you."

"You were supposed to keep him safe, that's it," my dad growled, and then added, "He can't see it happen again."

I expected Miles to redirect my dad so that we could begin to get to the bottom of his destroy-the-world schtick, or for Miles to give me some sort of direction about what we should do; however, what *did* happen next was entirely unexpected.

Before Miles could respond, my dad squeezed his eyes shut and repeated my mantra, "You're not real, go away."

"What are you—?" But I didn't have a chance to finish my question because the sight of Miles's body shimmering away took away my ability to speak.

Have you ever been in a free-falling elevator, not knowing whether the elevator car was going to come to a gut-wrenching halt mid-drop, or whether the car was going to crash-land into the base of the elevator shaft? I hope that your apartment's elevators work a lot better than mine, but if they don't, you know exactly how I felt at that moment.

With my mouth still open, I tried to say something, but all that came out were disjointed noises that sounded like a plain where words went to die. I had seen *a lot* of unbelievable things in my lifetime, but seeing Miles just cease to exist was something I never thought that I would experience. I wasn't delusional, I knew that one day he would die. Since he was a lot older than I was, the likelihood of him dying before me was significantly high, so it was not inconceivable that I would eventually have to mourn his death, but what had just happened was not a death. I'm not even sure if there was a name for what happened.

"What the *fuck*?" finally spilled out of my mouth, as I stared down at my dad, still tied up, but the satin ribbon was taut as my dad attempted to unpin his arms from his sides.

"What the hell did you do?" I screamed.

My scream must have been pretty loud, as I heard Griswold fall out of bed and cry "What the hell?" from behind me.

I spun around, and shouted, "Run!"

I had no idea whether or not my dad would target Griswold, but I didn't want to find out.

Griswold shook his head, as he bolted upright.

"I'm not leaving you," he asserted.

"Release me," my dad demanded. I spun back around to see my dad still struggling with the satin ribbons.

"Bring Miles back!" I commanded.

I balled my hands into fists, waiting for my dad's next move.

"No, he's not real."

I felt as if my pulse forgot its natural rhythm, skipping a beat, making me feel like *I* wasn't real for a moment.

"What do you mean *he's not real*?" I hissed.

"Untie me, and I'll explain," my dad hissed back.

"Bring him back," I growled.

"I'm not doing *a damn thing* until you untie me," my dad countered.

I stared into his gray eyes, bulging, practically screaming out of his sockets. His pale skin was overtaken by an angry rouge, which contrasted the sharp whiteness of his pajama shirt and matching pants.

"Bring. Him. Back," I said in a slow seething voice, pronouncing each word so that not one syllable was misunderstood.

Although my order was clear, my dad refused to obey. We both knew that this was a power struggle, and since I was the one asking for something, he knew that I *had* to be the one to relent. After all, what did he really have to lose?

Despite realizing this, we continued to stare at one another for a good five minutes until I very reluctantly surrendered.

However, before I let him go, I said, "Don't you dare run." He nodded, but I knew that this command was pointless. Closing my eyes, I silently repeated the same mantra to myself and felt Miles's satin ribbons dissipate into nothingness.

My eyes shot open to see my dad immediately bolt upright, and then stumble on unsteady legs.

"You're untied, now bring him back," I ordered.

Rubbing his upper arms, my dad looked around the motel room. His glance then fell to the floor, where he found his bare feet nestled in the Earth's gelatinous covering. Raising an eyebrow, he kneeled down to get a better look at Miles's creation. A lump formed in my throat at just the thought of Miles's fantastical creation outliving him.

Skimming the surface of the gelatinous covering, my dad asked, "Is this you?"

"Never mind that," I hissed, tightening my fists into fleshy balls ready to pulverize anything in their path. "Bring Miles back and explain."

My dad stood back up, searchingly looking into my glare, as if he were trying to read me, turning me over in his mind.

"He's not real. I shouldn't have even created him in the first place. I stupidly did it to cover up my own mess," he began, running his hands down his face. "That's what I create, Domino, messes."

I took a determined step toward my father and grabbed his collar with my left hand while my right was still balled up into a fist, poised to land an uppercut into his chin. I didn't give a damn about my dad's self-deprecation. He was right, he *did* make a mess out of everything, and because I was his son, apparently it was my job to clean it up.

My dad's nostrils flared as his glare shifted away from mine, as if he were ashamed to look into my eyes.

"Bring him back," I demanded again.

My dad sighed, and then sank back into the armchair while I was still holding onto his collar. Sinking with him, I released his shirt and stood back upright so that I was looking down at him, watching him cup his head in his hands.

Seeing as I was getting nowhere by demanding that my dad bring Miles back, I changed tactics.

"You said that if I untied you, you would explain, so explain," I barked.

As I waited for my dad to respond, I felt Griswold warily walk up beside me. His wide eyes stared at my father in fixation.

"Give me the word, I'll imagine something," Griswold whispered to me.

I nodded, mentally preparing for the high-pitched ringing. I would gladly put up with any side effects of this damn ability just to put an end to my dad's reign of terror, but before making any moves, I needed answers, and I needed my dad to bring Miles back. I cringed at the thought that I needed the man who abandoned me a decade ago for no apparent reason.

"Fine," my dad sighed. "He *used* to be real. Miles Godare really did own the bookstore where I worked when I was a kid. In fact, he was the only person who knew about my abilities. I didn't mean to tell him, he just kind of figured it out because I messed up. It wasn't the only time I messed up. I just didn't have a handle on them, so sometimes I accidentally imagined something into existence. The worst was probably that serial killer."

"Jack the Ripper," Griswold chimed in.

My dad nodded at Griswold, and continued, "Yeah, Jack the Ripper. I managed to wipe him out of existence, but not before he caused some damage. See, my stupid creation went after me. He was about to stab me with his knife, but Miles jumped in front of me just in time. Unfortunately, Miles didn't make it. He died right in my arms.

"After I managed to remove Jack the Ripper from existence, I had no idea what to do. I knew that I couldn't go to the police because who would believe me? I was covered in Miles's blood. So, I did the only thing that I could, I covered it up. I imagined Miles's corpse buried in the far depths of the Atlantic Ocean, and then reimagined a version of Miles, with everything that I could remember about him. I even changed the Jack the Ripper memory so he thought that I snuffed him out of existence. The only thing that I didn't have him remember was his death."

My throat suddenly went dry as if someone had wiped it down with extra-absorbent cotton balls.

I closed my eyes and gave my head a quick shake, just to make sure that I was fully awake and alert, before I said, "So let me get this straight, Miles was killed by *your* creation, a serial killer, and the Miles that *I knew* was a figment of *your* imagination?"

My dad gave an affirming nod as I continued, "And the *imagined* Miles, the one I worked for, created imaginary things, like that damn goo the Earth is covered in. How the hell is that possible?"

Wiggling his toes in the still-existent goo, my dad said, "I didn't know that he imagined it, but I guess that's possible. I imagined him decades ago."

"What does *that* have to do with anything?" I exclaimed.

"Look, when I imagine things into existence, they seem incredibly real. The longer they are in our world, the realer they become."

"Then why did you *unimagine him*?" I yelled, pointing at the spot where Miles was standing just a few moments ago.

In response, my dad blinked back at me, as if he were trying to figure out what he was going to say next.

Finally, he cryptically stated, "It's complicated."

"Then uncomplicate it," I said through gritted teeth, clenching my hands into fists again.

My dad roughly ran his fingers through his wavy hair, letting his hands settle on the back of his neck. After taking a deep breath, he said, "Because if I didn't, he was going to die again."

"What?" I unintentionally blurted out.

"It doesn't happen right away, but whenever I have seen someone die, and I imagine a living version of them, their death just comes back to me. And when that happens, I can't control it. It just breaks into reality, and the imagined versions wind up reliving their real-life counterparts' deaths."

"What?" I blurted out again, not really knowing what else to say.

"It's like a death loop that I can't control, so if I brought Miles back, he would just die. Maybe not right away, but it would have happened."

Even though I had literally just been asleep minutes ago, I suddenly felt very exhausted. I'm usually pretty good at processing a significant amount of information in a limited amount of time, but this was too much. The one stable adult, who I knew all of my life, was a figment of my dad's imagination, who he couldn't even bring back because if he did, he would accidentally kill him in some sort of psychotic death loop. Who the hell can digest all of that right when they just woke up?

I mean, one minute I am planning on getting to the bottom of how and why my dad is attempting to destroy the world, and the next I am discovering that a major part of my life is just a great pretense.

On top of that, my dad's so-called explanation only bred more questions. If he constantly saw Miles being killed, then why has Miles been alive my entire life? What did he mean when he said, "whenever I have seen *someone die*"? Does that mean that he had seen more people die, and reimagined them into existence? And why the hell was he trying to destroy the damn world? These questions are in no particular order; in fact, at this point, all of my thoughts, including these questions, felt like wild chinchillas frantically searching for the right spot to burrow in.

"Why hasn't Miles ever died before, then? Why only when you're around him?" I asked, scowling at my dad as he closed his eyes.

He sighed before he said, "Because I left, so I didn't picture their deaths. I also suppressed the ability through drinking, and when that eventually stopped working, I made sure that I was heavily sedated, so that I couldn't hurt anyone by imagining anything. It was the only way that I could keep them alive."

"What do you mean '*they*'? Who else did you reimagine?" Part of me didn't want to know the answer, but I was compelled to ask the question. I wouldn't call myself an inquisitive person, but when you find out that a large part of your life was a lie, you just need to peel everything away to get at the truth, however painful it may be.

He let out another sigh before he dropped the proverbial bomb. "Your mom."

CHAPTER 10

RESURRECTION

My body, no longer working in conjunction with my brain, took a few paces back and lowered itself onto the bed, gripping onto the already twisted sheets. My mouth hung open, as if it were waiting for the right words to just manifest, but I'm not sure if the right words existed for this occasion. Maybe Hallmark can get on that with a sympathy card stating, "I'm sorry that your mom is imaginary." Sure, probably no one else would buy it, but you never know. If my dad was able to pull his imaginings into reality, maybe there were other people in the world whose idiot fathers brought imagined versions of their mother into reality. Sure, it's pretty impossible, but then again, in my world, the impossible is unequivocally possible.

"My mom is *imaginary*?" I barely got the question out because my throat was unnaturally dry.

In response, my dad just nodded, unable to meet my gaze.

"Wow," Griswold whispered in disbelief. "That's...unbelievable."

"How?" I curtly asked. One simple word was meant to stand for so many others that I just couldn't get out. How could this be possible?

How did she die? Why did she die? Was she *always* imaginary? Was she *always* a drug addict? Is that what killed her? If she died, why didn't my dad stay? However, for now, "how" had to cover everything.

After a very long pause, my dad began his monologue: "Rosa Gomez was one of the bravest, fiercest women I ever met. In fact, when I first met her, some drunken idiot was trying to pick her up. The asshole kept pawing at her. Before I could step in, she twisted his arm behind his back, cursed at him in Spanish, shoved him into the counter and made him apologize. She didn't take any shit from any-one, and she lived life so intensely. Maybe that's why she needed the drugs, to dull some of that passion.

"When she almost ODed the first time, I begged her to quit. She really tried to go straight, but it was just too hard." He squeezed his eyes shut as if the sight of the room caused him pain.

"She was most successful when she was pregnant with you; well, in the beginning anyway. Toward the end, she used. She admitted it to me while she was in labor. That's why she put up a fight when I tried to take her to the hospital; she kept saying that they would take you away, but we should have gone to the hospital. After you were born, there was just so much blood. I didn't know what to do. I should have done something, but it all happened so fast, and I was left with you, completely unprepared for a world without her.

"The last thing that your mom said to me was to keep you safe. At the time, I thought that keeping you safe meant keeping you with me. I didn't realize at the time how stupid that thought was.

"I just acted fast, trying to do what I thought Rosa would want me to do. She always liked the idea of a Viking funeral, so I laid her body on a sailboat and imagined it lit aflame as it trailed farther down the Hudson River. She spoke about how she would raise you so often that I thought that she would want you to have both a father *and* a mother, but not just any mother, but *her*. So, after the funeral, I brought an imagined version of your mom into reality. This Rosa was just as fierce and brave as the original. In fact, I tried to make her exactly like the original, except without her fatal flaw, her drug addiction. For the first few weeks, she was fine. She took care of you like she was doing it all of her life. However, the longer she existed, the more she imitated her original, deceased self."

My dad opened his eyes, gaze cast down as if he couldn't handle looking anywhere else, especially at me.

"Sometimes, this thing works fine. Exactly what I imagine materializes, but sometimes it just doesn't. It was like my imaginary version of Rosa had gotten away from me and had taken on a life of her own. I guess it was too hard to imagine Rosa without the drugs, because the imaginary version started using, and it didn't take long for that usage to trigger the memory of Rosa's death. It was so vivid that I couldn't help but imagine it. The memory of Rosa was just as intense as she was, so I couldn't stop it from escaping into reality."

My dad took in a labored breath before he continued, as if this explanation were causing him physical pain.

"For five long years, my existence involved imagining Rosa's death, only to be followed by resurrecting her. No matter what I did, I always imagined her meeting the same end, only to try again. I was so stupidly determined to get it right, to just keep her alive, but even after five years, her death left this permanent mark on my mind that I just couldn't escape."

Finally looking up at me, his gray eyes were dull and wary as if recounting this story was depleting him of energy. Despite his exhaustion, he continued. "I couldn't keep watching her die. I couldn't keep making you see that, so I did the only thing that I could do, I left. I left the final imagined version of your mom to look after you. If I weren't around her, if I didn't see her every day, I knew that I wouldn't accidentally imagine her death on repeat. I knew that the only chance you had at having your mom back was for me to leave, so I did."

My dad swallowed as he wrung his hands. He continued to look into my eyes, waiting for me to respond or react, but there was just too much to react to, I didn't even know where to begin. How are you supposed to react to discovering that your mother is a figment of your father's imagination, who has been resurrected countless times because your father couldn't stop imagining your real, biological mother's death? Confused? Sure. Angry? Definitely. Simultaneously shocked and not shocked? That's a given. My mom may not be perfect, but I never doubted her existence. However, the fact that she *is* imaginary explains why she has never ODed. Still, though, my go-to explanation for this oddity was never, "Well, she's simply imaginary. That explains everything." Who even *thinks* that way? Well, maybe I should begin to, considering the fact that the two adults in my life who actually cared about me were not even real.

"Why don't I remember any of this?" It was as if the question was always on the tip of my tongue, just waiting for the right moment to be asked. While it's not uncommon to have your first memory when you are five years old, it's a little strange that I wouldn't remember something as impressive as my mom cyclically dying and being resurrected.

Part of me expected my dad to simply shrug, or to attribute my memory gap to the trauma of seeing my mom die only to come back to life a few moments later. Trauma can be vividly remembered or fervently suppressed. Maybe my mind just chose the latter. At least this would make sense.

"I didn't want you to remember," my dad admitted, continuing to wring his hands as if he could twist his past actions out of existence.

"What do you mean you *didn't want me to remember*?" I asked suspiciously, trying to prepare myself for the next bombshell that was bound to drop from his lips.

"I imagined that your memories were gone, except for your most basic memories, like how to walk, talk, eat on your own, and use the bathroom. You know, the basics. Everything else, your mom dying and coming back to life, was all gone."

I ran my fingers halfway through my hair before I grabbed large clumps and practically pulled them out, as I cried, "You *wiped* my memory? What the hell is wrong with you?"

"I was trying to protect you," he explained, his tone gentler, as if this would soften the blow. "I didn't want you to keep seeing their deaths, your mom's and Miles's. It was getting harder and harder for me *not* to imagine those moments. Eventually, these imaginary versions, they all fall, but you were too young to see that. The only way to stop it was to leave. I had to remove myself from your life so that Miles and your mom could live to take care of you."

"Is *that* what you were referring to?"

Looking at me with an eyebrow raised, he asked, "What?"

"When you said, 'Eventually, they all fall' before you left, that's what you meant? They all eventually *die*? *That's* the last thing you say to your kid before you leave?"

"Look, I did what I did to protect you, to keep you safe."

I scoffed as I stood up. Maybe it was the realization that most of my childhood was a lie, or maybe it was because I had just learned that I never really knew the real versions of the adults in my life who raised me. Either way, I just couldn't remain seated. I was compelled to get up and move around, so I paced the room as I said, "And your idea of *saving* me was to leave me with figments of *your* imagination? How is *that* saving me?"

I stopped pacing to stare at my dad, waiting for a response, but the only reply I got was from Griswold, who simply exclaimed what perfectly summed up every choice my dad made: "That's messed up."

In response, my dad cast his eyes down and shook his head.

"I did what I thought was best," he gruffly stated, and then looked into my eyes before saying, "Your life, everyone's life, is better without me. That's why I did what I did, to save you all."

"Well, your plan didn't exactly work, now did it?" I shot back.

My dad stood up, towering over me with his imposing mass. His neck muscles tightened as he stated, "Everything was working just fine until you broke me out."

I clenched my jaw and began to ball my hands into fists again.

"Trust me, we would have never come looking for you if it wasn't for the mess you caused," I seethed, feeling my nails dig into my damp palms.

My dad's eyes narrowed in confusion under his furrowed brow, bringing the cluster of beauty marks in the corners of his eyes together into one brown, bespeckled splatter.

"What are you talking about?" he asked.

"The reason why we *had* to break you out was to stop you. I don't know if you are doing this on purpose or if your fantasies have run amok, but you are causing a lot of havoc," I impatiently explained.

"That's impossible," he retorted, as if this alleged impossibility was a given fact.

"Look, if I've learned *anything* from the past twenty-four hours, it's that the impossible just doesn't exist."

"Well, what you're saying *is* impossible," he countered.

"Oh yeah? And how's that?"

"Because," my dad began, taking a seat and calmly placing his hands on the edges of the chair's armrests, "I was heavily sedated, and my abilities don't work when I'm out cold, they never have. That's why I created a doctor who would put me in that state, so that I could protect everyone from myself."

"Whoa," Griswold said, walking closer to the armchair and taking a seat on a corner of the bed. "So, is this your thing? To just imagine people into existence?"

"If it's necessary, yes," my dad stated, leaning back in the chair. "I tried to dull this thing by drinking. That and to just forget everything, even if it was for a little while, but that stopped working."

"That, and you got arrested," I interjected, taking a seat next to Griswold.

"Yeah, and that. But that last time I was arrested, when I was sent to the rehabilitation center, that's where I got my idea. I figured that if I were locked away and completely out of it, I couldn't use my abilities, and then everyone would be safe, so that's what I did. Unfortunately, that rehabilitation center that I was in wouldn't do that, so I created someone who would, a top-notch psychiatrist and neurosurgeon who had just the right paperwork and title to lock me up in a psychiatric hospital, in a room where I could just remain asleep."

"How do you know that your powers don't work when you're asleep?" Griswold eagerly asked, leaning in.

"They never have," my dad stated matter-of-factly, as if his word was all the proof that we needed. Before I could say anything, Griswold chimed in.

"That doesn't mean that it *can't* work. I mean, look at Domino. Just yesterday he thought that he could only see people's fantasies. Now, he discovers that he can *make* other people's fantasies real."

"Your friend is suddenly chatty," my dad said to me, as if Griswold was not a few feet away from him.

In response, Griswold shrugged and said, "What? Before you were having a pretty intense father revealing a whole bucket of secrets to his son moment. I wasn't going to interrupt that."

"He has a point," I said, pointing my thumb at Griswold. "Not about the revealing thing, but about not really knowing the limitations of your abilities. Maybe you just haven't realized what you can *actually* do. Maybe you're not consciously imagining random exotic animals breaking into zoos, record-breaking earthquakes, acidic black sludge, and detrimental snow boulders plowing into the Earth, but maybe you imagined them when you were unconscious."

My dad opened his mouth to respond, but before he could, we heard this jarring, loud thumping on the door, as if someone were thrashing their body into it, trying to break in.

"Open up!" I heard a familiar female voice scream from the other side of the door.

"Lucy," I whispered, jumping up from the bed and unlocking the door. I barely got the door open enough for her to slip in. She shoved past me as I opened the door a little wider to reveal a blackened sky, devoid of even a sliver of sunshine. Even the moon's illumination was missing, as if the moon itself had escaped into the expanse of the universe. In fact, the sky was devoid of any natural light, leaving us to fend for ourselves with our own artificial ones. It was as if we were in a perpetual state of nighttime, but one that was dipped in jet-black ink.

Descending from this blackened sky were lopsided forms that crash-landed into the Earth with a liquidy splat. I shakily held out a hand, seeing if I could catch one of the forms, to take a closer look, but before I could, Lucy gripped my forearm, pulled me into the room, and slammed the door shut.

"Frogs," Lucy huffed, locking the door and taking a seat on the corner of Miles's bed.

"Frogs?" Griswold questioned.

"Frogs," Lucy affirmed, and then added, "Raining from the pitch-black sky—in the morning—are frogs."

"Like, *real* frogs?" Griswold asked in disbelief, getting up from the bed and walking toward the door.

Lucy nodded as I opened the door again to reveal a shower of squishy blobs, dive bombing into the ground. Each landed with sickening, overlapping splats.

Turning away from the view and back toward Lucy, I said, "You can barely see anything. How do you know that they are frogs?"

Her face twisted into a grimace of disgust when she said, "One landed on me, right on top of my head, leading me to take my second shower of the morning."

"Sorry about that," I said, cringing at the thought of being pelted with a frog.

"Yeah, sorry," Griswold said, stifling a laugh.

Lucy narrowed her eyes at Griswold as he covered his mouth and said, "Sorry, but you should imagine what I'm imagining." I suppressed the visual so that I wouldn't see his mental image of the scene outside.

"Please don't, I lived it," Lucy said, holding up her hand. "So, do you think it's—?" Before she could finish her question, she caught herself, probably just noticing my dad, wide awake, looking in her direction.

Turning toward my dad, I asked with a heavy dose of accusation in my tone, "Is this you?"

In response, my dad simply asserted, "No, that definitely wasn't me."

"And why should I believe you?"

"Because," my dad said, leaning in, "when I imagine something and bring it into reality, I hear this little whistling sound, which makes it pretty difficult to have a conversation while I'm doing it."

"Like, a high-pitched ringing?" I asked in disbelief as I lowered myself back onto the bed.

"It used to be that intense, but it softened over time," my dad explained, and then added, "So I didn't do this, but someone did, and I think I know who it may be."

CHAPTER 11

LIGHTNING STRIKING TWICE

This may seem hypocritical for someone like me who has a pretty extraordinary secret, but I am just not a fan of secret keeping. It's just deceptive, and maintaining any level of deception eventually catches up to those keeping the secrets, whether or not it's their secret. Aside from what I can perceive, and apparently what I can pull into reality, I don't have any other secrets of my own. At this point, all the secrets that I have are inherited from my dad, like my mom's existence and my boss's disappearance. And these secrets I am forced to keep.

It's not exactly like I can tell the world that my former boss and mom were/are imaginary. I can't say for certain, but I can almost guarantee that that would not go over well. Well, it may go a little something like this: "Oh, officer, where is Miles Godare? Well, you see, he actually died decades ago. The Miles that everyone knew was a figment of my dad's imagination who was pulled into reality. Funny story, he was originally killed by Jack the Ripper—who was also a figment of my dad's imagination, not the *real one*—and then the imaginary Miles lived out the same death on a loop because my dad can't really control his abilities. For this reason, he can't bring back the version of Miles that he created because he will just imagine him dying. Oh, you want to talk to my mom? Well, she's imaginary too, but if you're looking for her, she's probably with one of her Jeffs or injecting herself with heroin, but don't worry, she can't technically OD or die unless my dad imagines it, which he most likely will if he sees her, so if you do find her, let's keep her away from her estranged husband/creator."

This is *my* life, but just hearing myself recount it makes me want to admit myself to a psychiatric hospital. That's the only way that I can see that scenario ending, with me being thrown into a padded cell in a brand-new straitjacket. Who knows? Maybe the psychiatric hospital where my dad was kept has a family discount plan.

Now, on top of all of my dad's other secrets, he has another. His past is like Griswold's magician's top hat, he just keeps pulling out an infinite supply of secrets, strung together into one long silk rope of deception.

"Are you saying that someone else can be responsible for...for whatever the hell is happening?" Lucy asked, throwing up her hands in frustration.

"Yes," my dad affirmed, tenting his fingers under his chin and nodding without another word.

"Are you saying someone else is responsible for what's happening outside through process of elimination or because you know for *certain* that there is someone else who is capable of doing *that*?" I fumed, my patience as thin as tissue paper.

"A little of both," my dad cryptically responded.

Before my dad had a chance to, Griswold encouraged him to continue. Elbows on shins, cupping his own face and leaning in, I thought

EVENTUALLY THEY ALL FALL

that any moment Griswold was going to faceplant into the dingy orange shag carpet.

"As far as you know, Domino and I are the only ones who can make something imaginary real, but there are others. I don't know why we're able to do what we can do, or exactly how it works, but I do know that it is inherited. You see, my dad had the same ability. Well, *almost* the same ability. He could only make what others imagined real, and not fully. You could see what he brought into existence but that was about it. You couldn't hear, smell, feel, or taste it. He was even worse at controlling his ability than I was. He couldn't do it very often, but when he did, it was usually accidental. I guess that's why he did what he did, he just couldn't take the suddenness and spontaneity of it."

Lowering his head and glancing down at the carpet, looking as if he was lost in thought. My stomach churned, a bad feeling curdling.

"What did he do? Did he learn to control it?" Griswold asked.

My dad slowly shook his head before he said, "No, I think he was done with trying. I think I was about ten, maybe eleven, when he committed suicide."

The room grew even quiet as Griswold leaned back a little, as if hearing about my grandfather's demise dampened his eagerness to learn more about my dad's frustratingly mysterious life.

"I'm sorry about your father," Lucy solemnly stated, and then after a pause continued, "But you said there are others who have the same, or a similar ability. Do you mean others outside of your family? Or do you have siblings or cousins who also have this power?"

"No brothers, no sisters. My dad was an only child, so the only first cousins I have are on my mom's side. My mom was normal, no powers that I knew of at least."

"Did she know about yours?" I asked.

After a pensive pause, my dad said, "Probably not, but I don't know if she knew about my dad either. After he was gone, we never spoke about him."

"Sounds familiar," I muttered a little too loudly, not caring if anyone heard. "So, who are these others who have a similar ability and how can we find them?"

"I don't know," my dad sighed. "And maybe I shouldn't have said 'others' because I only know of one other possible person who shares our ability. I didn't know that she was alive, but she must be."

"Who?" Lucy, Griswold, and I asked in unison.

Even though we all asked about this mysterious person's identity, my dad directed the answer at me.

"Your sister."

Well, I was glad I was already sitting down because if I wasn't, I definitely needed to be. *A sister?* What, was she imaginary too? At this point, I wouldn't have been surprised. Sure, an imaginary sister who has similar abilities. Why not? Oh, and instead of my dad being hell-bent on destroying the world with kamikaze frogs, it's my long-lost sister.

"The frogs!" I cried, shooting up. We were so distracted by unraveling my dad's past that we were doing absolutely nothing about the damn frogs and darkened sky.

"Dammit, we're slipping," Griswold exclaimed, slipping his phone out of his pocket, clicking it on, and scrolling through his screen. "It's all over the news feed. They originally thought it was an eclipse, but none are scheduled for today. Plus, there's not a ring of natural light, which according to this, you normally see in an eclipse. There are some postings about aliens and government experiments."

"Is it dark anywhere else?" Lucy asked, which prompted Griswold to scroll through his phone a bit more and open new tabs to find more information. After a minute or so, Griswold affirmed, "Yeah, pretty much, but in bursts? Oh wow, some are saying that this is the apocalypse."

"Okay, we need to stop this," I asserted, taking a deep breath to mentally prepare myself for the inevitable high-pitched ringing. "What can you imagine to stop this?" I asked Lucy and Griswold, but my dad was the one who responded.

"Why do they need to imagine something?"

I blinked at him a few times before I explained. "Well, that's how it works. I thought you knew that. *You* can imagine something and bring it into reality, but *I* can't. In fact, I pretty much can't imagine anything. I can make someone else's fantasies real, though, hence why I need Griswold or Lucy to imagine something that we can make everything seem normal. Well, normal for everyone else at least."

Throughout the explanation, my dad was giving me this quizzical look as if I had suddenly begun speaking to him in Arabic, midsentence.

"Firstly, I know how your abilities work. Remember, I was there during the first five years of your life. Secondly, *you* can do the same thing that I do. I know because I've seen you do it. And thirdly, because I know the extent of your abilities, I also know that you can control what other people imagine, so instead of just imagining something to combat a fantasy, just control *this* fantasy."

"I don't know how to control the fantasies," I asserted, completely ignoring my dad's second point for the time being.

"You did it before," Griswold reminded me. "With the snow."

"Yes, but if you remember, I had no idea how I did that. Even Miles had no idea how I did it; he had never even seen me do it before."

"Where is Miles?" Lucy asked, looking around the room as if Miles were hiding somewhere, waiting for the right moment to make his entrance.

"It's a long story," I quickly stated, mentally kicking myself for mentioning Miles.

Part of me wished that Miles *was* hiding in wait, working on a plan to bring the world back into the light and ensure that these kamikaze frogs returned to their rightful place in a swamp or on a lily pad, anywhere other than diving to their deaths.

"Look, *I've* seen you do it, so I know that you can do it now. You just need to concentrate," my dad instructed, placing his hands on the chair's armrests before standing up.

Walking past us, my dad pulled the door wide open to reveal the inky darkness of the sky, which was made that much more sinister by the sloppy sounds of squishy bodies splattering onto the ground.

"Gross," Lucy whined, cringing as a frog's body whizzed right by the door's opening before crash-landing on the gelatinous coated pavement.

Instinctively, I turned away from the door's opening, equally disgusted by the sight of the frog's slimy mucous film mixing with its thick maroon blood seeping from the flattened corpse, coating the sidewalk.

"Domino," my dad calmly said. Upon hearing my name, I turned to face him. He was still holding onto the doorframe with one hand and gesturing for me to come closer to the doorway with the other. "If you want this to stop, you need to control it. Just concentrate, see the scene for the illusion that it is and pull it apart."

I hesitantly walked toward him and took a deep breath, surveying the heavy blanket of smooth darkness, agitated by the sudden eruptions of artificial lights flickering on in the now visible motel parking lot. The illumination revealed flattened frog carcasses piling on top of car hoods, windshields, and in growing mounds dotting the pavement. I could not help but shudder as the mounds continued to amass from the frogs throwing themselves down to their deaths.

Taking in the scene, I tried to think of it as an illusion, that it was just a very intense, realistic film playing out in front of me on an expansive screen; however, it just seemed too real. While I knew that this was an unbelievable, fantastical image, I also knew that it had been pulled into our existence and was therefore now real. It was as if recognizing its new place in our reality made it that much more difficult to undo it.

I tried closing my eyes and repeating my mantra to myself, but when I opened my eyes again, the scene was unchanged. Tightly squeezing my eyes shut and taking a few deep breaths, I tried again but to no avail.

"It's no use," I huffed, stepping back from the doorway. "It's too real now. I just can't control it. I need someone to imagine something to stop it. That's the only way we're going to get rid of it."

"I've got this," Griswold said, standing behind me. I moved a little closer to the doorframe to make room so that he had a better view of the chaotic scene outside.

He bit his lip as he studied the scene; it looked like he was trying to figure out exactly what he could imagine so that the Earth looked normal once again.

After what felt like a solid minute, he closed his eyes. The second his eyelids closed, I felt the familiar sizzle in the air as diamond-shaped bright lights dotted the jet-black sky. The vibrant points expanded and shot through the blackness like hot white threads ripping through the sheet of black. The brilliant white threads raced through the darkness, forming what looked like intersecting cracks running through the pseudo night sky.

Soon the cracks thickened, overtaking the darkness as if it were absorbing it and turning it into sheer light. The brightness of the sky was almost immediate as I shielded my eyes from the luminescence.

No sooner than I felt bathed in the light did it peter out, softly drifting away to reveal the Earth as we knew it, just calmer and replete with frog carcasses.

"Okay, you see it?" Griswold asked, his eyes still closed.

"Yeah," I affirmed, and then added, "But can you do something about the frogs?"

"Got it," Griswold replied, squeezing his eyes shut even tighter as the piles of frog corpses formed into pixilated masses that dissipated into emerald green speckles.

"Pixilated cleanup?"

"Is there any other way?" Griswold replied, smirking.

"Guess not. Okay, I think I've got it," I said, taking a deep breath as I lifted up my arms, feeling the brightness break into reality.

"Why are you—?" my dad began, but I never heard the rest over the head-splitting, high-pitched ringing ripping through my eardrums. My knees buckled as the ringing intensified, growing into a piercing shriek that felt like it was ripping through my insides, turning organs, tendons, and muscles into thin, meaty strips.

Sinking to the ground, the pixilated burst of green corpses before my vision darken, helium filled my head and seeped into every crevice. The ringing subtly subsided just before I sank into complete darkness and my grasp on consciousness was snuffed out like a candle's wick.

"So, we were traveling with a nonexistent adult?" I heard Lucy ask, but her voice sounded low and distant, almost as if she wasn't in the same room, even though I felt that she was close by.

"What does it matter? He was kind of real," Griswold stated matter-of-factly.

"*Kind of real* isn't real."

"Well, we rode in on a kind of real dragon, and you're not complaining about that."

"I wasn't exactly thrilled about that either, but at least I knew about the dragon."

As Griswold and Lucy continued to go back and forth, their voices sounded clearer and more grounded in the room. I breathed a sigh of relief, realizing that the high-pitched ringing must have just temporarily dampened my hearing. Also, realizing that I had been laid out on one of the beds, I pressed my palms into the mattress, attempting to lift myself up to a sitting position.

I leaned back against the bedpost as I opened my eyes to see my dad sitting in the armchair, staring at me, while Griswold and Lucy were facing each other near the now closed door.

"Hey, he's awake," Lucy pointed out to Griswold, who then turned around to look at me.

Smiling, Griswold walked over to the bed and sat on the corner.

"Dude, you did it," Griswold excitedly informed me. "It's exactly like how I imagined it."

"No more falling frogs?" I asked, wincing, feeling the aftereffects of the high-pitched ringing.

"No more falling frogs, darkness, or anything," Griswold affirmed. And then, pulling out his phone, he added, "And people are saying it's a miracle. The news feed is all over the place with theories about what may have happened. Meteorologists are trying to figure it out."

"Well, they're definitely not going to attribute it to you, so we're in the clear," Lucy confirmed, sitting on the adjacent twin bed.

"But are we?" I questioned. "Yeah, maybe the world hasn't figured out what's going on *yet*, but who knows how long that's going to last? Secrets can't stay secrets for long, right, Dad?"

Still staring at me, my dad placed his arms on the chair's armrests and leaned back. He didn't nod or acknowledge that he had heard what I just said, as if he was waiting for me to continue, somehow knowing that I wasn't finished.

"If this supposed sister of mine is causing whatever the hell is happening in the world, then we need to find and stop her," I asserted, matching my dad's stare.

"That's easier said than done," my dad noted. "I thought that she died with her mother, but she must be alive. I can't think of any other explanation."

"Wait," Lucy said, waving her hands in front of her, as if she was trying to erase an invisible chalkboard. "Let's backtrack here. So, Domino has a sister who is probably alive, who is probably creating all of this chaos that is plaguing the world?"

"Yes," my dad affirmed, still looking at me.

After way too long of a pause, I finally said, "If we're going to do anything about this, you need to tell us more."

Placing his elbows on his shins, my dad leaned forward and laid his hands on the back of his neck.

"For almost a year, I lived without your mom. It may have been the worst year of my life, but I knew that was the only way to live now, without her. At the time, I didn't know what happened to her doppelgänger. I knew that I was no longer around to imagine her death, so she had to live, but beyond that, I knew nothing about yours, your mom's, or Miles's lives, only that they must have been better without me in them.

"My life became nomadic, just moving from place to place and finding whatever work I could. And in between jobs, I made time to forget my past. Without fail, I always found a bar in whatever city I was in, ordered the strongest liquor they had, and continued to throw back shots until everything was just blurry and numb. I did this for so long that it got to a point where when I entered a city, I found all the local bars before I started looking for my next job.

"The *liquid courage*, as they call it, helped to an extent, but not completely. The drinks just offered a moment of reprieve from the memories of your mom and Miles, but they flooded back in the morning along with the intense hangovers. But I didn't care. I still don't, really. Whatever I do to myself is fine, as long as I don't destroy Rosa.

"I thought that the alcohol could also push down my abilities, but instead it just caused me to lose any control I had over them. I only remember bits and pieces of what I brought into reality. It's only through stories passed from fellow bar patrons that I really understood how much damage I caused. Luckily, I don't think that anyone believed their stories because they all pretty much happened in a bar, so most people who listened to these stories but who were not present to see them unfold just chalked the fantastical images up to the storytellers having too much to drink that night. I don't even think that anyone believed the bartenders, who—I assume—were stone-cold sober.

"Well, I didn't stay anywhere that long, so I never found out if any story was believed to be true, or if anyone figured out that I was the root cause."

"Highly doubtful," Lucy interrupted, turning toward my dad. "What you and Domino can do is beyond reason, so I don't think that anyone would deduce the real cause of whatever you did in those bars." After a brief pause, she added, "Out of curiosity, what *did* you do?"

My dad chuckled before he said, "Well, I vaguely remember one night with swimming clowns dressed as mermaids."

"Don't you mean swimming mermaids dressed as clowns?" Griswold offered.

"That would make more sense, but no. And instead of swimming in water, they were just swimming in midair."

"So. Cool," Griswold exclaimed, which caused my dad to chuckle again.

"Yeah, it looked pretty damn cool, but it freaked out the bartenders and the customers. I think one of the bartenders actually quit that night. I recall that before he left, he declared the place haunted. Yeah, if only."

"I'm not sure what pseudo-haunted bars and you losing control of your abilities has to do with a long-lost sister," I stated. Normally, someone going off on a tangent doesn't really bother me, but my dad had vital information that could help us finally find the person responsible for the chaos messing up everyone's lives, so getting back on topic was necessary.

"Right," my dad said, removing his hands from the back of his neck to begin wringing them again. "Before my last arrest and creating a doctor who would institutionalize me, my life consisted of getting odd jobs and drinking. I was hell-bent on being alone, but I couldn't help but feel so damn *lonely*. So, there were nights, many nights, when I would find a...companion."

"What, like a hooker?" I asked, matter-of-factly.

In response, my dad nodded. "Yeah, sometimes. Actually, most times. But there was one woman, one who reminded me so much of your mom, I just kept going back. In fact, if it wasn't for the fact that I was somewhere in the Midwest—Illinois, I think?—I would have *sworn* that it *was* Rosa, except her skin was sallow, unlike the smooth caramel of your mom's skin tone. Even before your mom died, she never seemed to grow pale. But the icy blue eyes were practically identical, and she had your mom's spark. Unfortunately, she also had your mom's drug addiction problem, but I just didn't care. She resembled your mom so much that to be with her was like being with the original, except this one wouldn't die, or at least that's what I thought.

"Lightning struck twice, and this woman, Penny, became pregnant, like your mom. She insisted that it was mine, but I wasn't sure. After all, she'd been with many men; that was the job. But I stayed with her. We even moved into this small apartment, and I got a job at a construction company nearby. She quit hooking and got a job as a cashier, but that didn't last too long. She was too much like Rosa; she couldn't stop using. Except, unlike your mom, she didn't even attempt to try. She said that she wasn't strong enough, and in the end she was right.

"She was barely seven months pregnant when she was rushed to the hospital, but she was—what do they call it? DOA? dead on arrival? —well, she died. She ODed. And the doctors tried to get the baby out before it was too late, but when they finally did, her skin was practically as blue as her mother's eyes and the cord was wrapped around her neck. I couldn't even stay to hear them announce that she had died. I couldn't see her as anything but alive; I could picture it so clearly, so maybe she was. As impossible as it may seem, maybe she survived."

After he finished, he leaned back in the chair but continued to wring his hands. His gaze was no longer fixed on me, but on some indeterminate spot on the floor. Oddly enough, I felt more mentally prepared to process this story, as if the acute unbelievability of the other events in his past made this one not as shocking. You know your life is pretty messed up when you discover that you probably have a long-lost sister who was supposed to be dead but isn't, and find that you're not taken aback by the news.

"So, if she survived, then she may be in Illinois? Are you sure her mom, this Penny, is dead?" I asked, swinging my legs over the side of the bed and getting up. I steadied myself against the bedpost, not feeling entirely steady on my legs just yet.

"Yeah, she's dead. The doctor called it," my dad affirmed, still staring at the same spot on the carpet.

"Why should we believe you?" Lucy stated, standing up to face my dad.

"What do you mean?" Griswold asked, also standing up—not to face my dad, but to face Lucy, whose arms were firmly crossed in front of her chest.

"Look, I'm just saying that we are taking him at his word that everything that he says is true. We have no proof that he can't use his abilities while unconscious or while holding a conversation. We have no evidence that this Penny or Domino's supposed long-lost sister exists. We are taking the word of a man that was institutionalized only a few hours ago. No offense, Domino, I know that he's your father, but I think we need more evidence before we trust him."

We all stared at my dad, waiting for some sort of a reaction, either a defensive one or an admission that Lucy was right, but instead, my dad just stared at the same indeterminate spot. His eyelids lowered and his arms appeared limp, as if recounting his past zapped the life energy out of him.

"She's right, you know," I asserted, walking around Lucy and taking a few steps closer to my dad, feeling that my balance was steady enough now that I could walk without something to support my weight. "Why should we trust you?"

My dad looked up into my eyes and opened his mouth as if he were about to answer me, but he was interrupted by a succession of knocks on the door. Griswold moved toward the door, ready to answer it, but I shot him a look and held up my hand, indicating that he should pause.

"Who is it?" Griswold shouted from the spot where stood, just a few paces away from the door.

"Max Garrison! You need to come back, now!" a guttural voice roared from the other side of the door.

"He found me," my dad whispered, looking down again.

"Who?"

"The doctor. He found me and will stop at nothing to bring me back," my dad affirmed, as the knocking grew in volume to such an intensity that it sounded like the good doctor was beating a hammer against the door.

"What should we do?" Lucy asked, directing her question at no one in particular, but my dad must have felt that he was the only one who could respond.

"You need to run. He'll stop at nothing to get me back. That's how I designed him. And when I say he will stop at nothing, I mean *nothing*."

"Shit," I whispered as claws shot through the middle of the wooden door.

Instinctively, my arms shot up in front of me, elbows close to my body, palms spaced apart but parallel to each other. My knees were slightly bent, with my left leg farther out in front than my right. Griswold followed suit, except his hands were balled into fists, and he was standing closer to the door. Lucy had ripped a lamp's cord out of the wall and held the lamp by the neck, up above her head, repurposing it into a makeshift weapon.

While we were preparing for a fight, my dad simply stayed seated in the armchair and continued to look at an indeterminate spot on the carpet while he shook his head.

"How do we stop him?" I barked at my dad, annoyed that he was putting in zero effort to help us as his creation busted through the door.

"You can't," my dad whispered, barely audible over wood cracking.

"What do you mean we can't stop him? Why?" Lucy yelled, aiming the lamp at the door.

"He's created to get me back at all costs. He'll keep coming after me until he dies," my dad explained, not moving an inch.

"Make him disappear!" I growled as I stared at claws ripping through the door as if it were pliable cork, creating a hole so big that an arm could easily slide through it.

"Do it!" I commanded, turning away from the door to stare at the top of my dad's head.

"Just let him have me. It's better this way. You know all that I know, there's no more that I can give you," he whispered, and then, looking up, he added, "I can't help you. It's better that I remain asleep for as long as I am alive."

"If you feel that way, why don't you just kill yourself? Why go through the trouble of having a lunatic doctor sedate you?" I shouted, hearing Lucy scream. My eyes immediately darted back to the door to see the doctor's arm shoot through the gaping hole and grab onto the doorknob.

In what felt like an instant, the doctor turned the knob and flung the door open. He raised his bloody claws above his head, his eyes bulging and bloodshot, as if he hadn't slept for days. Foam was forming in the corners of his mouth as his lips turned in to reveal bright white, sharp, long canines.

"What the hell?" Lucy screamed, throwing the lamp at the doctor's head, which he swatted away as if it were a pesky fly buzzing nearby.

"Are those fangs?" Griswold yelped, turning toward me, as if I could provide confirmation.

"Dammit, is he a damn vampire or a werewolf?" I directed the question at my dad, but I kept my gaze firmly on the doctor, whose fangs seemed to grow and sharpen the longer he stood in the doorway.

"I told you, he will do anything to get me back. That's his sole purpose, to make sure that I remain asleep all of the time, at all costs," my dad explained.

"Even turning into a monster?" Lucy yelled, looking around the room, probably trying to find another makeshift weapon.

"Whatever it takes," the doctor affirmed, his timbre gravelly, yet penetrating, as if his voice were trying to burrow itself inside your head, just so he could plant something detrimental in your brain.

My dad's sadistic creation smirked as it lunged toward me, claws aimed at my throat, but before he could reach me, I let out a guttural cry, my arms shooting farther out in front of me. Even though I wasn't holding anything in my hands, the creation's eyes widened in terror as if I were gripping a grenade in my right hand and holding its pin in my left.

"What the—?" I began, but then I caught myself when I felt it. I did not know how, but I knew that the doctor couldn't move or really do anything unless I willed him to do so. It was like this invisible tether bound him to my mind.

"What? What's going on? Why isn't he attacking?" Lucy asked, still standing in a defensive pose.

"You're controlling him now, aren't you?" my dad said, standing up to face me.

"I'm not letting him hurt anyone," I asserted, remaining in the same pose, afraid that if I moved even a centimeter, I would lose my power over the doctor.

"You need to let him take me," my dad said, his tone flat but firm. "It's the only way to keep everyone safe."

"I don't think so," I stated, my tone defiant.

Before my dad could even argue, I closed my eyes and repeated my mantra, "You're not real, go away." By the time I opened my eyes, the vampiric or lycanthropic doctor had faded into nothingness, as if he had never existed.

"Damn, you did it," Griswold said in amazement, lowering his arms.

"You didn't have to wipe him out of existence. He would have just taken me if you would have let him," my dad scolded me.

Lowering my arms but balling my fists, I narrowed my eyes at my dad as I said, "That *thing* that you created to capture you at all costs was going to attack me! Do you get it? He would have *killed me*," I yelled. Then, unballing my fists, I turned toward the bathroom door and muttered, "But you don't care. All you care about is hiding from your past."

"That's not true," my dad asserted, my back now turned to him. "I care about you. You're my son."

"Yeah, right," I said, as I opened the bathroom door and closed it behind me.

CHAPTER 12

REFUSING GREAT POWER

The cool water running down my face felt revitalizing. I pushed down the sink's stopper so that the water could pool in the basin; once it filled to the brim, I turned off the faucet, cupped my hands, dipped them in and splashed more refreshing water on my face. After I felt thoroughly drenched, I gripped the edges of the sink and looked into the mirror.

Under my slightly furrowed brows, I saw echoes of my mom's edgy stare. It was only now that I realized that my features were a mixture of them both. His thick eyebrows and dark hair, her icy blue eyes, his thin lips, her sharper cheekbones, the bridge of his nose. The skin tone, a combination of the two. Like it or not, their genetic makeup was splayed all over me. However, I'd like to think that I didn't, and wouldn't, make their poor choices. I may look like my parents, but that doesn't mean that I am doomed to replicate their disasters. In fact, at this point, it had kind of become my job to clean them up, especially my dad's. It was difficult not to be furious at him, but I still needed him to find my sister, that is *if* she existed and was really the cause of the chaos. As Lucy said, we still did not have enough evidence to confirm that my dad's stories were true.

"Domino, are you okay?" I heard Lucy ask from the other side of the door. Her tone was unnervingly sympathetic. I cringed at the thought of someone feeling bad for me, but I guess when you have parents like mine, that's unavoidable. It's even *more* unavoidable when one of your dad's creations tries to attack you.

"Yeah, I'm fine," I replied, still staring at my reflection.

Before leaving the bathroom, I pulled up the sink's stopper and watched the pool of water drain until there was nothing left but wet residue on the basin.

When I opened the door, everyone was facing me.

"I'm fine," I repeated, closing the bathroom door behind me, then added, looking at my dad, "No thanks to you."

"I told you, you should have let him take me. I designed Dr. Sutai to stop at nothing to bring me back should anyone try to break me out."

"Wait, Dr. Sutai? Isn't that, that guy's partner?" Griswold asked, pointing at the spot where I—what? vanquished? dematerialized? erased out of existence? yeah, let's go with that—erased my dad's creation out of existence.

"Yeah, when we were in your room, at the psychiatric hospital, the doctor mentioned that Dr. Sutai was the only other person with a key that granted him access to the floor where they were keeping you," Lucy confirmed.

"They are *both* Dr. Sutai. He can clone himself. I made him that way in case anything happened to one of them," my dad explained.

"Oh, that's just great! So, we're not done with him," I exclaimed, running my hand down my damp face.

"You would be done with him if you just brought me back," my dad calmly stated. He paused for a moment before he added, "You asked why I didn't just kill myself. Why didn't I just end my life instead of creating a fictional human guard dog to keep me locked up. Do you really want to know why?"

I could feel Lucy and Griswold's eyes on me as I sharply nodded.

"When my dad killed himself, everything that he brought into the world just disappeared. It was like their existence was dependent on his, so without him alive, none of them could go on living. So, I could have just ended my life, but if I did, Rosa would be gone for good."

An intangible heaviness settled in the room, as if a palpable tension were born from the silence that followed my dad's admission.

I still had doubts about whether or not my dad was causing the recent chaos in the world, but when he spoke about my mom, his tone was so sincere, I just couldn't help but believe him.

"So, the only way to get rid of Dr. Sutai is to hand you over?" Griswold asked, turning to my dad.

As my dad nodded, I asserted, "We're not going to do that. If I really do have this sister, and she is the one causing all of this to happen in the world, then we need him to find her."

"I told you everything that I know," my dad contended.

"Well, maybe a trip to Illinois will jog your memory," I replied.

"What makes you think that I will go? I created Dr. Sutai for a reason," my dad said; his tone was low but firm.

"You owe me," I stated, matching his tone. "You owe me for everything that you did, so just go ahead and unimagine your doctor."

My dad shook his head as he said, "I can't remove anyone or anything from existence without them or it being in my sights."

"So, we're going to Illinois, knowing that we are being hunted by a mad, imaginary doctor with supernatural powers?" Lucy asked, raising an eyebrow and crossing her arms over her chest.

"Yeah, I guess so. We don't really have any other choice," I confirmed.

I know what you're thinking—Domino, if your dad told you every-thing that he knows, then why not just let Dr. Sutai take him? After all, a nonexistent-now-existent, supernaturally juiced-up psychiatrist/neu-rosurgeon will hunt you down just to capture your father. Why elect to be hunted? Yeah, you make some great points, and under normal cir-cumstances, I would try to avoid being hunted down at all costs, but we still couldn't trust my dad. *Maybe* he was telling the truth about my long-lost sister, but as Lucy pointed out, we don't have any evidence to support his claims. So, until we could be sure that I *do* have a long-lost sister, and that she *is* the cause of the fantasies running amok in the real world, my dad was just going to have to come along for the ride.

"You rode here on a dragon?" my dad asked as I pushed back Hermon the Third's hood to reveal his series of dark brown horns, emerald green face, and purple fangs. My dad didn't really seem shocked or frightened, as most people would be when confronted by the sight of a dragon standing a few feet away from them. Rather, he just seemed curious about our mode of travel. I guess when you are used to pulling your fantasies into reality, very little surprises you.

As my dad draped Miles's cloak over his shoulders, I turned to Griswold and Lucy, who were just about to put their cloaks on.

"Look, this is my family's mess, so I should be the one to fix it. I've already put you both in a lot of danger, so you don't have to come with us to Illinois."

They both looked at each other, as if they were mentally conferring with one another, and then they looked back at me.

"There's no way I'm abandoning this adventure," Griswold stated, smirking. And then, wrapping his arm around my shoulder, he added, "Plus, who else has an imagination like mine that you can tap into?

Think of all of the possibilities! My imagination and your powers? We'll find and stop your sister in no time!"

"It may not be that cut and dried. We still are not sure if she exists."

"Yeah, which is also why you need us," Lucy began to explain, turning around to watch my dad climbing on top of Hermon the Third. "You could use the backup. Plus, we are your friends."

"More than that," Griswold interjected. Lowering his arm, Griswold took a step closer to Lucy and turned to face me. "You are my *best* friend, Domino. I'm not letting you do this alone."

Griswold was rarely serious, so when he was, I knew to take him seriously.

"Well, I guess there's no talking the both of you out of coming."

As if they had a hive mind, they simultaneously shook their heads and chirped, "Nope."

I sighed, resigned to their decision. I would not admit this to them, but a small part of me was glad that they wanted to continue going down this crazy rabbit hole. After all, they were the only people that I could trust, and as far as I knew, they were the only two people who were *actually* real.

As Griswold fastened his cloak and walked toward Hermon the Third, Lucy lingered behind, looking at me as I adjusted my cloak.

"We *are* friends," Lucy stated, and then looked down as she began to twist the edges of her cloak in her fingertips. "But maybe, you know, maybe—"

"Maybe there's more there?" I finished, reaching out to hold her left hand.

Our palms kissed, parallel to one another as our fingers interlocked.

Her bright smile revealed her vibrant, multicolored elastics. She brushed a strand of wavy brown hair behind her ear as she looked down at our hands.

"Yeah, maybe more."

Before we could say anything else, we heard Griswold shouting, mounted on top of Hermon the Third's back.

"Hey, love birds, are we going or not!"

"Coming," I said, smirking, still holding onto Lucy's hand as we made our way toward Hermon the Third.

Before I had a chance to react, we landed only a few feet away from one of the two mint green bronze lions in front of the Art Institute of Chicago. The lions' firmly defiant stance and powerfully framed manes revealing their ever-vigilant, belligerent glare perfectly matched Mr. Humphries's imagined twin lions. Maybe this is where he got his inspiration for his fantasies.

"Are you crazy?" Lucy hissed from behind me. "Griswold, why in the world would you land right in front of a museum? What, do you want everyone to see that we are riding on a dragon!"

"First of all, Hermon the Third is currently invisible, so no one can see us or him. Secondly, Hermon the Third is just going to stay here for a few seconds so that we can get off," Griswold began, and then I picked up where he left off.

"And finally, I am pretty sure that it's more likely that someone is going to hear disembodied voices than see an invisible dragon, so maybe we should just dismount and then figure out where to hide Hermon the Third."

"Fine, but it was still stupid to land right in front of a museum," Lucy huffed as I felt her dismounting.

After we were all on the ground, I heard my dad whisper, "If you are all afraid that your dragon will be discovered, why doesn't Domino just make him disappear?"

"You mean erase him from existence?" I asked, and then shook my head. Realizing that I was still cloaked in invisibility, I added, "I can't do that to Hermon the Third. He's not technically my creation, even though I brought him into reality, and he's gotten us to where we needed to go. I'm not you, I can't just erase something—except for homicidal monsters—from existence at the drop of a hat."

I cringed at the memory of Miles just fading from existence. I know that he wasn't real, that he was *never* real, but he was the only version of the real Miles that I knew. Even though he was a figment of my dad's imagination, Miles was very real to me. Hermon the Third may have also been the imagining of a very high junkie, but he was still the most reliable dragon-sometimes-Pegasus that I knew. Well, he was the *only* one that I knew, but still, I would never erase him from existence as if he was just a pithy construct that I was only using for my own ends.

I walked toward Hermon the Third's head, and said, "Hermon the Third, I think it's time to set you free. We can't keep hiding you."

It didn't take a lot of convincing before I felt Hermon the Third flapping his expansive wings as he flew away.

"Where do you think he's going?" Griswold asked.

"Not sure, but hopefully it's by a vending machine or convenience store because he really seemed to like his chips and chocolate bars."

"That dragon's got good taste," Griswold affirmed.

"So, how are we supposed to get back to New York once all of this is over?" Lucy asked.

"We'll cross that bridge when we come to it. Let's just find my sister first," I replied evasively. She had a point, but I definitely was not prepared to think that far ahead. Also, there was a very distinct possibility that if this sister *did* exist, she may put up a fight. And without knowing how powerful she was, I had no idea if this were a fight that I could win.

After we crouched in the bushes to remove our cloaks and decided to hide them there, we emerged to survey the area. With the line of towering skyscrapers and fast-paced pedestrians, Chicago eerily felt a lot like home.

"So where to now?" Lucy asked, pulling her foot out of the bushes.

"Can it be a diner, or a fast-food joint?" Griswold asked, placing his hand on his stomach for added effect. "I haven't had anything since last night, and that was just a bag of chips from the vending machine."

As I pulled out my phone to find the nearest fast-food place, in my peripheral vision I saw my dad squinting at something on the ground as he raised his fingertips to his temples. Suddenly, at our feet, a small pile of plain burgers began to form. It was as if they were springing up from the ground and multiplying at an exceedingly alarming rate.

My eyes darted from left to right to see if anyone else could see the growing hill of burgers just magically forming at our feet. For the time being, passersby seemed to ignore the small burger spout that was growing in volume and intensity.

"Stop doing that," I hissed at my dad, as the burgers were practically jumping up from the middle of the pile and landing on top of one another.

"I didn't mean to," my dad admitted, his eyes widening at the multiplying burgers. "It just happened, and I can't make it stop."

"Shit," I hissed through gritted teeth.

"We've gotta do something, we can't hide that," Lucy said, pointing at the burgers, which were now toppling over one another and spreading out, covering our feet.

"Does anyone have a bag? We can try piling them in," Griswold offered, as he crouched down and began to pick up the burgers.

"We've gotta do something," I repeated Lucy's sentiment; my eyes continued to dart around, as if an effective plan was in the area but just out of reach.

My gaze finally landed on my dad, who had shut his eyes as he pressed his fingertips deeper into his temples. However, this action did not seem to be doing anything because the burger pile continued to grow. However, seeing his eyes squeezed shut did give me an idea.

"I hope that he wasn't lying about the whole being sedated thing," I said, as I balled my hand into a fist. I pulled my right elbow closer to my body with my fist clenched as I twisted my hips so that I was facing my dad.

"This better work," I said as I pulled my arm back and threw it forward with all of the force that I could muster. My punch landed squarely on my dad's chin, causing him to instantly fall back slightly to the left, with his head landing just near the bushes.

The second that my dad's head touched the ground, the burgers stopped multiplying, as if they were merely a part of a magic trick that had come to its satisfying conclusion. The medium-sized pile of burgers stood like a McDonald's or a Burger King shrine.

Part of me wondered if the ground's gelatinous coating softened the impact of my dad's body landing onto the ground. Well, even if it didn't, at least knocking him out put an end to his fantasy.

"Dude, did you just knock out your dad?" Griswold asked in disbelief.

With my hand still balled into a fist, I exclaimed, "Well, I needed to do something."

"Yeah, but wow, that's harsh."

"Well, at least we know that he wasn't lying about not being able to project his fantasies into reality when he is unconscious," Lucy offered.

"Silver lining," Griswold exclaimed, grinning, and then added, "And we have lunch."

"Yeah, I'm not eating that," Lucy said in disgust.

"Suit yourself," Griswold said, shrugging as he bit down into one of the burgers that he had picked up before.

Maybe Lucy was right and my dad was telling the truth about when he could use his abilities, but I was not completely convinced. It's possible that he can't sustain a fantasy that was already in motion when he was conscious, but that doesn't mean that he can't project a new fantasy into reality when he is unconscious.

Plus, this small incident shed light on a problem that we should have acknowledged before—my dad still did not have control over his powers. Who knew what else he would pull into this world and when?

"Nothing to see here folks," Griswold announced to the forming crowd. It's a true testament to human nature that a spouting burger hill didn't seem to grab a single person's attention, but a teenager knocking out a grown man causes pedestrians to crane their necks and take a detour on their journey to wherever they were headed just to determine what happened.

Some members of the crowd began to hold up their cell phones, as if they were preparing to take a picture of the scene or to record it for their social media pages. I dragged my dad to the museum steps, trying to evade their cameras.

"Ladies and gentlemen, it's all a part of the show. No photography, please," Griswold continued as he fanned out his arms, standing in front of my dad and me.

"Show? What show?" someone from the crowd asked.

With her back turned away from the crowd and standing about an arm's length away from me, Lucy mouthed, *Show?* to which I shrugged and mouthed back, *I don't know.*

"Ah, the show. The magic show!" Griswold eagerly exclaimed. "Excuse me for one moment, folks."

Griswold suddenly appeared to my left and leaned in to whisper, "I'm going to need your help."

"Why would you tell them that this is a magic show?" I whispered back.

"I don't know. That's the first thought that popped into my head. Would you prefer that they knew the truth?"

"Fine," I grumbled, peering around to see the small crowd waiting for an impromptu magic show. "What do you need me to do?"

"You know, just use your," Griswold began, and then wiggled his fingers near his temple, "your *thing* and we'll be golden."

"Grizz, think of a different plan," I shot back.

"Too late. Get ready," Griswold enthusiastically instructed as he pivoted back toward the crowd.

"Ladies and gentlemen! Thank you for your patience. Now that one of my assistants is unconscious, with a dramatic flair, of course," Griswold began, pointing at my dad, who was sprawled out onto the museum steps. "We will begin the greatest magic feat you will ever see, the levitating man!"

"Oh, you've gotta be kidding me," I muttered under my breath.

"What?" Lucy asked, not fully realizing Griswold's plan.

"Ladies and gentlemen, please turn your attention to the stairs."

As members of the crowd craned their necks to look at my dad, I felt the sizzle in the air. As if someone or something slid an invisible plank with transparent tethers under my dad's body, he began to float up from the ground. His arms were perfectly clipped at his sides, and his legs were pulled together as if he needed to be kept completely straight and narrow in order to defy gravity.

Once the fantasy was fully realized, Griswold gave me a firm nod.

Without fail, the unnerving high-pitched ringing resounded throughout the open space as I pulled Griswold's vision into reality. I could barely hear the gasps from the crowd as reality caught up with Griswold's fantasy and my dad's body was about four feet off the ground.

Griswold grinned as his hand slowly sliced through the air above and underneath my dad's body to prove the stupendousness of his trick.

As the crowd erupted into applause loud enough to overcome the intensifying high-pitched ringing, Griswold took several bows, thanking his audience.

After a few more bows, Griswold stared at my dad's floating body, imagining it being gently lowered back to the ground. Following suit, the high-pitched ringing cut through my eardrums as my dad's actual body slowly lowered to the ground. Once gravity had safely taken hold, I sank to the floor, feeling that my legs were going to give out at any second.

The ringing began to dampen as the crowd's applause reached its crescendo, and then unraveled into fading individual claps as individuals began to disperse.

"Thank you, folks, that's all. Thank you for your attention," Griswold announced, soaking up the limelight for a few moments before kneeling down next to me.

"That. Was. Awesome!" Griswold whispered-shouted with enthusiasm.

I was rubbing my temples as if the sheer clockwise motion would make the high-pitched ringing subside even faster. It didn't, but it felt better than just sitting on the ground, waiting for the pseudo-tinnitus to go away on its own.

"Awesome for you, excruciating for me."

"Well, if you would just prac—" Before Griswold could finish, I held up my hand.

"I know, I know, *practice*. I get it. I don't have to keep hearing about it," I curtly shot back.

Griswold settled into a sitting position as I continued to rub my temples more vigorously, feeling the guilt from snapping at my best friend begin to seep in.

Sighing, I turned toward Griswold, who was looking down at an indeterminate spot on the ground.

"Look, I didn't mean to sound...well, you know. It's just that I don't want to get *better* at this. I just need it to work so that I can stop my sister, dad, or whoever from destroying the world. That's it. Beyond that, I am not interested in any superhero comic book training montage."

Lifting his head, Griswold turned toward me and asked, "Why not? Firstly, those montages are *super* awesome—pun intended—and secondly, why don't you want to get better? As a very wise comic book man said, *with great power comes great responsibility.* Rest in peace, Peter Parker. So, isn't it responsible to practice?"

Of course, Griswold would reference a comic book character's famed words in an effort to convince me to practice using my powers. However, even the late great Peter Parker could not persuade me. Yes, Peter and Griswold were absolutely right, *with great power comes great responsibility*, but what happens when you have omnipotent power? Peter Parker is basically the human embodiment of a spider. How much trouble did he get into scaling walls and swinging from one skyscraper to the next? Okay, maybe he caused some damage to his fictional city's infrastructure in some epic battles, but as far as I knew, he couldn't alter the very fabric of reality. That is, unless there is a lost issue that Griswold didn't force me to read like he did with the others.

The truth is, Lucy was right, my abilities are "godlike." It's like John Emerich Edward Dalberg-Acton said, "Power corrupts; absolute power corrupts absolutely." That's right, Mr. Humphries's imagined predators may be distracting, but I still pay attention in history. I don't know about you, but I think that pulling fantasies into reality and having the ability to bend them to your will is as close to absolute power as you can get.

What if I learn to master this absolute power and it changes who I am? What if it actually corrupts me? What if, similar to comic book and real-life villains, this absolute power consumes me? Right now, I can say that that would never happen, but who knows? Given the right circumstances, anyone can become evil, right?

How could I possibly explain my reasoning to Griswold, Lucy, or anyone? They just didn't understand what it was like to have all of this power at their fingertips.

"Look, these *powers* are just a means to an end. I just need to know how to use them to prevent my dad, my sister, or whoever from destroying the world. I don't need to *master* them to do that, I just need to know how to use them, which I do," I explained.

Okay, I wasn't being entirely truthful. I kind of knew how to use them. The whole controlling-people's-fantasies schtick didn't always work, and then there was what my dad claimed that I could do—bring my *own* fantasies into reality. As far as I was aware, I was never able to imagine anything. I never had a daydream, nor do I remember dreaming at all, period. However, if I *was* able to tap into my imagination and bring my fantasies to life, then that was a power I couldn't even access. Still, I was almost certain I was able to do enough to stop my dad, sister, or whoever we needed to stop from creating even more reality-defying havoc.

"Yes, but if you *mastered* them, then you wouldn't keep feeling sick after using them," Lucy said, settling herself into a sitting position next to me.

I began to shake my head as I said, "You just don't get it."

"Then explain it to us," Lucy insisted, resting her hand on my forearm.

"Yeah, explain it to us, because I really don't see the problem with using such an awesome ability," Griswold added.

I scoffed before stating, "Yeah, *awesome.* It's awesome to know that you can pretty much do *anything.* I mean, *literally* anything, as long as someone is able to imagine it. Oh, and I can control what they imagine once I make it real. It's just too much power. No one should have that much power, so why try to hone it? Aside from stopping one of my crazed family members, why else would I need these abilities?"

Lucy and Griswold looked at one another as if they were mentally voting on who would speak next. I guess Lucy was the elected speaker because she was the one who began.

"We're just concerned, Domino. We've seen you pass out multiple times after using your abilities, and your nose has even started bleeding. We just think that if you practiced, maybe you wouldn't get so sick afterward. Your dad even said that the sounds he heard when using his abilities weren't as intense after he had been using them for a while."

"Yeah, and even after *years* of using his abilities, he still can't control what he can do," I said, and then I turned toward Lucy's concerned gaze to continue. "He has used his godlike ability who knows how many times, and he may be the cause of the havoc we are trying to stop. I mean, the man created a self-cloning, psychotic psychiatrist/ neurosurgeon to put him in a coma *just* so he couldn't use his erratic abilities, so I am definitely not going to look to him as a role model."

"I'm not saying that you should. I am just saying that whatever intense sounds he heard seemed to subside as he used his abilities," Lucy explained.

Before Lucy could continue, we heard groaning from the museum stairs. The three of us stood up and walked toward my dad, who was rubbing his chin, which already had the deep purple outlines of a freshly forming bruise.

Lifting himself to a sitting position, my dad looked up at me and simply said, "Thanks."

"Well, that's not a weird thing to say after being punched in the face," I stated sarcastically, raising an eyebrow.

"I know why you did it; it's something that needed to be done to stop this," my dad explained, pointing his index finger at his temple.

"Well, at least we now know that you're not lying about not being able to use your abilities while you are unconscious," Lucy stated.

My dad nodded as he stood up, still rubbing his chin.

"That's why you should have just let Dr. Sutai take me. I am no help to you; if anything, my being awake is just going to make the situation worse."

"Look, we'll deal with whatever your mind throws our way, even if it means knocking you out again," I began, opening and closing my right fist, feeling the pain in my knuckles begin to intensify. "If my sister is alive and is using her abilities to release chaos on the world, then we need you to help us find her."

My dad gave a sharp nod as he lowered his hands to his sides.

"What hospital did they take Penny to?" Lucy asked my dad.

Turning toward her, he tilted his head up toward the sky as if the answer were written in the clouds.

"I think it was Northwestern Medicine?" my dad said, his timbre too hesitant to exude any semblance of certainty.

"Well, then that's the first place we look," Lucy affirmed, and then added, "The hospital must have records of Penny and the baby. It may be a long shot, but it's our only lead."

CHAPTER 13

HACKING THE SYSTEM AND OTHER OBSTACLES

As we neared the elongated, wood-veneer front desk, we were confronted by a series of healthcare professionals in matching aquamarine scrubs and N95 masks, either staring at their desktops, checking charts, or looking everywhere else but at us.

"Excuse me," I said, leaning over the desk to look down at one of the healthcare workers, whose eyes were fixed on the glowing desktop screen in front of her. "We are looking for a patient that died in this hospital about nine years ago. Can you help us?"

The healthcare worker, whose name tag read Carmela Scara, Registered Nurse, peeled her eyes away from the computer screen to look up at me.

"Are you looking for the patient's death certificate?"

In my peripheral vision, I saw Lucy nod, so I followed suit.

"Hmm," Nurse Scara uttered as her gaze drifted back to the computer screen. With her brows slightly furrowed, she quickly typed something on her keyboard and then said, "You'll need to contact the Illinois Department of Public Health to get the death certificate."

"And they'll just give us the death certificate?" Griswold asked.

"Not exactly, you'll have to complete an online application. Are you a relative of the deceased?"

"Ummm," I began, looking over at my dad, who was lingering behind us. "Kind of?"

"Hmmm, well, if you're not a relative of the deceased, you'll need a form of documentation from the office or agency that needs the death certificate."

Lucy shook her head and pulled me away from the desk.

"I think we're getting nowhere fast. We just need to know if Penny's baby lived, right?" Lucy whispered in my ear.

Nodding, I whispered back, "Yeah, but it's not like we can just hack into their system and find the information that we need."

"Why not?" Griswold asked, causing both Lucy and me to jump. "Sorry, I saw a pow-wow and thought that I would join."

Looking over Griswold's shoulder, I saw Nurse Scara continue to study whatever was on the computer screen. I pulled Lucy and Griswold a little closer to the hospital's entrance, so that the nurse was out of earshot before I continued.

"Grizz, none of us know how to hack into a computer. Don't get me wrong, you're great with CGI, but that's not the same as hacking."

"You are thinking *so* inside the box," Griswold stated, tracing an imaginary box with his index fingers in midair. "You know that this is an outside-the-box type of plan."

"Oh no," I began, holding up my hands. "We can just find the information that we need the old-fashioned way."

Lucy's hand found mine as she gave it a light, affirming squeeze.

"We know that you are reluctant to use your abilities, but you want to find your sister, right?"

"If she exists," I interjected, nodding.

Lucy smiled, revealing her elastics. "Right, if she exists. And we want to find her as soon as possible because who knows when the next catastrophic event will happen, right?"

"And when it happens, you will have to use your abilities to stop it, right?" Griswold added.

I reluctantly agreed, nodding again.

"So, doesn't it make sense to just get your sister's information as quickly as possible? Or, in the case where your dad is lying and she doesn't exist, to confirm that as soon as possible?"

Looking into Lucy's gentle amber eyes, I nodded once again, sighing.

"Okay, I'll do it," I reluctantly stated.

"Hold on. Maybe before you do anything, you should sit down," Lucy quickly said, still holding my hand, walking me toward three adjacent gray vinyl-covered chairs facing the hospital's front desk.

As the three of us sat down, my dad pulled one of the chairs from behind us around, sat down, and then said, "What now?"

"Now," I began, turning toward Griswold, "we work out of the box."

Griswold grinned as he nodded, and then added, "Exactly. You ready, Domino?"

"Go for it," I sighed, already feeling the sizzle in the air around us.

Along with the sizzle, I sensed this spark in the atmosphere, as if shots of energy were emanating from...where? From Griswold's forehead? No, not exactly. It felt more embedded, far past his skull, as if lightning were igniting in rapid-fire bursts underneath his gray matter, in his frontal lobe.

Although I couldn't see it, I perceived a surge of numerical values and images coursing through spidery, translucent tendrils in electrified shivers.

"Whoa," I exhaled a breath I didn't even realize that I was holding in.

"What?" Griswold asked.

"I don't know how to describe it, but I think that I've got it," I said, hesitantly.

Instinctively holding my hands out toward Griswold, my muscles tensed up as I braced myself for the high-pitched ringing. It quickly crescendoed to the treble shrieks of a mythical banshee's battle cry as I took in a deep breath, trying to focus on bringing absolute truth to Griswold's hacker fantasy.

At the same time that I felt the electricity coursing through Griswold's frontal lobe, I also felt a stream of warm liquid slither down my nostrils. The scene in front of me began to fade to black as vibrant pixilation fizzled around the edges of my sight, bringing with it a cloak of darkness.

Before I plummeted into unconsciousness, I felt myself mouth *Laptop* as if this were an afterthought, something in the periphery of the fantasy that I perceived but was just now remembering to bring into reality. Darkness shrouded my vision as I flexed my wrists and used every ounce of strength that I had left to pull this device into reality.

"Just get me more tissues," I heard Lucy order. Although I could feel her hand on my forearm, she sounded like she was speaking from a distance, as if she were able to throw her voice.

"It looks like the bleeding stopped, but I am more concerned about him passing out," a familiar voice said, also from a distance.

"It's okay, he just hasn't had anything to eat for a while," Griswold asserted.

Gripping the chair's metal armrests, I began to lift myself up from the slumped position that my unconscious body had apparently sunk into. I hesitantly opened my eyes to the harshly bright LED lights of the waiting room. Wincing, I felt my pupils retract as the deafening thrumming in my brain persisted like a sadistic, steadily beating drum.

"He'll be fine. He just needs to see his doctor when we get home," Lucy confidently stated, looking up at Nurse Scara, whose dark eyes were brimming with doubt.

Nurse Scara opened her mouth to say something, but before she could respond, she looked down at the small beeping black device on her waist.

She furrowed her brow and studied me for a moment before she stated, "Get him something to eat before he faints again. I want to make sure he gets checked out, so *don't leave*."

Lucy and Griswold nodded before Nurse Scara sprinted down the hall, her dark brown ponytail bouncing along to the urgency of her step.

"You've got it?" I asked, squeezing my eyes shut at the reverberation of my own vocal cords vibrating in my ears.

"Jeez, I know we've asked this before, but are you *okay*?" Griswold asked, his voice sounding a little closer than before.

"Yeah, you look like you are in more pain than the other times," Lucy added, taking my hand in hers and lacing her fingers through mine.

I nodded, opening my eyes again to take in Lucy and Griswold's concerned looks.

"I'm fine," I uttered, picking up one of the tissues on my lap and pressing it under my nose. "How long was I out?"

"Longer than you should have been," I heard my dad say from the corner of the waiting room.

Lucy gave him the side-eye as she said, "You weren't out for *that* long..." Her voice drifted off, as if there was something else that she wanted to say but she just didn't know exactly how to articulate it.

"What?" I asked, pulling the tissue away only to find flakes of dried blood sprinkled on the white material. I gave my nose another good rub with the tissue before shoving it into my pocket.

Lucy's gaze drifted to Griswold, who lifted up a sleek, black laptop from his lap.

"Yeah, so? I don't get it," I admitted.

"When I imagined myself as a hacker, I imagined that I could break into any database, but I didn't imagine myself having a *specific* computer to use."

"Okay, but I remember a laptop," I said, looking down at the device that Griswold held in his hands. It was identical to the one that I had pulled into reality.

"What Griswold is saying is that he didn't imagine *any* laptop. The one he has just appeared in his lap," Lucy cut in.

"I remember bringing *that* laptop," I began, pointing at the device for added emphasis, "into reality, so if Griswold didn't imagine it, then who did?"

"You," my dad said, walking closer to our chairs.

"Excuse me?"

"That *does* make sense because before you fainted, you mouthed the word "laptop", which was odd," Griswold said, lowering the laptop back onto his lap.

"I can't—"

"But you can," my dad interrupted me. "As I told you before, I've seen you do it, when you were little. That's how I knew that you had inherited my abilities in the first place. When you were a baby—around two years old—these random toys would just appear out of nowhere. Maybe that's why you were so content; whatever you wanted, you just created out of thin air."

"So, Domino has the ability to bring others' fantasies *and his own fantasies into reality*?" Griswold exclaimed.

"Say it a little louder, I don't think the coma patients heard you," I chided him, glancing around to determine if anyone overheard us.

There were a fair number of people sprinkled around the waiting room, all of whom were staring down at their phones, as if the screens displayed vital instructions that they were expected to memorize.

"Sorry, but seriously, dude, that is so awesome."

"Whatever, let's just do what we came here to do," I said, squashing Griswold's excitement.

His usual smile faded a little as he nodded, opening up the laptop and typing something on the keyboard in a flurry of determined taps.

"He's just excited," Lucy uttered, which barely sounded like a whisper to me since my hearing still was not at 100 percent.

"I know," I sighed, watching Griswold's brow furrow as he scanned the screen while he typed. "I am just getting tired of discovering that I can bend reality in new and unique ways."

"Look, it's obvious that you think of your abilities as some sort of curse, but that's *your* perception. If you just changed that perception, then you would understand that you have this incredible, unbelievable *gift*," Lucy insisted, giving my hand a gentle squeeze at the word "gift."

"Lucy, you can say that it's a gift because you aren't the one who has it," I said, unweaving my fingers from hers and holding my hands up to my face, looking at them as if they were new weapons that I now possessed. "Just a few days ago, I only needed to contend with seeing what other people imagined. No big deal. I mean, it was distracting at times, but I could deal. But now? Having the ability to pull any fantasy into reality, and bend it to my will? Who knows what that type of power could do to a person?"

"You're right," my dad began, placing a hand on my shoulder as he took a knee so that he was directly in my sight line, "These abilities do affect who you are and the choices that you make. Look at me, I would have had a completely different life if not for what I can do. But what *you* could do, that I just *can't*, is control them, and learn how to control them even better because if you can *completely* control them, then they can't control you."

I lowered my hands to look into my dad's steady gaze, rife with the conviction of his speech. Whether or not my dad was the cause of the chaos wreaking havoc on the world, he had a point. Maybe there was some truth to what he said. Whether I liked it or not, I had these damn powers, so if I took an if-you-can't-beat-'em-join-'em approach toward them, maybe they wouldn't overpower me.

"I'm in," Griswold asserted, still typing on the keyboard. "I'm going to check the databases for any information on Penny. I'll need her last name and the date that Domino's sister was born."

Still kneeling, my dad turned slightly toward Griswold with this glazed look on his face, as if Griswold had asked him for the exact value of pi and he was trying to place all of the digits in the correct order.

"Don't tell me you don't know," Lucy hissed.

"No, it's not that, it's just that I don't know if Penny's last name was her *real* last name," my dad asserted, and then added, "It was Lane. And she died on January 22nd."

"Ummm, her name was Penny *Lane*? Like the Beatles song?" I scoffed, shaking my head. "Jeez, that couldn't be her real name."

"Probably not, but the date I gave, that was definitely the day that she died," he asserted.

"Well, there was a Penelope Sasso who died on that day," Griswold stated before he looked up and stopped typing. "And she had a baby."

"That must be her," I said, leaning forward, intent on learning more.

"According to this, the baby lived. She was in the NICU for a few months before she was turned over to social services."

"She lived," my dad said in disbelief. By this time, my hearing was practically back to normal so I heard the full force of his shock.

"Isn't that what you suspected? That she was the one causing the destruction that we have encountered?" Lucy questioned.

"Yes, but still—"

"But it's still unnerving to have your suspicions confirmed," I finished for him, to which he nodded in agreement. Turning my attention back to the task at hand, I asked, "Grizz, can you hack into the social services database to find out what happened to my sister?"

Without saying a word, Griswold directed his attention back to the computer screen as the tip of his tongue poked out from between his lips.

"I'll take that as a yes," Lucy affirmed, watching Griswold type away at an impressive speed. "You know, this much power in Griswold's hands could be dangerous," Lucy joked, at which Griswold grinned.

"Yeah, but I follow Peter Parker's words pretty closely," Griswold rebutted, not looking up from the screen.

"What's that supposed to mean?" Lucy asked me, continuing to watch Griswold.

"Spiderman, the whole 'with great power comes great responsibility' schtick," I explained.

Although Lucy was kidding, having the ability to hack into any system could potentially be dangerous in the wrong hands, but I knew Griswold well enough to know that he would never use his skills to a nefarious end. Maybe, similar to how I trusted Griswold, I needed to trust myself. While my confidence in myself could never match Griswold's self-assurance, maybe if I just gave myself more credit, then I could learn to use these abilities without them corrupting my mind and causing me such pain.

"Got it!" I heard Griswold excitedly cry; however, his triumphant exclamation was dampened by the roar of a familiar guttural voice.

"Found you!" The grating sounds of the two syllables were like miniblasts that reverberated throughout the waiting room.

"Shit," I hissed, looking around to see those in the waiting room begin to look up and direct their attention to the deranged, fantastical psychiatrist/neurosurgeon, clad in a ripped lab coat. With fangs and claws drawn, crouched in an attack position, the good doctor looked like a bona fide classic horror film monster come to life. And, following the classic horror film trope, the first shrill scream sent the hospital waiting room into a frenzy of flailing limbs and clumsily running people making their way to the hospital's exits.

I rose to a standing position so that I was better able to face the doctor, head on.

"You can't take him," I asserted, balling both hands into fists. I could feel both my dad and Lucy rise to standing positions, only a few feet behind me. Without looking at my dad, I addressed him, "Make him disappear."

Before my dad could respond, Dr. Sutai growled, "I don't think so" as he sped to my dad's side at lightning-fast speed and sank his claws into my dad's neck.

"What the—?" Before I could finish, my dad fainted into the doctor's arms.

"Propofol," Dr. Sutai asserted, digging his claws deeper into my dad's neck. "Instead of blood, your father imagined me with a liquid sedative coursing through my veins. Mine is fast-acting, instantaneously putting your father back to sleep so that I can transport him back."

"How do you know that he wouldn't have gone willingly?" Lucy asked, taking a decisive step forward, her grimace focused on the doctor's malicious grin.

"I couldn't take the risk. Max Garrison designed me to keep him under sedation at all costs."

"Yeah, we already know, but that doesn't mean that I'm going to let you take him without a fight." Still feeling a bit shaky on my legs, I didn't want to risk running at him and face planting, so I did the only other crazy thing that I could think of doing. I turned to Griswold and asked, "Where can you imagine him?"

"How does Antarctica sound?" I could practically hear Griswold's smirk as the familiar sizzle in the air made its way into the hospital's atmosphere.

"Perfect," I whispered, extending my arms and uncurling my fingers, bracing myself for the inevitable surge of high-pitched ringing that would once again mar my eardrums; however, it was totally worth it as I saw the doctor's pupils dilate at the realization that he was being transported to a winter wonderland.

"At least your nose isn't bleeding," I heard Lucy say as she stood over me.

"That's progress," I grunted, pushing myself up from the linoleum floor that smelled like it was drenched in ammonia.

I gripped the arm of the waiting room chair, lifting myself to a standing position, which I quickly regretted. To avoid blacking out, I quickly sat down in the chair. With the darkness fading, I turned to my left to see my dad's unconscious body, head slumped forward, sitting next to me.

"Great," I said over the remnants of the high-pitched ringing still echoing in my ears.

"Do you think sending that doctor to Antarctica will stop him?" Griswold asked, gripping onto the corners of the laptop.

"Knowing his mission, it may slow him down."

"I just don't know why he insists on turning himself into a creature. What's the purpose of the fangs and claws?" Lucy asked as I looked over at the series of half-moon puncture wounds in my dad's neck, which had already begun to scab over.

"Well, if his body is coursing with a sedative instead of blood, and he could use his claws like a makeshift syringe to inject said sedative into my dad's neck, his fangs probably serve the same purpose," I postulated.

"That, and he just looks like a villain," Griswold added.

"Yeah, that too. So, Grizz, what did you find out about my long-lost, not-so-dead sister?"

"That was a quick subject change," he quipped.

"Yeah, well, the doctor isn't a problem right now, but my sister is, so what did you find out?"

Before Griswold could respond, over the subsiding ringing in my ears, I heard a blaring alarm.

"*Now* they trip the alarm?" I groused.

"We've gotta get outta here," Lucy whisper-shouted, as she bolted up from her seat.

Eyeing Griswold's laptop, I ordered him to hand it over to Lucy so that he and I could lift my dad's unconscious body and drag him out of the hospital.

"Are you crazy? You just passed out!" Lucy exclaimed. As if my body was trying to prove her point, as soon as I stood up, a spray of vibrant pixilation and darkness obstructed my field of vision.

Shaking my head, I gestured for Lucy to hand me the laptop.

"I'll take the laptop, and you two get my dad out of here."

Simultaneously nodding, Griswold and Lucy grabbed my dad's limp arms and pulled him up, at which he barely moved. They tried again, but to no avail.

"It's like lifting a giant punching bag with limbs," Griswold stated, and then added, "I think we are going to need a little magical intervention."

I grimaced as I asked, "Where to?"

Before Griswold could name a location, I saw a series of security guards running toward the waiting room from the end of the hall.

"Shit," I whispered as I closed my eyes, and similar to Dorothy, I thought *There's no place like home.*

CHAPTER 14

THE SEARCH FOR DORA

The firmness of the wood felt good against my back, as if this one tangible object were necessary amid the fluidity that had become my reality. Ironically enough, my very existence and what I was capable of doing made my reality malleable.

Eyes still closed and ears still ringing with the pseudotinnitus, I was still able to hear Lucy exclaim, "Central Park! But why?"

"What about Central Park?" I groaned as I sat up and opened my eyes to the scene where Griswold and I first met, with the familiar chain link climbing net in full view. Still gripping Griswold's laptop, I placed it beside me on the bench as I rubbed my eyes.

"Dude, why did you take us back to New York?"

"I don't know," I sighed, removing my hands from my eyes to take in the scene again. "I am not even sure how I am able to do anything that I do. I just wanted to find a way out of there, thought of Manhattan, and I guess I just imagined us here."

"Well, Central Park may just be a pit stop because your sister is probably still in Chicago, that is unless you can teleport her here too?" Griswold asked.

"Impossible," I stated with finality, wincing as I felt the rhythmic thrumming in my head make its way through my body.

"I don't know, Domino, with you, nothing really seems impossible."

"Fine," I conceded, and then added, "For the time being, it's not gonna happen. So, what else did you find out about my sister?"

"Well," Griswold began as he picked up the laptop from the bench. The second he sat down next to me, he flipped the laptop open and proceeded to type something on the keyboard.

"I was able to access Dora's—that's Penny's daughter's name, by the way—caseworker's files. I wasn't really able to read anything, but when I skimmed through, it looked like the caseworker had a lot to say about Dora Sasso."

Lucy sat on Griswold's other side as we both leaned in to look at the screen.

As Griswold scrolled through the pages of text, I said, "Grizz, I cannot even believe that you found this so fast. I mean, how?"

In response, Griswold shrugged.

"I don't know, I just followed the digital breadcrumbs. You know? Penelope Sasso's medical files, to Dora's, to the social worker on file, to the social services database—as you said to hack into—to, well, this," Griswold explained, pointing at the screen.

"That seems...impossibly easy," I responded in awe.

Again, he shrugged and said, "Not as easy as you would think. I had to break into quite a few systems to access that information."

"See, I told you. Dangerous," Lucy joked.

"More like *very useful*," Griswold rebutted, grinning.

I nodded in agreement, as I scrolled back up to the top of the screen.

"Yeah, useful, but it's going to take us a ton of time to read through all of this," I admitted, reading the first line to myself. *Dora Sasso, three months old, was released from the NICU after doctors concluded that she was in perfect health.*

I reread that line just to make sure that I had read it correctly. I could have sworn that my dad said that Dora was born with the umbilical cord wrapped around her neck, and that her skin was practically blue. How in the world did she survive that? It was damn near impossible that three months later she was in "perfect health," but defying the impossible seemed to be a Garrison family trait.

I will spare you the mundane details, but Griswold, Lucy, and I spent who knows how many hours reading through the files on Dora. Well, the details pretty much amount to us staring at a computer screen and realizing that Lucy was a much faster reader than Griswold or I was.

Apparently, when Dora was younger, she was almost adopted, but as the paperwork was underway, she was abruptly returned to the foster care system without any explanation from the family as to why they decided not to adopt her. This occurred when Dora was about two years old. After this incident, she went to and from a string of foster homes. While she only spent a few months at each home, she seemed to stay the longest with Vincent and Marla Decicco. In fact, the latter half of the caseworker's files were filled with the mention of the Decicco family, specifically Vincent Decicco.

While she was never removed from the home, the caseworker listed suspected cases of child abuse that were never confirmed. The file commented on allegations of inadequate guardianship and included an interview with a next-door neighbor and babysitter, Bernadette Norris, who stated that "the girl was very accident prone and imaginative." But it didn't say anything about Dora being removed from the home, despite the fact that she was sent to the hospital several times. One incident on record indicated that when Dora was taken to the hospital, the EMTs assumed that her right arm was broken, but once she was examined by a doctor, it was confirmed that not only was Dora's arm not broken, but it wasn't even bruised. In fact, the case-worker recorded additional strange incidents where Dora was sent to the hospital with a supposedly serious injury only to discover that she had a minor cut, a bruise, or nothing at all.

"How is it possible that she went to the hospital with an injury but when she was checked out, they found nothing?" I asked no one in particular. However, no one needed to respond because I already knew the answer. Dora imagined her injuries away. While that conclusion may seem far-fetched, it makes complete sense when you consider my sister's lineage. *If* I were right, that would also confirm that Dora was probably the cause of the disastrous events that had taken place. It also raises the question, why would Dora hide her injuries? Was she trying to protect her foster family, and if so, why?

"Wait until you get to the last entry," Lucy stated, pointing to the last paragraph on the page, dated August 2nd, 2021.

Prior to a home visit, Dora Sasso was reported missing by her foster mother, Marla Decicco. Vincent Decicco was found deceased in his bed after suffering from a fatal heart attack. ACS was involved in several reports of suspected child abuse, where Decicco was the alleged perpetrator, but without sufficient evidence, no pending cases are on file. Marla Decicco, Bernadette Norris, and staff at the school where Dora was enrolled, Norwood Park Elementary School, were interviewed by ACS and the Chicago PD about Dora, but so far there are no leads to her whereabouts.

"Is there anything else?" I asked, turning to Griswold, who in response shook his head.

"So, if she went missing over a month ago, there need to be some updates," Lucy explained, pointing to the keyboard. "Open up a new tab and try to find anything on the Dora Sasso case."

Griswold found articles in local Chicago newspapers about Dora's disappearance, but none conclusively stated whether or not she ran away or was kidnapped. Griswold then hacked into the police records, and the report confirmed that Dora ran away since there was no evidence that a kidnapping had occurred, and that this was still an "open investigation."

"So, no one knows anything," I concluded, leaning back from the screen.

"Well, let's look at what we *do* know," Lucy pointed out, her hand raised, fingers splayed in a calculated gesture, prepared to count off the facts.

"One, Dora was removed from several foster homes for some unknown reason only to find herself placed in the Decicco household. Two, while in this home, the caseworker suspected that Dora was being abused, but there was no definitive proof because every time she went to the hospital, her wounds were either not severe or non-existent. Three, Vincent Decicco, the assumed abuser, died of a heart attack around the time that Dora went missing. Four, only the foster mother, babysitter, and staff at Dora's elementary school were interviewed to determine her whereabouts. And five, the case is still open," Lucy explained, lowering a finger as she noted each fact.

"It's a good thing there were only five facts," Griswold stated, eyeing her raised fist.

Lowering her fist, Lucy rolled her eyes at Griswold before she said, "Yeah, but there's a lot that we *don't* know that could also help us find Dora."

Raising her hand again, she counted.

"One, why was Dora passed from foster home to foster home? The caseworker never gave a definitive answer. Two, *if* Dora was abused, then what happened between the moment that she was hurt and when she arrived at the hospital? Three, who called in the suspected abuse? Was this from the home visits? Did Marla call them in? Maybe the neighbor or a school official? Maybe someone else? Four, what *exact* information did these individuals provide in these interviews, and were there any witnesses—or anyone else who knew Dora—who should have also been interviewed? And finally, five, if the case is still open, what are the Chicago PD doing to try to close it?"

"And of course, the most important question of all, where is Dora now?" Griswold interjected, holding up six fingers.

"You need to go back to Chicago to find out." Griswold, Lucy, and I gave a little jump at the baritone voice coming from my dad, sitting on a nearby bench.

"Jeez, give us a heart attack, why don't ya?" Griswold said, pressing his hand to his chest.

"What do you mean by 'you'? *We* need to go back," I corrected, turning toward him.

My dad subtly shook his head.

In response, I shot up from the bench and quickly found my footing before I walked over to him. Standing in front of him, I looked down at his slumped shoulders and his dull gray eyes staring up at me.

"Look, I am not going to listen to you ramble on about how you should just let Dr. Sutai take you away, especially after I just sent him to Antarctica. I'm just getting tired of it, all right?"

Shaking his head again, my dad said, "I can't help you. I can't help anyone."

"Enough with the self-deprecation," I sharply exclaimed. "You're coming because you not only owe it to me, but you owe it to Dora. Maybe you are not the *direct* cause of whatever is happening in the world, but if Dora is responsible, you have a part in that responsibility."

My dad lowered his gaze as I continued.

"You weren't there for me, fine, but for your daughter? Who you had abandoned at the hospital? Yeah, maybe you thought that she was dead, but how long did you stick around to confirm whether or not that was true?"

Pointing to Griswold's laptop, I continued, "Do you even *know* what type of life she had without her parents? I mean, Penny died, but you didn't. You should have stuck around, and don't give me that crap about her life being better off without you in it, because if you read what I read, well, you'd know that a life with an unstable, self-disparaging parent who can barely control his abilities is better than being tossed from home to home to and being *allegedly* abused by a foster father."

I stood over him, waiting for a reaction, but he just continued to look down at the gelatinous coated ground. He didn't even attempt to defend himself.

After what felt like too tense of a moment, I turned to face Lucy and Griswold, who had quickly looked away from my dad and me, trying to appear as if they had been focused on something on the screen the entire time.

"You're right," Lucy stated, her gaze shifting from the computer screen to me. "We *do* have to go back to Chicago if we're ever going to find Dora."

"Yeah, and we should probably get there sooner rather than later," Griswold said, staring at the screen, his fingertips gliding down the trackpad.

"Why?" I asked, sitting back in my original seat so that I could get a better look at the screen.

I didn't even need to read the headline over the images of the white swirling cyclones to know that these were no ordinary hurricanes. Groaning, I resigned myself to reading the following: "Unexpected hurricanes making landfall on the United States' West Coast."

"Great," I said flatly, not bothering to read the article.

I pulled out my phone, unlocked it, and scrolled to a map app to find out how long it would take us to get from NYC to Chicago. "Over eighteen hours," I muttered to myself, as I tapped my phone and shoved it back into my pocket. Realizing that Lucy and Griswold didn't hear me, I repeated, "If we take a bunch of trains and buses, it'll take over eighteen hours to get there."

"Uh, Domino, you know there's a quicker way to get there, right?" Griswold hesitantly offered, slowly closing the laptop.

"I know," I reluctantly admitted, running my fingers through my hair. "So much for my hearing. Grizz, just imagine us there, fast."

Grinning, Griswold quipped, "Your wish is my command."

"Why did you imagine us *in* the bushes!" Lucy yelped, roughly picking out the leaves that became entangled in her hair.

"While it would have been totally awesome for us to just magically appear in front of the museum steps, I am pretty sure that we would have drawn some unnecessary attention to ourselves," Griswold explained, standing up.

"He's right, and at least we're here," I said, wiping my nose with the back of my hand just to make sure that it wasn't bleeding. When I pulled my hand away, surprisingly, there was no trace of blood. I wish that I could say the same for the high-pitched ringing, the remnants of which were still attempting to eviscerate my eardrums.

With nothing to hold onto, I took a deep breath as I rose to a standing position. While I was woozy, at least my legs weren't giving out.

"Hey, you didn't pass out!" Griswold chirped, stepping out of the bushes.

"Hurray for small miracles," I responded distractedly, looking around for my dad, who I found just a few feet away, already brushing some leaves out of his hair.

"You're getting used to using it," my dad noted.

"Grizz, how's the laptop?" I asked.

Griswold took a moment to study the device, and then gave me a thumb's up. Okay, maybe I asked about the laptop to completely ignore my dad's observation about my abilities, or just to ignore him in general, but that laptop has really come in handy. Sure, if it broke, I *could* just imagine a new one into existence, but if given the choice, I'd rather not. I'm pretty sure that I am causing permanent damage to my hearing by constantly pulling fantasies into reality. Actually, I'm surprised that my ears aren't literally bleeding by this point.

"So where to now?" Griswold asked.

"We need to begin where Dora was last seen, at her house," Lucy asserted, gesturing for Griswold to open the laptop. "Can you find her location?"

Griswold's ever-present grin crept up as he said, "Can I ever."

He nestled the laptop in the crook of his arm while he typed something onto the keyboard.

"Not too far away," Griswold muttered, still typing. "No need for *magical* intervention, I guess."

Rolling my eyes at the term "magical intervention," I gestured for us to begin walking as Griswold sent the address to my phone.

"Got it," I confirmed, seeing that we were only a few blocks away from the Decicco household.

"Umm, does anyone else see the silhouettes of zoo animals painted on the windows, or is it just me?" I asked, head tilted up, looking at the second story of the house. The silhouettes of what resembled tigers and lions starkly contrasted with the white window frame and the house's bright yellow exterior, as if the house were covered in a chipper color to completely contrast with the assumed abuse that occurred within.

"Yeah, I see it too," Lucy affirmed, and then added, "Do you think that was Dora's room?"

"Well, only one way to find out," Griswold stated as he walked toward the front door.

He rang the doorbell a few times before the door creaked open, only slightly ajar, fastened to the doorframe by a rusted chain. From the opening, we were met with a beady blue eye that looked us up and down.

"Who are you?" we heard a female voice croak.

While my dad looked straight through the opening, not uttering a word, Griswold, Lucy, and I looked at each other. It's at times like these that I wished that Miles were still around because he wouldn't have knocked on the door without a plan.

"Are you Marla Decicco?" I asked, which was followed by a curt "Yes" from the voice behind the door.

"Umm, we are involved in the Dora Sasso investigation. We have a few questions to ask you about your foster daughter," I explained.

The beady eye narrowed, as if behind those dark blues was a lie detector and everything that I was saying was coming up false. Well, technically, I wasn't really lying. Sure, I was bending the truth a bit, but at least that was better than bending reality.

"Where are your badges?" the voice croaked, her tone becoming sharper as if she were on high alert.

"We are actually private investigators, ma'am, who have a high success rate with runaway cases. We are familiar with the case, but we have a few additional questions for you that may help us find Dora," Lucy confidently explained.

Brilliant, I mouthed to her as the door closed, and we heard the chain slide, which was quickly followed by the door swinging open to reveal a middle-aged woman wearing a dull blue house dress that hung loosely on her thin frame. Her skin was almost as gray as the streaks in her frizzy blonde hair that hung just above her bony shoulders. Her lips were pursed as if she was in a perpetual state of sourness and suspicion.

"You look far too young to be investigators," Marla stated suspiciously, studying us again with her beady eyes.

"We just look young for our age; we have actually been doing this for a long time. Here, take my card," Griswold offered as he reached into his pocket and the air sizzled.

I rolled my eyes as I saw the imagined business card. The cartoonish drawings of the four of us standing in black trench coats were stamped with the phrase "Griffin's Gumshoes" followed by falsified phone numbers.

I swayed a bit as the high-pitched ringing came and went like a freight train speeding by.

Griswold, now feeling the card in his grasp, handed it over to Marla, who studied it as if it was the Rosetta Stone.

"So, what questions do you have for me?" Marla asked cautiously, looking up from the card.

From this woman's reaction to us, I could not help but wonder if she knew more about Dora's whereabouts than she had let on to the police. The caseworker's files did not mention that Marla had any involvement in the alleged abuse, or in Dora's disappearance, but she was acting a little too paranoid to be completely innocent.

"Yes, can you take us through the day when Dora disappeared?" Lucy asked, searching her pockets for something to write on and with. When she found nothing, she just tucked her hands in her pockets as we listened.

Crossing her arms in front of her defensively, Marla said, "I'm not sure what I can tell you that I haven't already told the police."

"We just want to hear the story firsthand," Lucy explained, looking over Marla's shoulder to the living room. "Do you mind if we sit down?"

Without a word, Marla gestured for us to follow her down the narrow hallway. Except for two end tables that framed the floral printed couch, a worn, brown leather recliner and a TV that seemed to be transported from the 1980s to the Deciccos' living room, the room was pretty bare.

On the end table next to where I chose to sit stood a framed picture of a woman with long blonde hair, smiling up at a man with salt and pepper hair, wearing a matching gray suit. His upturned, chestnut brown eyes practically sparkled as he stared into the camera lens, as if daring it to find any fault in that perfect moment.

"That was Vincent and me a few years ago," Marla stated, nodding toward the picture. "It was our fifth anniversary and the day that he got a job as a weatherman. I think the last day that I saw him that happy was on our wedding day."

Marla let a small smile escape as she lowered herself onto the recliner and smoothed out her dress.

"We weren't foster parents yet. That would come a few years later," Marla began, still looking at the picture. She then shook her head as if she were shaking herself out of a reverie. "You wanted to know about the day that Dora disappeared, right? Well, it's like I told the police and that caseworker, the day wasn't unusual at all. I was making breakfast in the kitchen around 7 AM, like I always do. Vincent usually doesn't come down until 7:30 AM, the same time that I take Dora to school, so I didn't suspect that anything had happened, until it was 7:30 AM and there was no sign of Dora or Vincent. That's what made me go upstairs to see what was going on. When I got upstairs, I found Vincent in bed, already cold, and Dora was nowhere to be found. That's pretty much it."

After recounting that morning, Marla leaned back in the recliner as if reliving the events took something out of her.

I don't know what prompted me to say what I said next, maybe just pure curiosity, maybe something more, but the next thing that came out of my mouth was, "Do you have a picture of Dora?"

Marla nodded as she fished in her pockets for something, and pulled out a frayed photograph that she passed to me.

"That's her school picture. It's a few months old, but it's the most recent picture that I have of her. It's a copy of the one that I gave to the police."

I gingerly held the corners of the picture as I looked it over. Dora's black, curly hair hung neatly above her shoulders; the color made her fair skin look that much lighter. Her round gray eyes stared into the camera, similar to Vincent's, but unlike Vincent, she seemed to be daring the viewer to try to look away. Remnants of our dad punctuated the corners of her eyes, which were painted with more than a few beauty marks. She also inherited his cheekbones and thin nose. I had no idea what Penny looked like, but from appearances alone, it was obvious that Dora was my dad's daughter.

"Can I see?" my dad asked.

Without a second thought, I passed the picture down to him. He cupped the photograph in his hands as if it were a miniature version of the baby that he had lost.

"Dora," my dad whispered, as he continued to stare down at the picture.

"Where was the last place that you saw Dora before she disappeared?" Lucy asked, leaning in.

Marla opened her mouth to respond, but before she could give an answer, in my peripheral vision, I caught my dad rubbing his temples.

"Shit," I muttered under my breath as I shot up from my seat, but before I could do anything a figure with curly black shoulder-length hair and daring gray eyes magically appeared in the middle of the living room.

My dad continued to rub his temples, as his fantasy wildly looked around. Marla's beady blue eyes grew to three times their size as she screeched Dora's name.

"Stop it!" I ordered, my eyes darting all over the room, determining if there was anything that I could use to knock him out.

"I can't!" my dad helplessly cried back as he continued to rub his temples.

"Stop it!" I shouted again, my voice booming much louder than I expected it to. That's when I felt it, that familiar invisible tether, as if I had lassoed my dad's creation and claimed it as my own.

Quickly, I whispered my mantra, "You're not real, go away," and watched with sickening curiosity as my sister's fantastical doppelgänger faded from existence.

I let out a breath that I didn't even realize I was holding in as I lowered myself back onto the couch and turned toward a wide-eyed Marla.

I took another deep breath before I said, "I can explain."

"You don't need to explain," Marla calmly stated. "You're like her. I should have seen it," Marla continued, looking from my dad to me. "You look so much like her. Now it makes sense. You are related, aren't you?"

I glanced over at my dad, who merely stood in stupefaction, jaw slightly slack, his gaze quickly shifting to avoid my glare.

I sighed, resigned to telling the truth. At this point, there was no point to having a cover. "Yes. I am her biological brother—well, half-brother—and this is her father. We need to find her because there have been a lot of strange occurrences and we think that Dora may be responsible for them."

Marla once again looked us over before she said, "I think so too, which is why I will tell you what *really* happened."

CHAPTER 15

WHAT HAPPENED

"Wait, so are you saying that you *knew* about Dora's abilities for *years*?" Lucy asked.

Marla nodded as she tucked strands of gray-streaked blonde hair behind her ears.

"I didn't know right away, but after Dora had been with us for a while, I knew that she was different. She always played by herself, even at school, and when she got home, she used to love watching commercials. Not TV shows, mind you, but the commercials, specifically commercials for toys. At first, I had no idea how she had so many toys, especially when I didn't buy them for her. It wasn't until I saw the Barbie dolls advertised on TV magically appear in front of her that I realized what was going on," Marla explained. Like brother, like sister, I guess.

"And you just accepted that Dora had the ability to make her fantasies come true?" Lucy asked in disbelief.

Marla immediately shook her head and blinked a few times before she continued. "I didn't know that *that* was what she was doing. I thought it was some sort of magic, but no, that's just not something that you accept right away. In fact, at first, I thought that I was going crazy, seeing hallucinations. That's until Vincent saw it too. That's when I knew it couldn't just be me. It was Dora—she could do *unimaginable* things."

My dad nodded in understanding, knowing all too well what we were capable of doing, the type of damage we could inflict with our abilities.

"When you discovered the truth about Dora, what did you do?" Lucy asked, leaning in.

Marla took a deep breath before she continued. "At first I didn't really know *what* to do. When Dora first came to live with us, the caseworker filled us in about Dora's past, but she *never* told us what Dora was capable of doing. It was just so unbelievable how one minute there is nothing in front of you, and the next whatever Dora was thinking about just magically appeared. It was just so much to handle. Vincent wanted to give her back, but when I thought about her being returned so many times, and how Dora would look up at me with that toothy smile, well, I just couldn't take her back. I didn't get into many fights with Vincent, but when we did fight, and I felt strongly about my opinion, well, I usually won. So, Dora stayed. Looking back, that was the worst decision that I made."

My mind drifted back to the caseworker's report, citing the suspected but unsubstantiated accounts of abuse.

"It's true," I asserted, shifting my body slightly to the left so that I was facing Marla. "Vincent was abusing Dora, like the caseworker suspected."

Marla's gaze drifted from me to the floor as she gave a subtle nod. She shoved the photo of Dora in her pocket and began wringing her hands as she continued.

"It did come to that, yes. Vincent was no saint, but I had never seen him raise his hand to a child, that is until Dora made things appear. We were both afraid, but I never thought that Dora was evil, unlike Vincent, who swore that Dora was possessed. He scolded her any time she made something magically appear. He told her that she was giving herself up to demonic forces. He yelled at her to stop, and made these odd threats about hailstorms or black tar covering the Earth if she didn't stop."

I leaned back on the couch as Marla's words sank in. Vincent's threats to Dora were far too similar to the strange occurrences. Was it possible that this was a self-fulfilling prophecy, that Dora was imagining Vincent's threats and pulling them into reality? What would compel her to do something like that?

"So, he told her that apocalyptic events, like the sky turning pitch black, or record-breaking earthquakes, would occur if she didn't stop?" I asked, at which Lucy sharply inhaled. In my peripheral vision, I could see her eyes widening in realization.

"But why? Why would she *do* that? Why would she imagine his threats and pull them into reality?" I asked Marla

"Out of guilt," Marla asserted, pursing her lips again, as she slightly rocked back and forth on the recliner, continuing to wring her hands.

"Guilt? Guilt for *what*?" Lucy asked.

Without a moment's hesitation, Marla replied, "Guilt for killing Vincent."

My brain kept asking "how," but my mouth did not seem to comply. I am no forensic scientist, but I am sure it's possible for someone to induce a heart attack in another person using some sort of poisonous assistance. However, in Dora's case, that wouldn't have been necessary, because her paranormal abilities could just do the trick. I'm not saying that Dora was not capable of giving Vincent a heart attack, because under the right circumstances, anyone could be capable of doing anything, but how could Marla just come to that conclusion?

"Didn't he die of a heart attack? How could you blame Dora for that?" Lucy asked, furrowing her brow.

"I didn't tell the police, but I *know* that Dora killed him because I watched her do it that morning. Most of what I told the police about what happened that day was true. I was in the kitchen making breakfast at 7 AM, and normally Dora and Vincent didn't come down until 7:30 AM, except I didn't wait to go upstairs. In fact, I went upstairs a little after 7 AM when I heard Vincent screaming at Dora.

"When I made it to the top of the stairs, I found Vincent in his pajamas, standing in Dora's doorway, screaming at her to remove animals from her window. I didn't realize what he meant until I stood behind him and saw the images painted on the windowpane. I looked around for the paint can but quickly realized that Dora had just made them appear for her own entertainment.

"I don't know why this set him off. Maybe it had just gotten to be too much for him. Either way, I could tell that he was at his breaking point. I told him that what she had done was harmless, but he wouldn't listen. He kept accusing her of being evil, and saying that we should have never kept her.

"I should have just left him alone. I should have gone back to making breakfast and allowed him to just calm down in his own time, but I saw how he lashed out at Dora. She always came out of it pretty unscathed, but that was after a while. I am not even sure how it was possible. One time, I even saw her arm break, but by the time she got to the hospital, it was healed. If he hurt her again, she would have healed—she is an extraordinarily fast healer—but I just couldn't watch it again, so I kept going at it, trying to get Vincent to back off."

For some reason, my dad, who hadn't made a sound since he brought a doppelgänger of Dora into existence, suddenly gasped.

When he noticed Marla looking over at him, he quickly shook his head and tried to cover up the gasp by clearing his throat.

"Sorry, you were saying?" I asked, urging Marla to continue.

"Well, I told Vincent, 'Come on, honey, she's just playing,' and then I made the mistake of putting my hand on his arm. Enraged, he spun around and raised his hand to me. I winced, waiting for the blow, but I never felt his hand. Instead of slapping me in the face, he pressed his hand to his chest as he sank to the floor. His eyes were wide with terror as he struggled to speak. It was like he was a fish out of water, gasping, feeling the life force drain out of him.

"I kneeled next to him. With my hand on his chest, I quickly looked up, about to tell Dora to call 9-1-1, but I stopped myself. Dora's hands were extended out in front of her, with her fingers gripping something that wasn't there. That's when I realized what she was doing.

"I tried to tell her to stop, but when I opened my mouth, nothing came out. I think I was too shocked by what I was seeing. It wasn't long before Vincent became still and the light went out of his eyes. I brought my fingers to his neck to check for a pulse, but there was no use in confirming what I already knew—he was dead.

"I can't really explain what I did next. Maybe Vincent had changed too much, or maybe I cared for Dora too much. It's possible that it was both, but instead of leaving Vincent where he was, I mustered up all of my strength to pull him back into our bedroom and hoist him onto the bed, so it looked like he died in his sleep. After tucking his body under the covers, I walked back to Dora's room. She hadn't moved an inch, as if she had been petrified by what happened.

"I kneeled down to her, placed my hands on her shoulders, and said the only thing that I could think of. I told her to run, to run away from this house, just in case the police suspected her of killing Vincent.

"It's only now that I realize how stupid that was because no one would have suspected that she killed him. Without knowing about Dora's abilities, no one would accuse her of making Vincent have a heart attack, but at the time I just wasn't thinking straight. The only thing on my mind was that I had to protect Dora, even if that meant sending her away. That's the last time I saw her."

As Marla recounted the last day that she saw Dora, I tried to hold back my reactions until she finished. However, once she was done, I didn't really know exactly *how* to react, not that there was a specific way *to* react when someone tells you that your sister—who you didn't even know about until recently—imagined her foster father was having a heart attack in order to protect her foster mother from being hit by said foster father. Sure, murder was illegal and, in most cases immoral, but I couldn't blame Dora for how she reacted. As I remembered my younger self, that day when my bat was poised at the small of Jeff's back, I felt an overwhelming instinct to protect someone that I cared about wash over me. Self-preservation is powerful, but the urge to defend your loved one was infinitely more powerful.

Sure, she could have just manifested a weapon that would have left a nasty mark on dear ol' Vincent, like, oh, say a baseball bat, instead of making him have a heart attack, but maybe her actions were two-fold: she was trying to protect her foster mother *and* stop Vincent from hurting her ever again. So maybe what she did was a form of self-defense. That, and maybe she wasn't a baseball fan.

I'm not trying to make excuses for Dora, but I cannot help but empathize. Again, given the right circumstances, we are capable of doing anything. For Dora, when Vincent was attacking her, and about to physically assault Marla, that must have pushed her over the edge. Now our mission was to get her back from that edge before she did any more damage.

"Do you have any idea where she may have gone?" Lucy asked, to which Marla just gazed down at her hands and subtly shook her head.

"She could be anywhere," Marla admitted. "That's what I told the police—I have no idea where she is. I sent that poor child out into the world to fend for herself, and..." Marla's voice caught in her throat as she shivered and wiped her eyes with the backs of her hands.

"Hey," Lucy began, her tone especially gentle and soothing. "If Dora can do anything close to what Domino can do, and it sounds and looks like she can, then she is fine."

"We're pretty certain that she's fine, or at least that she's alive, but from what you've told us, she is definitely bringing Vincent's threats into reality," I noted.

"There's no way that you could have known that she would have created natural disasters and made zoo animals appear out of nowhere," Lucy explained.

At the mention of "zoo animals," Marla's head shot up and she straightened in her seat, as if someone unexpectedly poked her in the back with a stick. She touched her lips with her fingertips as she looked from Lucy to me.

"Did you say zoo animals?" Marla asked, anxiously.

"Yeaaah, why?" I responded, trying to determine where she was going with this question.

"The zoo, that's where she is!" Marla exclaimed with utmost certainty, as if, in that very instant, she was able to actually see Dora at the zoo.

"And you're saying this because she made zoo animals appear in various zoos?" I questioned, skeptically.

"Is that what she did? Never mind, yes, Dora loved animals, but not just any animals. Hold on, I'll be right back," Marla quickly stated as she got up and went upstairs.

"Do you think that she could really be at the zoo?" Griswold asked, to which I shrugged.

"It's possible," Lucy admitted, to which I added, "Anything's possible."

"Why the zoo?" Lucy asked, to which I nodded toward the staircase as I heard Marla descending the stairs. "I think we're about to find out."

Once she was in view, I noticed a sizable stack of books in her arms.

Instead of walking back into the living room, she headed into the kitchen, which was just a few feet away from where we were sitting.

Lucy, Griswold, and I immediately followed her, but my dad just remained seated on the couch, as if he didn't want to see what Marla had to show us.

Fanned out on the kitchen table were several worn paperback books with vibrant images of exotic animals, one of which was entitled *Zoo Animals from around the Globe.* This was the book that Marla pointed to as she said, "She loved reading about zoo animals, but she absolutely *loved* this one."

"Did you go to the zoo often?" I asked as I picked up the book and examined the beige cracks in the spine.

"Unfortunately, no. When Dora first came to live with us, we did take her, but after she imagined a goat in her bedroom, Vincent forbade her from going ever again."

Picking up Dora's favorite book, I flipped through the pages to find images and captions of exotic zoo animals. It wasn't until I found photographs of a white lion, a Tasmanian devil, and a Bengal tiger that looked identical to the one that pursued us at the Central Park Zoo that I knew that Dora was pulling the animals that she had read about into reality.

"That's where she is," I asserted, slamming the book shut and placing it back on the table. "Which zoo did you and Vincent take her to that one time?"

"The Lincoln Park Zoo."

"That's where you think she is?" Lucy asked. After I nodded, Lucy continued, "Okay, but what if she's not there? What if she's imagining these animals and these natural disasters from somewhere on the Chicago streets, or maybe somewhere else in the world?"

I took a deep breath before I responded. It was entirely possible that Dora was anywhere in the world, or at least in the Chicago area. However, I also knew that she was probably scared and felt isolated. She probably sought the comfort of one of the few things that brought her joy, these zoo animals, and although she had the memory of the book to guide her, the zoo setting would provide her with more inspiration. That's at least what my gut was telling me. I hoped that I was right because this was our only lead.

"If she's not there, then we are back to square one."

CHAPTER 16

NOT SQUARE ONE

Bears carved out of limestone peered over the giant beige cube, looking down at the copper capitalized bold type mounted on the granite. Underneath our limestone friends was what could only be described as twin pairs of copper formed into bowing bamboo shoots, intersecting and forming into what a lazy, lopsided tic-tac-toe board must look like. This—what? symbol? —was perched just above the zoo's name with the assumed motto just below, which read "For Wildlife. For All." While this message was very welcoming, it should have included a footnote, such as *"However, you can't hide out here and cause worldwide destruction through the power of your mind. Not cool."* Sure, that message would only apply to my sister, but maybe the footnote would have been effective.

As we walked past the entrance's prominent cube, I could not help but notice how peaceful it felt. Autumn's golden and auburn foliage lined the concrete path, which was strewn with crisp, fallen leaves. Aside from the distant calls of animals in their habitats and visitors exiting the closing zoo, you could barely hear a sound.

I could understand why Dora would see this zoo as a sanctuary. Being surrounded by animals tucked away in their pseudo-homes, which were replicas of their real natural habitats to give them a sense of comfort, and with visitors paying more attention to the wildlife they came to see rather than a child wandering around, I figured that Dora was pretty much left alone. On second thought, the security cameras were probably tracking any suspicious activity. If this were the case, how could the zookeepers not notice a girl hiding out in their zoo? Sure, during the day, it didn't seem weird for a kid to be walking around a zoo by herself. Maybe she was trying to find her class, maybe she was looking for her parents, or maybe she forged ahead of her parents to see one of her favorite attractions and they were trailing far behind her. There were too many unknown variables in the equation to suspect that she was a runaway. The police did have a somewhat recent photo of Dora, so if she were skulking around the grounds at night, how could you not notice that?

I didn't know anything about the training needed to become a security guard at a zoo, but I was pretty sure they knew how to watch a monitor. I mean, who didn't? Could it be possible that she was able to avoid the cameras, or that the cameras were broken? Both scenarios seemed unlikely. Nevertheless, let's say that both were true; if the security guards did their rounds, at some point, wouldn't they have come across a girl hiding out near one of the habitats, by a concession stand, or something? It's doubtful that they would have missed her unless she is the Olympic gold medalist of hide-and-seek. Suffice to say, I'm sure the US Olympic Committee probably would not elevate hide-and-seek to Olympic game status, but that doesn't mean that my sister isn't damn good at it.

"I don't see her anywhere," Griswold announced, craning his neck as he looked around.

"I don't think that she would be hiding in plain sight," Lucy stated, crossing her arms over her chest and lowering her head so that strands of wavy brown hair fell over her eyes.

"Hey, are you okay?" I asked as we continued to walk on the path.

"Yeah, it's just pretty fresh, you know?"

I nodded, recalling the tiger break-out at the Central Park Zoo, how Lucy's shirt sleeves were ripped off, revealing a splay of fresh bruises up and down her arms. Reaching for her hand, I laced my fingers through hers and gave her hand a light, reassuring squeeze.

"It's okay, I won't let anything happen to you," I said, and then quickly regretted it when I realized that I sounded like a cliché hero who was going to protect the damsel in distress. I cringed at the thought of becoming the imagined Harlequin romance version of myself; briskly brushing away that notion, I added, "Just as I know that you wouldn't let anything happen to me either."

"Umm, before we have a 'we're all in this together' moment, should we split up to look for your sister?" Griswold asked.

"Considering that I have no idea what she will do when we find her, let's stick together," I responded.

"Okay, then we should probably try to find out where she's hiding because it looks like we're going to be kicked out any second," Griswold stated, nodding at one of the security guards who was eyeing us.

Pulling out my phone, I looked up the zoo's visiting hours. We were a couple of minutes away from the closing time, 5 PM.

"Shit," I muttered, sliding my phone back into my pocket.

"Do we need an escape plan?" Griswold asked.

"No, we need a distraction," I quickly responded, at which Griswold grinned.

"Then I'm your guy," Griswold declared, staring at the path as that all-too-familiar sizzle in the air produced a swarm of rabbits.

Now, I know that rabbits normally do not swarm, but these furry mammals did.

Taking a deep breath, I spread my legs apart and straightened my spine, hoping that my posture alone would prevent me from passing out. I extended my arms toward the ground, feeling these fluffy bunnies manifest into existence.

I fought against a reeling sensation as the high-pitched ringing reverberated in my ears with a vengeance. I felt twin palms pressed into my back, like someone was trying to hold me up, as I finished pulling the rabbits into reality.

"What the—?" I heard someone shout over the high-pitched ringing still blasting in my eardrums.

"Herb, who the hell let the rabbits out of the Farm-in-the-Zoo?" someone else yelled back.

"Do we even have this many rabbits in here?" the other guy shouted in return.

"We better get outta here before the security guards remember that we are here," Lucy shouted-whispered to me, and then added, "Are you okay to walk?"

Nodding, I felt the hands on my back pull away, as my dad came around from behind me. Without a word, he quickly threw my arm around his shoulders and hunched over so that he was almost my height as we briskly walked away from the confused security guards.

Letting go of my hand, Lucy wrapped my other arm around her shoulders as our quick walk turned into a run.

The four of us ran right through one of a few metal archways leading into a tree-lined dome made out of thin intersecting metal vines. Sprays of bursting, vibrant light obstructed my vision as I slowed down.

"I just need a second," I said, planting my feet on the ground as Lucy, Griswold, and my dad came to a stop. I took a deep breath before I removed my arms from Lucy and my dad's shoulders as I made my way to one of the white, concrete slabs that, I assumed, were meant to serve as really hard benches.

As soon as I sat down, the miniature fireworks show playing out in front of my eyes began to dissipate. While festive, I was glad that my vision was returning to normal, because I needed all of my senses to find Dora, who could literally be anywhere in that zoo.

"Okay," Lucy began, speaking with a decisive lilt. "In order to find Dora, we need to do what any good investigator would do."

"Umm, get backup?" Griswold guessed, to which Lucy responded with an overt eye roll.

"No, a good investigator would put him/herself in Dora's shoes. If she's in this zoo, where would she go? What would she do?" Lucy asked.

"I mean, she could be anywhere," I admitted, slowly standing up.

"True, but let's think about how Dora is feeling right now. She's obviously scared, and probably thinks that the police are after her, so she would probably go somewhere enclosed, where she can't be spotted," Lucy worked out.

"We need a map of the zoo," I concluded, pulling out my phone, and pulling up the zoo's website again. Griswold and Lucy crowded around me as I clicked on the "Visit" tab, and then tapped on the interactive map. I enlarged the green and beige map, so we had a better look at the grounds.

"Where are we now?" I asked myself as I moved my fingertip along the screen.

"Could we be here?" Griswold asked, pointing at a picture that resembled a crown made out of intersecting vines.

Lucy shook her head and then said, "No, because there is no entrance near that place. We are probably close by one of these entrances." She pointed at each white space with a double arrow line drawn in the middle.

However, Lucy didn't have a chance to continue because she was interrupted by a growing wave of squeaky, nasally honking sounds, which were increasing in frequency and potency.

"What the hell is that?" Lucy mouthed, her body suddenly becoming rigid, her eyes darting from side to side in acute vigilance.

My dad also looked around, trying to locate the mysterious noise, but his body didn't seem as tense, as if he knew that we didn't need to prepare to go up against anything of consequence, because we didn't.

"Grizz?"

"Yeah, Domino."

"Do the rabbits recognize you as their leader?"

Griswold looked everywhere else but directly in my sight line before he said "Maybe."

"Grizz!" I exclaimed. "Why would you do that?"

"What? They need a leader!" he insisted.

"Well, *leader*, your army of rabbits are going to lead the security guards right to us," I explained, quickly looking for an escape. It didn't take long for me to find one; only a few feet away, I spotted a very short tunnel, which resembled what a large, hollowed-out tree trunk might look like if someone had cut up a tree into chunks, peeled one of the chunks, and placed this peel inside of the dome.

"Come on," I said, pointing down the passage as the rabbit calls grew in volume.

Leading the way, I speedily crawled through the tunnel and into the foliage, but before I could go any further, I felt someone grab my foot. Quickly spinning around, I saw one of Lucy's hands gripping my sneaker.

"What are you doing?" I whispered. "We need to get out of here."

"You don't know where that leads," Lucy shot back, and then settled herself into a sitting position. "You could be headed into some exhibit with a predator and get yourself killed."

Realizing that she had a point and that I couldn't move with her vise-like grip on my foot, I crawled back toward the lip of the passage and sat across from Lucy, Griswold, and my dad. With our knees pulled in, the four of us tried to be as still as possible as we just waited like ridiculous sitting ducks.

However, we didn't have to wait long, because Griswold's swarm of loyal rabbits quickly pooled into the dome, closely followed by a small crowd of security guards holding walkie-talkies up to their mouths.

"We've gotta—" I began as I poked my head out of the tunnel's opening, but before I could finish my sentence I saw a small figure wearing a black hoodie pulled up over his/her head with matching black pants, crouched near one of the archways. It was difficult to make out exactly who the person was since the hood was pulled up, obscuring his/her face, but the figure seemed too small and quiet to be a security guard; plus, the actual security guards were frantically trying to round up the eagerly hopping bunnies.

Still crouched, this mystery person extended its arms toward something on the ground, or the ground itself. I watched as the once pale pink ground morphed into soft brown dirt, bedding neat rows of feathery carrot tops.

Without missing a beat, the larger rabbits in the swarm enthusiastically dug into the dirt to loosen the newly created carrots that were firmly rooted in the ground, while some of the smaller bunnies sniffed around the carrot tops as if they were wary of the vegetables that just magically appeared under their paws. While the rabbits quickly got to work, the security guards screamed. From their screeches, you would think that the ground had suddenly turned into a graveyard infested with zombies breaking out of their tombs instead of just a plain old not-real-now-real carrot field.

The hooded figure did not seem to move, even after the security guards yelled something into their walkie-talkies and ran out of the dome.

"Is that—?" Lucy began, but before she finished, I affirmed, "Yeah, we found her." Still looking at the crouching figure, who had begun to stand up, I added, "Actually, she found us."

I looked over at my dad, whose skin was so pale that you would think he saw zombies rising out of the ground too. Note to self, don't tell him about that because he could accidentally make that happen. Staring at me, he shook his head, as if I had asked him to do something that he would never be caught dead doing.

"Well, what now?" Lucy whispered.

Great question. Well, I want to say *We stop my sister from causing any additional damage*, but how exactly do I go about doing that? Yes, if she creates something monstrous, it's pretty much up to me to combat it, but does it have to get to that point? Maybe she isn't even fully aware of what she is doing. It's not like she's your stereotypical malicious villain bent on world domination. She's just a scared kid who was only trying to protect her foster mother. Sure, things got way out of hand, but that doesn't make her evil.

I closed my eyes and took a deep breath before I crawled out of the passage to face Dora, and Griswold's army of bunnies, who were too hyperfocused on unearthing carrots to notice me. However, I could not say the same for Dora, who immediately disappeared. So that's how she evaded capture.

"Dora!" I shouted, potentially to no one because Dora could have run away for all I knew.

"Where'd she go?" Lucy asked as she crawled out of the tunnel, followed by Griswold.

"I don't know," I huffed. "She literally disappeared. And when I say literally, I mean *literally*."

"So, she made herself invisible?"

"Yup."

"Cool."

"Umm, not cool, Grizz, especially when we are trying to find her," I explained, looking down at the hungry rabbits diligently munching on ripe orange carrots. Aside from the field she imagined, there was no sign of my sister anywhere, or any clue as to where she may have gone.

"Well, she couldn't have gone far," Lucy insisted, looking around the dome. "We just need to figure out where she ran off to."

"And how to make her visible again," Griswold added, bending down to pet some of the bunnies stepping on his sneakers.

"Well, is that something that you could do?" Lucy asked, turning to me.

"Probably, but we'd need to find her for me to make her visible again, otherwise I run the risk of just making a visible version of her, which definitely won't help," I admitted.

"*Or* we can create something that would make her *appear* visible to us," Griswold interjected, smirking.

Before I could agree, I felt the sizzle in the air as pairs of black-framed eyeglasses appeared on the bridges of Lucy, Griswold, and my noses. Taking a decided stance, and a deep breath, I held out my arms as I felt the thick plastic of the frames begin to form. Although the high-pitched ringing was intense, the volume seemed to be at a semi-manageable decibel level. As much as I didn't want to use my abilities, the more I did use them, the less painful the side effects seemed to be.

"Nice, these babies should do the trick," Griswold asserted, tapping on the lens with his fingertip.

"What are these?" Lucy asked, removing the frames to inspect the thick black plastic.

"They just make what is invisible visible. At least, that's how I imagined them," Griswold explained.

"Well, at least this will help us find her," I acknowledged, looking through the red-tinted lenses, fighting to remain standing. "But we still need to remain hidden. Grizz, can you hack into the security cameras and make sure that we aren't seen?"

"On it," Griswold said, opening his laptop nestled in the crook of his arm. Lucy put the glasses back on as she looked over Griswold's shoulder.

With Griswold and Lucy both preoccupied, I crouched down to look back into the tree bark tunnel to find my dad still sitting in the same position, as if he were frozen to that spot.

"Ever going to come out?"

My dad opened his mouth to say something, but then quickly closed it, peered down, and then shook his head.

"Okay, whatever," I returned, standing up.

I did not know why I expected anything more from the father who abandoned both of his children. What? Did I expect him to help me help the daughter who he had left for dead? How in the world could I expect any help from a man who cannot help himself to such a degree that he literally created a sadistic doctor whose sole mission in life was to put my dad into a drug-induced coma.

"We're all set, the security cameras are on a loop so they won't detect us," Griswold exclaimed, closing the laptop.

"Ready to find your sister?" Lucy asked.

I took one last look at the tree trunk passageway before I turned toward Lucy and Griswold and nodded, leaving my dad to wallow in his own self-pity.

CHAPTER 17

TOO MANY DAMN BATS

"You don't think that we should go back for your dad?" Lucy tentatively asked, adjusting her new glasses, which kept sliding down the bridge of her nose.

"Nope," I stated simply, continuing to move forward, trying to remain as vigilant as possible in the hopes of spotting my now invisible sister.

"Okay," Lucy responded, and then after a palpable beat, she said, "It's going to be dark soon, Griswold, will these work in the dark?" I slid my glasses off and looked up at dusk's amber light bathing the sky. We must have been walking around the zoo for well over an hour by now.

"Yup," Griswold chirped, his head gliding from side to side like a periscope. "I imagined that we would be able to see anything invisible in any kind of light."

"Okay, but what about that video loop that you created? I think the guards will notice the discrepancy between the video feed and the actual night sky," Lucy pointed out.

"It's fine, I will just create another loop when—"

"Hold it. Did you hear that?" I asked, holding up my hand at the faint sound of crying.

The three of us stood in place, straining to listen. It was very soft, and somewhat muffled, but there was no mistaking it.

I scanned the stone bleachers, looking for anything that resembled a human being. It didn't take long before I saw a small figure sitting on one of the bleachers, with her hood firmly pulled over her face. With the heatwave still going strong, I had no idea how she wasn't dying of heat exhaustion in that hoodie. She wiped her eyes with the backs of her hands as she looked out onto the still seal pool.

"You see her too, right?" Griswold whispered to me, which prompted me to press my index finger to my lips. In turn, Griswold made the my-lips-are-sealed gesture.

Without really having a solid plan, I took a few tentative steps toward the bleachers.

"Dora?" At the mention of her name, Dora immediately went rigid and shot up out of her seat, ready to run.

"Stop!" I shouted, reaching out as if I were going to grab her.

Dora turned to leave, but she didn't. Instead, she turned her hooded head to look at me.

"Dora, I just want to talk," I said, trying to make my tone as calm and gentle as possible while I held up my hands like I was surrendering.

"You can see me?" she asked. Her tone was a mixture of paranoia and genuine curiosity, as if she didn't trust me, but at the same time she was intrigued by what I might know about her, which wasn't much.

I nodded, tapping on the side of my new eyeglasses.

"They make invisible light visible, and they allow me to see in the dark," I explained, and then took a small step forward. Noticing her flinch, I took a step back.

"Dora, I'm—we're—" I began, pointing to Lucy and Griswold, who were a few feet behind me, "not going to hurt you. We're here to help you."

With her hood obstructing her face, I couldn't tell if she believed me or not, but because she still had not moved, I knew that she was at least listening.

"You can't help me," Dora said, her voice catching in her throat. "No one can."

Even though there was absolutely no sign of rain a few moments ago, the sky suddenly went dark and it began to pour. Streaks of lightning cracked across the sky in spindly electrified veins, followed by rumbling, guttural thunder.

"That's not true," I asserted, spreading my legs apart so that I was in a firm, balanced stance. "*I* can."

As soon as I said "can," a rush of thunder echoed overhead, practically drowning out all of the sound around us.

"No," Dora insisted, pulling on the strings of her hoodie so that it cinched around her face so tightly that the opening looked like the mouth from that painting *The Scream.* It was a miracle that she could even breathe in that thing.

"Dora, I know what happened with you and Vincent! I know that Marla told you to run!" I screamed over the onslaught of thunder and lightning. Cracks of electrified light shot down from the sky, one blasting into a tree nearby, severely scorching the thick tree trunk and withering most of its leaves, now shriveled, black char.

"I'm bad!" Dora cried, her scream punctuated by another lightning strike shooting across the sky.

"No, you're not bad, Dora, you're just different," I reasoned, taking a tentative step closer to the bleachers. I continued to look at Dora's hidden face, not daring to look anywhere else.

"It's all my fault," Dora cried, crumpling to the position she was in when we found her, sitting, knees pulled up to her chest, as if she were trying to fold in on herself.

"It's *not*," I insisted, gingerly taking another step forward, almost able to touch the bleachers. "What Vincent said, and what he did to you, *that* was bad. He should've never hurt you or Marla. You were just trying to defend her. I know that you never meant to kill him."

The thickest streak of lightning went hurtling through the sky, crushing into something metallic from the sound of it. When the zoo suddenly went dark, I knew that it had caused a blackout. Luckily, the eyeglasses Griswold imagined had infrared lenses so that I was still able to see Dora in the dark.

Whether Dora was whimpering or silently crying, I couldn't tell because the thunder created an explosive roar that, coupled with the thick cascading rain, obliterated all other sounds, or so I thought, until I heard my name screamed in a skin-crawling high-pitched screech.

I spun around to see Lucy and Griswold lunging out of the way of a lightning bolt headed straight for them. Instinctively, I threw out my arm and grabbed hold of air, screaming for the lightning to stop as it was careening toward them. Every muscle in my body tensed as I felt that instant connection, as if I were linked to that lightning streak.

Gritting my teeth, I pulled my arm back as if I were holding an invisible arrow on a bowstring, poised to shoot it. At my command, the lightning froze; still suspended in midair, it drew back. Aiming my arm toward the sky, I released my grip, splaying my fingers. The lightning bolt spun upward and shot into the sky, ending its ascent in a display of fireworks that fizzled out in sprays of golden light.

"Are you okay?" I shouted to Lucy and Griswold, who were hunched over on the ground, covering their heads for protection.

They looked around, as if expecting to find the lightning bolt to be somewhere within the vicinity. As soon as they must have assumed that they were in the clear and began to stand up, another lightning bolt shot down into the ground, slicing through the gelatinous coating covering the Earth.

Spinning back toward Dora, I pleaded, "Stop, Dora! I know that you don't want to hurt anyone."

Dora gripped the edges of her hoodie and pulled it off, making herself visible once again, revealing her wide, puffy gray eyes and damp cheeks.

"How did you do that?" Dora asked. The thunder subsided and the rain thinned out as if her curiosity were quelling the storm that she had created.

"You're different, Dora, but you're not so different from me. I know who you are," I explained.

"You don't know anything about me," Dora cried.

"I know more about you than you think," I continued to explain, taking another step forward so that I was within arm's reach. "I know that you spent most of your life without a family because your mom died giving birth to you. I know that you never had a dad because your real one left when you were born. I know what it's like to be abandoned by your dad, and I know what it's like to be different, to be able to do the impossible, because I'm your brother."

The rain continued to taper until it was a subtle drizzle; all that remained of the lightning and the thunder was what was left in its aftermath, a charred tree and a slew of terrified animals cowering in their habitats.

"My brother?" she whimpered, wiping her cheeks with the backs of her hands.

I nodded as I inched closer, but I paused as she pulled back, scurrying further down the bleacher like a frightened animal about to be captured.

"Why should I believe you?" she questioned, eyes narrowed at me, hugging her body.

"It's true," a voice asserted from the other side of the bleachers. Looking over Dora's shoulder, I saw my dad, shoulders broad, arms firmly at his sides, appearing much more composed than he had over an hour ago. He was too far away, but I knew that he was staring into Dora's eyes.

"Why should I believe *you*?" Dora repeated, her question accentuated with a streak of lightning cracking the darkened sky.

"You're right to be suspicious. I haven't earned your trust, but I really know what you are," my dad began as he walked toward Dora, who was hugging herself so tightly that she looked like she was in a makeshift straitjacket.

He *really* knew her? What, was he trying to one-up me? I didn't really take him as a competitive person, especially about who knew Dora better; however, if we were going to play that game, at least I had read the caseworker's reports and had an actual conversation with Marla. Nevertheless, with a very scared, unstable kid with the ability to bring infinite chaos into the world, now was not the time to argue.

"And it's my fault," he admitted, stepping over one of the metal railings and onto a stone bleacher. "When Penny told me that we were going to have a baby, I was terrified. I didn't even know if the baby was mine, but after a while, I believed that it was. I didn't mean to become a father again. I had already left that life to protect my son from me, and here I was, creating that life for myself once again.

"However, over time I thought that this situation was different. Penny was alive, so maybe together we could raise this child, and if she or he shared my abilities, then I could work really hard to show my child how to control them. Maybe that would help me control mine too. Maybe that's all I really needed. I began to become hopeful, really believing that this time around would be different, that is until it wasn't."

My dad paused, both in pace and in speech, only a few feet away from Dora. She did not move an inch, but just continued to hug herself, like if she were to let go, she might fall apart.

"When the baby was born, I was so certain that she was dead. Penny had already died, and now it looked like the baby had died too. I don't know, maybe I just couldn't take another death. I so desperately wanted her to live, maybe too desperately. I just saw the lifeless blue baby disappearing, as if she had never existed, and a living one in its place."

Oh shit. Of course, that's what he meant by "really" knowing "what" she is.

"Are you saying what I *think* you're saying?" I asked, already knowing the answer but still needing confirmation. He paused before his gaze shifted to me; his nod was subtle but unmistakable.

You would think that I would have been shocked by this revelation. And maybe I was, but I didn't feel shocked. I didn't feel anything, like the truth hadn't completely sunk in, not just yet.

"I don't get it. What's he getting at, Domino?" I heard Griswold ask from behind me. I turned around to see Lucy and Griswold standing only a few feet away.

Looking over my shoulder, I stated, "He imagined a living Dora into existence. The real Dora died in that hospital, right after her mother."

Without waiting to see Lucy and Griswold's reactions, I looked back at my dad and asked, "But how can you be sure that you really did that?"

"Because she's like every other person I imagined. Even though our creations are real, there's just one thing that makes them different, they don't really get hurt. Their bones may break, they may get cut, but they heal too quickly, as if any bruise, cut, or break has been erased."

Do you know how when an epiphany just hits, and you feel simultaneously enlightened yet utterly stupid that you didn't realize something sooner? Yup, that's exactly how I felt at that moment. The clues were all there: Dora's broken arm healed way too quickly, my mom never ODed, and the bruise on her cheekbone faded faster than it should have that time when one of her Jeffs punched her. I had never seen Miles hurt, so I couldn't confirm this about him, but it made sense. Not that I was an expert on bringing fantasies to life, considering that I had only very recently discovered that I could do it, but it stood to reason that there had to be one distinction between what was actually real and what my dad, Dora, or I made real, otherwise it would all seem too flawless.

"Are you saying that I'm not *real*?" Dora cried, shooting up from her seat, facing my dad.

He opened his mouth to say something, but must have decided against it.

"Dora," I began, but I had no idea where I was going to go with this. She was already terrified of what she was capable of doing, and saw herself as an abomination. *Now* she had to deal with the fact that she didn't even really exist. Okay, she did, but only because of my dad's grief. What can you say to help someone—let alone a scared kid—deal with that? It's okay, you're still real, you were just imagined instead of being born? Oh, and now that we got that out of the way, can you stop pulling Vincent's apocalyptic threats into reality? I'm pretty sure none of that would go over well. What we needed here was a therapist who specialized in daddy and reality-warping issues. I am pretty sure that person doesn't exist, but then again that doesn't mean that person *can't* exist.

Well, it's not like I had any time to pull anything or anyone into existence, because in the next second I heard a voice shout from the other side of the seal pool, "Hey! What are you doing here?"

Luckily, I was still wearing my eyeglasses because I saw exactly where the six security guards were standing, all aiming their glaring flashlights at us. Yeah, I almost forgot about them too.

"We—" That's all I got out before six 7' -foot-tall, silver pods shimmered around each guard, sealing them inside.

Looking back at my dad, I saw his right hand raised to his temple as he stared at the newly formed pods. Dora looked from my dad to the guards and back again, as if she were processing what he had just done.

"What *exactly* did you do to them?" I asked, pointing at the pods.

Lowering his hand, my dad asserted, "They're fine. They are just unconscious, so they can't interfere."

"Interfere in *what*?"

My dad took a deep breath as he looked from Dora to me before saying, "In righting a wrong. This is my fault, so I have to make it right."

"And what does that mean?"

"This," my dad stated, pressing his fingertips to his temples as he looked at Dora.

Dora raised her fingers to her head as she crumpled onto the bleachers. Blood trickled down her nose as she squeezed her eyes shut and let out a high-pitched shriek.

"What the hell are you doing to her?!" I screamed at my dad, but he didn't move. He just continued to stare at Dora as she gripped her head.

"Stop!" I commanded, thrusting out my arms, imagining a gust of wind throwing him off balance.

I heard a whooshing sound before my dad flew back, looking like he had been hit by an invisible cannonball. He didn't have time to break his fall as he fell backward. As I rushed over to Dora, I heard the thud of my dad's head smacking into the concrete bleacher.

"Dora?" I asked as I tentatively placed my hand on her shoulder.

I expected her to recoil under my touch, but instead she just removed her hands from her head, opened her eyes, and looked up at me, slightly squinting as if she were trying to place me but couldn't quite do so.

"Who's Dora?" she asked, wiping her nose with the sleeve of her sweatshirt.

I spun around to look at Lucy and Griswold, who were just looking back at me, with the same lost expression I must have had.

Turning back to Dora, I affirmed, "Umm, that's your name," and then I added, "You don't know who you are?"

She wiped her nose again as she shook her head.

"What do you remember?" Lucy asked, as she and Griswold walked toward us.

"N—nothing," Dora stammered, her eyes widening at this realization. "I don't remember anything."

"Oh damn, that's messed up," Griswold asserted.

Gripping our arms, Lucy pulled Griswold and me away from Dora, so that she was out of earshot.

"Your dad wiped her memories clean," Lucy confirmed, looking over my shoulder, probably to see whether or not Dora was listening to her.

"Yeah, that's exactly what he did to me when I was five, to make me forget," I explained.

What I didn't say but I knew to be true was that he could have just wiped her from existence. It would have been pretty simple. All he needed to do was just believe that she wasn't real. In fact, it was probably far more mentally draining to erase her memories, so why didn't he choose the easier route? Could it have been that she seemed too real to erase, or that he couldn't bear to erase someone from existence who had lived for nearly nine years? He didn't seem to have that problem when he erased Miles from existence, the doppelgänger living far longer than Dora, but that was only because my dad was afraid of imagining Miles's death again.

Maybe this was different. Whether Dora was created from his mind or the old-fashioned way, she was still his daughter.

"Do you think that he wiped away *everything*?" Lucy asked, tapping her temple.

"It's possible, but when he did it to me, I still had my abilities."

"Yeah, but you were only able to see other people's fantasies for as long as I knew you," Griswold noted.

"That's true," I acknowledged, and then added, "But I just didn't realize what else I was able to do because I never tried to do it before. I mean, no one wakes up and says, 'Hey, maybe I should try to pull the imaginary into reality.'"

"Could you imagine if they did? So cool!" Griswold exclaimed, grinning.

"Umm, not if they are anything like Dora," Lucy countered, and then quickly added, "I mean, not that Dora is ba—"

"No, I get what you mean," I responded. "That type of power is dangerous in the wrong hands, especially in the hands of a traumatized kid."

"Should we test her to see whether or not she still has her abilities?"

"Can I go home?" Dora asked, who was now standing a few feet away from us, her hands tucked into her pockets. "Wherever that is, I just want to go home."

I took a few steps closer to Dora as I knelt down, and looked into her wide, gray eyes.

"Dora, I need you to do something, okay? I need you to imagine—" I began, and then Griswold interjected with the word "Rabbit." Of course he would choose a rabbit. Fine, rabbit.

"I need you to imagine a rabbit. Do you see it in your head?" I asked, at which Dora nodded.

"Okay, now really see the rabbit right at your feet. Imagine every little detail of that rabbit. See the heart-shaped, damp pink nose sniffing the air. Feel the soft, fluffy fur. Literally imagine every aspect of that rabbit as if it really existed, beyond your imagination. Can you do that for me, Dora?"

Once again, she nodded, staring down at her feet. As she stared, I felt that familiar sizzle in the air as the fluffiest miniature rabbit appeared at the tips of her sneakers.

"Do you see the rabbit?" I asked, turning to Lucy and Griswold, who peered down at the floor as if they were looking for a needle in a haystack. After a beat, they shook their heads.

"Wiped completely clean," I affirmed, looking back at Dora, who was still staring down at the ground, which was still covered in a gelatinous coating.

I closed my eyes and imagined the gelatinous coating melting away, knowing that the Earth no longer needed to be protected from black sludge. After I felt it dissipate, I stood up and took a breath.

"Should I keep imagining the rabbit?" Dora asked.

"No, it's okay, you can stop. It's over. We'll take you home," I stated, and then, looking over her shoulder, I remembered our unconscious dad still lying on the pavement.

"Umm, but first I need to—"

Before I could complete my sentence, I heard a wave of flapping wings and a series of high-pitched squeaks, as if a flood of mice were flying overhead. Well, I was close, because when I looked up, the sky was obscured by what appeared to be thousands of bats soaring through the air. It was out of a scene from Alfred Hitchcock's *Birds,* except remade into a far more disturbing film—*Bats.*

"What the—!" Lucy yelled, ducking as random bats began to descend, swooping right over the seal pool. Griswold followed suit, holding his laptop over his head, using it as a makeshift shield.

Some of the bats landed atop the silver pods, while others perched on the seal pool's metal railing. They eerily stared in our direction, as if they were watching us.

Dora's scream was much shriller than the one she released when my dad wiped her mind clean as she dove to the ground, covering her head with her hands.

This scene was far too bizarre to be real, but who could possibly have pulled this nightmare into reality? I looked from Dora to my dad, the only other people I knew who could have brought this horrific fantasy into existence. Both were lying on the bleachers, one unconscious and the other now powerless, so neither of them could have possibly done this. Well, if not them, then who?

Without even releasing my question into the universe, it was answered when the rest of the bats descended to the ground, flying in a circle just over the seal pool, forming into a squeaking funnel. The bats that were already perched joined in what quickly became a small cyclone, all of their wings beating against the air at such a velocity that their wings seemed to blur into one another. However, it didn't seem like an optical illusion, but rather that the bats were literally melding into one another.

As the sounds of individual flapping wings morphed into what sounded like a giant top whirring over water, I realized that the bats *did* meld into one another, transforming into a black, spinning mass.

"What the hell," I said to myself, as the black mass's acceleration began to decline, until it came to a complete stop, hovering just over the water. It looked like a cocoon floating in midair, waiting to release its metamorphosed creature; however, I did not have to wait long for the transformation to take place, because not even a few seconds later the black cocoon cracked open to reveal a creature with bulging and bloodshot eyes, razor-sharp claws, and bright white canines that perfectly matched the white coat it was wearing.

"Damn it," I growled, clenching my hands into fists.

Dr. Sutai retracted his canines and claws as he grinned. Then, looking over at my dad's unconscious body still lying in the same spot, he growled, "I'll be taking what's mine now."

"Leave him alone," I hissed, staring at the doctor's hungry, impossibly dilated pupils. It appeared as if the whites of his eyes were overtaken by a menacing, liquidy black abyss.

"Or what?" the doctor hissed back, gliding so quickly to my dad that it barely registered in my vision until he was there, almost like he ran at hypersonic speed. "I know your tricks," the doctor said, arm extended and fingers splayed. "But I have a few of my own."

"Domino!" Lucy screeched, cowering closer to the ground as the once black cocoon rematerialized into a series of bats that swarmed around Lucy and Griswold, enclosing them into another melded black cocoon.

"No!" I screamed, as the cocoon lifted off of the ground, ascending faster into the air until they were about twenty feet above the ground. From within the cocoon, I could hear faint muffled cries and fists beating the inside of the hideous black shell.

Spinning toward Dr. Sutai, I gritted my teeth as I seethed, "Let them go, now!"

"Stay out of my way, and I'll let your friends go," Dr. Sutai stated, lifting up my dad and throwing his arm over his shoulder.

I scowled at the doctor, considering my options, which were not many. I could trust this supernatural, insidious doctor and let him take my father away so that he would release Griswold and Lucy, or I could take my chances and try to go up against him and rescue my dad from his clutches, possibly risking Griswold and Lucy's lives in the process. Now, the former seemed like the logical choice. It's not like the doctor was created to kill my dad, but just to put him in a permanent coma. There was a distinct difference between a permanent coma and death, but not much of one. However, at least my dad would be a living organism in a permanent coma, and my mom would still exist.

Nevertheless, the first option involved a quintessential factor that I just can't wrap my mind around—trusting the doctor. This man—no, *creation*—can form into thousands of bats and horror-film creatures at the drop of a hat, and I am supposed to trust him to let my friends go? How naïve does he think I am? Well, I guess I will just have to go with option three. Damn, option three was going to suck.

"Fine, you can have him," I said, holding my hands up in surrender.

The doctor grinned as he began to move forward but didn't move an inch. Oh, correction, he *couldn't* move an inch.

I winced as I extended my both arms out to my sides; one was aimed at the beige concrete slithering up Dr. Sutai's leg, hardening and thickening in its ascent, while my other arm was aimed at the giant concrete hand molding itself to form underneath the levitating black cocoon, extending its newly formed fingers to pluck the cocoon from the air and place it on the ground.

"You little bastard!" Dr. Sutai roared as the concrete ascended up his arm, holding it in place.

Spreading my legs firmly apart, I fought against the high-pitched ringing as I concentrated on my creations.

"Let him go, or live forever as a statue," I threatened, taking deep breaths after every other word, feeling my strength waning.

"Never," Dr. Sutai sneered, opening his mouth to release his sharp canines. Before I could react, he sank his fangs deep into my dad's neck. He hesitated for a moment, jerking from side to side before he pulled his head back, after which a thick trail of blood flowed down my dad's neck.

"Dad!" I screamed as he fell to the ground, his body limp, blood pooling out of his neck and onto the concrete. Shakily I knelt down, and pressed my fingers to his slippery neck to feel a pulse; it was barely beating, but it was still there.

"Let me go, and I'll save him," Dr. Sutai demanded.

My head snapped up as I felt the concrete continuing to engulf him in his stone encasement.

"I don't think so," I said, raising my blood-coated hand in the air to form a fist, beckoning the concrete to finish the job. Above the high-pitched ringing, I heard the guttural cry of Dr. Sutai as the concrete shell formed around him and began to seep into his body, turning his innards into nothing more than anatomically correct boulders.

As soon as his screaming faded away, his bat cocoon creation cracked open, and disintegrated into ash inside the concrete hand I created.

I could hardly hear Griswold and Lucy calling out for me as I pressed my hand to my dad's neck, applying as much pressure as I possibly could to stop the blood.

"Dammit, you can't die," I hissed, barely hearing myself over the high-pitched ringing still resounding in my eardrums. "You have to live for me, for Dora—Dora!" My head shot up at the realization that if he died, so would she. Everything he ever created would die with him.

"Dora!" I yelled again. While pressing on his neck with one hand, I was reaching out to my cowering sister with the other.

I took a deep breath, gritting my teeth against the high-pitched ringing, concentrating on taking control of Dora with my mind. If I could create that tether on instinct, then there was no reason why I couldn't will it to happen.

As I felt my dad's pulse dimming, I extended my other arm out even farther, forcing my mind to take hold of Dora.

"Come on, you can do this," I mouthed, focusing on Dora's still body. The thumping under my fingertips faded away until all I could feel was slippery, still flesh.

"No!" I yelled, extending both of my hands out to Dora. As soon as both of my arms shot out, I felt this release in my mind, as if it had been in a vise, and was now liberated.

I closed my eyes as images flashed in my mind, like someone was holding up a thousand-page flip book in front of my face. Pictures of my mom and dad hugging one another on the couch, or kissing in the park, flooded in front of me. Flashes of birthday candles and a baseball bat wrapped in a red bow suddenly appeared. Memories of my mom hemorrhaging on the ground, and my dad crying over her corpse played on repeat. I remember feeling this intense sense of confusion, as if the scene were entirely out of context, but now I knew better.

The last flash was by the water. My dad looked at me so pleadingly with his gray eyes, the cluster of beauty marks etched on the corners of his eyelids so prominent.

"I have to go away, Domino. It's for the best," he said.

"I don't understand, Daddy, where are you going?" my five-year-old self asked.

My dad sighed, and then explained. "It doesn't matter. All that matters is that you will have your mother. You will both be safe. That's what's important." He looked from his car to the keys in his hand, making a light metallic ringing sound. "Domino, in life, a lot is going to fall around you, whether you like it or not. Sometimes, you won't be able to control it, even with the powers that you have, but I know that you will make it through, even if I can't. Like a domino, even if you fall, you'll always get back up. Eventually, they'll all fall, but you are strong enough to just get back up. But the only way that you'll have a fighting chance is if you start fresh."

He placed his fingertips to his temples, and stared into my eyes. My eyes glazed over as he repeated, "Eventually, they all fall." As he turned away, I could hear him murmur, "But you are strong enough to just get back up."

"Dad," I whispered, as my vision began to dim. Before the darkness descended, I felt this invisible force reach out of me as everything faded to black.

CHAPTER 18

HOSPITAL GOWNS AND LAVENDER

The rhythmic beeping only intensified my massive headache. It felt like what I imagined someone poking you with a pencil nonstop would feel like, except in the brain and with the force of sound. I think it goes without saying, but imagining things is becoming easier. Now, bringing them into creation? That's a whole different story, hence the massive headache.

I don't know what compelled me to do it, but before opening my eyes, I took a moment to feel around. I seemed to be lying on something soft, like a thin mattress but without any springs. My head was propped up on something even softer and smoother. I seemed to be wearing a very thin, long shirt and a tube with a plastic base was sticking out of the crook of my arm.

"Domino? Are you awake?" I heard Lucy ask from a corner of the room.

I opened my eyes to see her sitting in a beige armchair in the small windowless room; aside from that armchair, the bed I was lying on and the steadily beeping EKG machine, the room was pretty bare.

Lucy's wavy brown hair was pulled back into a tight ponytail, and she was wearing a completely different outfit from the one I had just seen her in. The flower pattern of her dress matched the vibrancy of her elastics, which she revealed as she smiled.

"Good, you're awake," Lucy said, sounding relieved.

"Where am—?" But before I could get the question out, the last few hours that I was awake flooded back. The zoo, the bats and those bats forming into a giant cocoon, my dad, Dora. It all plummeted into me like a giant wave crashing into the shore.

"Shit!" I exclaimed, shooting up out of bed and pulling the tightly tucked covers off of me. Oh, perfect, I was wearing a hospital gown. "I've gotta get outta here," I asserted, cringing as I ripped off the transparent tape on my arm holding the needle to the IV in place.

"You don't need to go anywhere," Lucy assured me, putting out her hands like she was trying to calm down a hyperenergetic puppy.

"Yes, I do," I maintained, jimmying the needle out of my arm. Jeez, they really had it jammed in there. Once it was out, I pressed my hand to the inside of my arm, swung my legs over to the other side of the bed, planted my feet on the floor, and took a step forward, only to be met by a spray of vibrant fireworks clouding my vision.

"Dammit," I exclaimed, sitting back on the bed and rubbing my eyes.

"The doctor said that you should rest. Your head hit the pavement pretty hard when you passed out. We had no idea when you were going to wake up," Lucy explained.

I touched my forehead to feel the bandage securely wrapped around my head.

"How long have I been out?"

"Two days."

"*Two days?*" I shouted. At the same time, the door swung open, revealing Griswold with a backpack swung over his shoulder and wearing a black T-shirt imprinted with a splayed deck of cards with the caption "Pick a card, any card" underneath, and faded black jeans. Now the outfit changes made sense; how the hell had I been unconscious for two days?

"Good, you're awake," Griswold said as he sat on the corner of the bed. "You had us worried there. Well, I knew that you would be okay, but still, you didn't wake up for a while."

I took another go at getting out of bed, but to no avail.

"Where's Dora and my dad?"

Lucy and Griswold shot each other a look, and then Lucy reached over to place her hand on top of mine.

"Dora's fine, but your dad...He didn't make it, Domino. The doctors said that his carotid artery had been sliced open. He was gone before the EMTs made it to the zoo."

The feeling of his pulse waning under my fingertips rushed back with a bitterness that only the memory of someone's death can have. I had no idea how Dr. Sutai sliced my dad's carotid artery open with a vampiric bite, but then again, the guy did some pretty impossible things, like creating a bat army that tried to capture my friends.

He was willing to risk being permanently erased from existence, betting on me freeing him from his concrete shell so that he could save my dad from bleeding out. I don't know if I made the right decision, or if there was even a "right" decision, but if I had released the doctor, I just *knew* that my dad would be gone anyway. Maybe I should have allowed Dr. Sutai to save my dad only to force him back into a permanent coma, because there was no way that he was ever going to let it go, and I doubt that my dad would have erased him from existence. Even if my dad did erase him, he may have just created another doctor to put him in a medically induced coma. My dad's self-deprecation was so deeply rooted, he might actually be more at peace now, but I'll never know, and I just have to live with that.

My dad only remained alive so that he could keep his fantasies alive, so that raised the question, how was Dora "fine"?

"Did you say that Dora is *fine*?" I asked.

Griswold nodded, and then stated, "Yeah, she's in Chicago with her mom, well, her foster mom."

How is that possible? My dad made it clear that everything that he had created—no matter how long it had been in existence—would fade if he were no longer alive. It's like they were connected to him, so if that connection broke, then his creations had nothing tethering them to reality.

That's it! The tether. Afterall, I made the same connection with his clone in the hotel room to prevent him from attacking us. Maybe that connection extended to every version of him. I must have done it; I must have taken hold of Dora so that I could keep her alive even after my dad's passing. But if I was able to keep Dora alive after connecting with her, then did that mean that I could have erased Dr. Sutai from existence? After all, I made the same connection with him in the hotel room to prevent him from attacking us. However, I may have just had a temporary hold on him. Well, I'll never know because there is no way that I am going to break open that statue to find out.

At least Dora was alive, but there was one thing I needed to confirm about her, otherwise everything that we did may have been for nothing.

"Is her mind still wiped clean?" I asked, looking from Griswold to Lucy and back again.

Both Griswold and Lucy nodded.

"Yeah, she doesn't remember anything before that evening," Lucy affirmed.

"And I also checked to make sure that she can't," Griswold began, and then wiggled his fingers near his temple and narrowed his eyes as he focused on an indiscriminate spot on the bed, "you know. She can't. Whatever your dad did to her stuck."

Raising my eyebrow, I asked, "What look was that?"

"What?" Griswold stated, throwing up his hands. "That was my I'm-bringing-a-fantasy-into-reality look, or as I call it, the Domino stare."

"I *definitely* don't look like that," I countered.

Griswold smirked, and then said, "You can't exactly see your face when you're doing it, can you?"

"Fair, but no."

When I took hold of Dora, I was just trying to keep her alive, but I didn't realize that I had kept her memories and powers bound. However, maybe it was better that they were. After all, her memories only caused her mental anguish, and she saw her powers as a burden more than anything else. Plus, she was wreaking havoc on the world with them, so maybe it was best that she didn't have her abilities, so that she could finally live in peace with Marla.

"Wait, did you say she's in Chicago?"

"Yup."

"Suggesting that we're not?" I asked, ridiculously looking around for a view to locate myself in a clearly windowless room.

"Nope, we're back in New York," Griswold announced.

"Wait, how is that possible?"

"Well, after your dad passed away," Lucy began, and then paused, looking around awkwardly, sensing the rawness of that statement, "the pods he trapped the security guards in disappeared. Naturally, they were very confused. However, I think they got past that when they saw two bodies lying on the ground, one of whom was bleeding out. One of the guards called 9-1-1, while the others started questioning us about what had happened. Then, when the police arrived, they started questioning us *and* the guards.

"Dora was still shaken from Dr. Sutai's attack, and she kept saying that she didn't know anything, and that this monster came out of nowhere and began to attack us."

"That was pretty ingenious," Griswold interjected. "So, we played along. We said that we didn't know anything about the pods or loose rabbits that the guards mentioned. We admitted to staying in the zoo after hours, but we were trying to find our way out. That's when we ran into this monstrous man who was trying to hurt Dora. When your dad heroically tried to stop him, this evil man bit into your dad's throat, killing him instantly."

"And they believed you?" I asked, skeptically.

"It seems like it," Griswold answered, pulling his backpack off and unzipping it to pull out his laptop. "That, and I hacked into the cameras to erase any video footage of that evening."

"But didn't you have it on a loop?"

"Yeah, but dude, it was coming down in *buckets*. If that weren't on the feed, they would be suspicious," Griswold explained, giving his laptop a light tap before sliding it back in and zipping up the backpack.

"Okay, but erasing the video footage doesn't mean that they believed you," I countered.

"No, but other than us being there, they don't have any proof that Griswold and I were involved," Lucy noted.

"That, and I *may* have made it seem like the guy who killed your dad also abducted Dora," Griswold added.

Rolling her eyes at him, Lucy stated, "You didn't just 'make it seem' like he abducted Dora, you literally said, 'The man who killed Max Garrison also kidnapped Dora.'" She winced at the mention of my dad's murder and then murmured "Sorry."

"So, despite the fact that the Chicago police determined that Dora *wasn't* kidnapped, you managed to convince them that she *was*? How?" I asked in disbelief.

Griswold shrugged and then added, "They couldn't prove otherwise, could they? Dora couldn't remember whether or not she was kidnapped, so she was convinced, and I don't think that Marla contradicted our story."

"Fine, but that still doesn't explain how we got to New York," I pointed out.

"Well, they brought you and your dad to the nearest hospital right away, in Chicago. Griswold and I never made it to that hospital because we were being questioned, but we were able to make a few calls," Lucy explained, and then nodded to Griswold. "He called his parents, who pulled some strings and managed to get you transferred from a Chicago hospital to one in New York."

"How?"

"You know country club people. They know someone, who knows someone, who knows someone in hospital administration. You know how it goes," Griswold explained, matter-of-factly.

"Okay, but why would your parents do that for you? Weren't they furious with you for leaving and never getting back to them?"

"Yeah," Griswold admitted, looking down at the bedsheet and pinching the fabric between his fingertips, "But, surprisingly, they just seemed relieved that I was okay. Plus, you're like family. It didn't take that much convincing," he concluded, and then after a beat, he added, "I *did* have to promise that I wouldn't wear a magician's outfit to school anymore, and I'm grounded for eternity, but it was worth it."

"Thanks, Grizz," I said, giving him an appreciative smile.

However, I felt my smile fading as a very bitter realization dawned on me. Griswold had his parents, but did I still have mine? Clearly, my dad was dead, but what about my mom? If she was yet another figment of his imagination, and he was no longer alive to keep her real, then did that mean that she had been erased from existence?

"Has anyone tried to contact my mom?" I asked, anxiously.

Before either of them could answer, someone wearing light blue scrubs—presumably, a nurse—burst into the room and announced that visiting hours had ended.

"Wait, has anyone tried getting in touch with my mom?" I asked once again, finding it very hard to keep my voice steady. There was a very real possibility that my mom no longer existed, but I needed this confirmed before I could...what? Plan my life as an orphan? Well, maybe the foster care system wouldn't be as bad for me as it was for Dora, but that didn't mean that I wanted to be in it, or that I wanted my mom to disappear from the face of the Earth. Her drug abuse and parade of Jeffs were irritating, but she was still my mom, real or not, and I needed to know that she was alive.

"I'd have to check our records, but right now, I am going to get the doctor to check you out," the nurse explained.

As soon as she walked back out the door, I raised my arms.

"Screw this," I said, gritting my teeth against the high-pitched ringing, feeling my molecules shift.

I leaned on the green moss-covered brick wall of my apartment build-ing, taking deep breaths, hoping that the extra intakes of oxygen would bring my vision back into focus. After a few minutes, my head no lon-ger felt like it was filled with helium, so I took a few steps away from the wall. As I felt the night's humid wind on my skin, I regretted not imagining myself standing here wearing pants.

Cinching the back of my hospital gown by gripping the material with my hands, I closed my eyes as the high-pitched ringing subsided.

Although the ringing seemed to lessen the more I used my abilities, it was still extremely disorienting.

I took another deep breath before I opened my eyes and pulled open the entrance door with one hand while still holding the back of the hospital gown with the other. I rolled my eyes at the strips of bright yellow police tape still strewn over the elevator doors. Yeah, that was never getting fixed.

"We have to live on the damn fifth floor," I muttered as I headed for the stairs.

Yeah, instead of scaling the stairs, I could have imagined myself in my apartment, but I still felt light-headed, so I wasn't going to risk passing out. Okay, going up five flights of stairs definitely wasn't helping the "no passing out" goal, but at least I could take a break while climbing the stairs to recuperate. That's definitely not something you can do when you are disrupting reality.

When I finally made it to the fifth floor, there was a distinct lack of marijuana fumes and BO in the air. In fact, the hallway smelled faintly of lavender, which couldn't be a good sign, because not one scent emanating from this building even came close to resembling that of a flower.

I shoved this thought aside as I marched—well, gradually walked while trying to steady myself against the wall—up to my front door. I kicked up the dingy welcome mat to find the key taped to the bottom. How no one had broken in yet, I will never know.

Once inside, I surveyed the empty space. Well, it wasn't completely empty. The same grimy couch and chair were still adjacent to one another, but that musty fragrance was gone. The coffee table was also completely spotless; for as long as I could remember, it was always covered in something, either newspapers or my mom's drug paraphernalia. I hadn't even realized that it was made of mahogany.

"You're home," I heard a voice state. I turned to my right to see my mom stepping out from my bedroom, hair pulled into her signature sleek, neat bun, which is usually how she styled it for work, but she wasn't wearing her waitress uniform. Instead, she was wearing a plain black T-shirt and jeans.

"Mom?" I asked, almost as if I had to confirm that it was her.

Then she did something that she had never done—she walked over and pulled me in for a hug. It just wasn't her style to embrace anyone, so I was kind of taken aback when she wrapped her arms around me; that, and the fact that she still existed. Don't get me wrong, I was relieved that she was alive, but I couldn't help questioning how it was possible.

Still hugging me, my mom said, "When the hospital called, that scared the hell out of me. I was worried about you, kid."

So, they *did* call. Well, no need to check the records now.

"Mom," I said, pulling away, "you probably have a lot of questions about where I was."

My mom took a step back and furrowed her brow, as if she were considering what she was going to say next.

"Yes, I do, but right now, I only care about the fact that you're okay. See? I even cleaned up so that you would have somewhere clean to recover when you came home."

"Mom, there's something that you should know...I found Dad, but he...he died. I know that we haven't seen him in a decade, and we never talk about him, but I just thought that you should know," I explained.

I don't know what compelled me to tell her about my dad, but whether she was the real version of Rosa Gomez Garrison or not, she still had a right to know that her husband/creator was dead.

She looked down and slightly nodded before she said, "I'm surprised he survived this long."

In response, I nodded back, wondering if I was the only one who knew *why* he chose to live.

"Mom, what do you know about Dad?" I asked.

"I know that your dad loved you very much," she responded.

"Okay, but do you know what he was capable of doing?" I pressed.

The crease in her brow deepened as she was trying to work out the deeper meaning of my question.

"To be honest, that part of my life is a blur. It's in the past. But what I *do* know is what you are capable of doing, and that you would do *anything* to protect the people that you care about," she explained.

"Well, yeah, that's just what you need to do," I stated, matter-of-factly. I mean, why wouldn't you protect those you care about?

"Sure, but not everyone thinks like that. You know, even as a kid, I *knew* that you would do anything to make sure that I was okay. You did protect me, but I just took it as a fact. I can't explain it, it's just this strong feeling that I had, like we were connected," my mom explained.

I had always felt connected to her as well, but I never thought anything of it, except that she was my mom, the person who raised me, so why wouldn't I feel connected to her? I mean, most people feel connected to the person or people who raised them, that is unless they were abusive and/or cruel. However, maybe this was a *different* sort of connection. Maybe I mentally connected with my mom in the same way that I connected with Dora. I couldn't remember when, but whenever it happened, this tether that I created with my mom must have kept her alive.

So, does that mean that my dad kept himself in a permanent coma for nothing? What if we had discovered that I was keeping my mom alive sooner? Would his life have turned out completely different? Knowing him, he probably would have committed suicide, so maybe it was for the best that he never found out. However, in the end, not knowing didn't save his life anyway. This was just something else that I would have to live with. We all have our burdens, right? I just needed to deal with mine and move on. At least I had people in my life who could help me through it all.

"You're my mom, I'd protect you no matter what," I affirmed.

"Yeah, but not the one that you deserve. I can change, though, no more drugs," my mom asserted, gesturing toward the clean mahogany coffee table. "I got rid of everything. I'm gonna quit cold turkey, once and for all, I promise."

I suppressed the urge to roll my eyes, knowing that the promise wouldn't stick. Well, at least one advantage to knowing that she was really imaginary was that I *knew* that she wouldn't OD from her drug use; that didn't make it okay, but I could at least take comfort in the fact that she would survive.

"Right, Mom," I said, and then quickly changing the subject, I asked, "So, pizza for dinner?"

"Sounds good," my mom said, walking over to the landline on the wall in the kitchen. Without me asking, she stated, "Something's wrong with my cell phone. It died days ago. Can you grab a takeout menu from the drawer?"

Ah, well, no wonder I just received that one text from her.

"Got it," I said, as I pulled out the first menu in the bloated drawer.

As she dialed, she said, "Maybe over pizza, we can discuss where you were and what happened."

"What happened to only caring about the fact that I was okay?" I joked.

"Yeah, but I can see that you are, so spill, kid."

I took a deep breath before I began, "It's a long story, but let's just say that it all started with a roaming Bengal tiger."

EPILOGUE

ADVENTURE PART II

"I thought you said no zoo dates," Lucy reminded me as we stood under the red brick-laden archway covered in a new sheet of snow. Yeah, I unimagined the heat wave by now.

Taking hold of her gloved hand, I corrected, "No, after our *first* date, what I said was that we shouldn't go to the zoo for our *next* date. I mean, how many dates have we been on now, like twenty?"

"You're counting free periods and lunch, right? Because my three-month grounding doesn't end for another week," Lucy countered, giving my hand a light squeeze.

"You're lucky. Grizz has a life sentence. Well, I doubt his parents can ground him when he's eighteen, but I'm sure they'll try. I can't believe they even informed Dr. Wexler about his grounding; that's intense. Plus, school's only been open for a couple weeks. They only just finished the repairs. And, I imagined you out of your house plenty of times, so it's close to twenty dates. Well, regardless, this is not the second. Also, I'm 95 percent positive that we won't be attacked by a roaming Bengal tiger."

I know, you must be surprised that I am using my abilities, especially when they are so infuriatingly painful. However, Grizz and Lucy made compelling arguments about why I should practice, and they were annoyingly insistent. That, and my dad said that there are *others* who share our ability. Even though nothing extra strange has happened in the last few months, I wasn't taking any chances.

Believe it or not, the practice was helping. Now the high-pitched ringing had become somewhat tolerable. I mean, at least I wasn't passing out anymore. It still hurt though, and I still hated the idea of having this much power, but I just had to deal with that and believe that my abilities would only corrupt me if I let them.

Lucy gave my ribs a playful jab, and then asked, "And that other 5 percent?"

"You can never be 100 percent certain of anything," I teased.

"Especially when it comes to what is real and not real, right?" Lucy countered, and then she added, "Speaking of which, how's your mom dealing with the whole 'my son has the powers' deal?"

That's right, the night I came home I told my mom everything. Well, *almost* everything. Sometimes some things are better left hidden, like the fact that my mom is actually imaginary and my abilities are what's keeping her alive. I know what you're going to say: *Domino, she has a right to know.* Maybe you're right, but how would knowing really help her? Knowledge is power, sure, but *too much* knowledge could be downright burdensome.

I shrugged as I said, "She's adjusting. Between not abusing drugs and discovering that your son has really strange abilities, she has a lot to adjust to."

Yeah, I know, I'm as shocked as you are; I didn't think that she would keep her promise either. I was going to have to rethink that

Teflon metaphor I normally use to describe her. Actually, scratch that, she is still like Teflon when it comes to her parade of Jeffs.

Lucy and I continued to walk, the fresh sheet of snow crunching under our boots, until we found a nearby bench. I wrapped my arm around Lucy's shoulders, and she leaned in.

We sat like that in a serene moment of silence, just watching the pristine snowflakes drift to the ground in a graceful descent.

"Domino?" Lucy asked, breaking the silence.

"Yeah?"

"I've been meaning to tell you," Lucy began, taking a deep breath. "I read something on my newsfeed earlier today. It was about the Lincoln Park Zoo."

I sat up a little straighter, more alert, sensing that this couldn't be good news.

"What did it say?" I reluctantly asked.

"It may be nothing, but the story reported on one of the mysterious new statues—the one we know as Dr. Sutai—just breaking, like someone took a sledgehammer to it. The police suspect that it was just vandals, and the zoo director doesn't really seem bothered because they had no idea who authorized the statue being put there in the first place, so it's not really being pursued."

Perfect. Maybe the zoo director and the police thought nothing of that statue being destroyed, and maybe it *was* nothing, but we had to err on the side of caution because we knew the potential ramifications of Dr. Sutai escaping his concrete tomb. Maybe he just faded away from existence the second my dad died, but maybe he didn't. Maybe that tether I created with his clone connected to all of the versions of him *was* a permanent one; it's possible that I kept this sadistic creation alive. If his former life's mission were over, then wouldn't his new one be vengeance?

Taking a deep breath, I unwrapped my arm from Lucy's shoulders and stood up. Turning toward her, I gestured for her to take my hand.

The second I felt her gloved hand in mine, I determinedly marched forward. She quickened her pace to catch up with me as she asked, "Where are we going?"

Eyes straight ahead, I stated, "To Grizz's place. If Dr. Sutai escaped, then he's probably coming for us, and I'm not taking any chances."

For months, I didn't understand why I didn't remember my dad telling me that I was strong enough to get back up. I don't know, maybe it was because I saw him as a jerk all of my life for abandoning my mom and me, so I couldn't give him any redeeming qualities. Maybe it's because memories—even your first ones—become naturally fragmented, and not remembering that part was completely random. I'm not sure, but whatever the reason, my dad was right. Well, in part.

Yes, eventually, everyone and everything *will* fall, even peace falls away. Even when you *thought* that you defeated an enemy or overcame an obstacle, another adversary—or the same damn one in my case—or another barrier could—and probably will—get in your way. Yes, I was strong enough to get back up, but why do it alone? I finally figured out that my first name was a reminder of all the falls I must endure, but I did not have to endure them by myself.

Sure, my life was incredibly weird, but at least I had people that I could rely on, like Griswold, Lucy, and my mom, to get me through. And that support was why I was strong. Sure, I would rather not use my abilities, but what choice did I have when I knew that what seemed impossible was entirely and unequivocally possible? Like it or not, I needed my abilities to face anything and *everything.*

So, yeah, crazy adventure part two, here we come. Well, at least I knew the perfect dragon-sometimes-Pegasus that we could count on for a ride.

ABOUT THE AUTHOR

 Jenna Marcus is an academic leader and published author of the YA novels *My Unusual Talent* and *Breathe Deep and Swim*. She has a fervent passion for leveraging her decade of expertise to robustly enhance and redefine the quality of teaching and learning. As an avid reader, she believes that every child should find a narrative to love and hopes to inspire our younger generation to discover stories that truly move and inspire them.

Currently, she lives in New Rochelle, New York, and she works in New York City as a Literacy Coordinator at a charter school. Until June 2020, she held the combined roles of Director of Student Achievement and IGCSE Coordinator at a private international boarding school in New York. She holds an MSEd in Educational Leadership, an MSEd in Middle Childhood and Adolescent English Education, and a BA in Literature; she is also a certified in School Building Leadership and ELA.

When she is not writing or teaching, you can find her in a café with the largest cup of coffee, catching up with friends, reading a good book, or both.

Made in the USA
Middletown, DE
01 May 2022